Dan McGirt was born ~~~~~~~~~~~~~~~~~
received a BA in Poli~~~~~~~~~~~~~~~~~
of Georgia in 1989 and is currently studying law. He
enjoys reading, fencing, acting and watching live
coverage of Congress on C-SPAN. *Jason Cosmo* is his
first novel.

Also by Dan McGirt in Pan Books

Royal Chaos

Dan McGirt

Jason Cosmo

Pan Books
London, Sydney and Auckland

First published in the USA in 1989 by
Signet Books, a division of New American Library
First published in Great Britain 1990 by
Pan Books Ltd, Cavaye Place, London SW10 9PG
9 8 7 6 5 4 3
© Dan McGirt 1989
ISBN 0 330 31243 X

Typeset by Selectmove Ltd, London
Printed and bound in Great Britain by
Richard Clay Ltd, Bungay, Suffolk

1

The arrival of the stranger was quite a shock. My humble village of Lower Hicksnittle was normally a quiet place, which was natural enough considering its location on the northern fringe of the backward kingdom of Darnk. Its inhabitants plodded thickly through life, considering all things beyond the confines of their clustered hovels and rocky turnip fields to be alien, hostile, and ultimately unimportant. We knew little of events elsewhere in the Eleven Kingdoms, for travellers from the south were rare. To the north lay endless leagues of empty wasteland and the black wall of a distant, unexplored mountain range. Lower Hicksnittle was as isolated and uninteresting a place as could be found. Hence our amazement when the stranger appeared in our midst.

He strode into the Festering Wart Tavern like an insult and stopped in the middle of the common room with his hands on his hips and arrogance on his face. All the village men were there that spring evening, drinking stale rutabaga beer and gossiping about the recent rash of mottled pig pox going around. We ceased our talk to stare at him in sullen, suspicious silence. The only sound was the sputtering of the smoky pig fat lanterns which hung from the dangerously bowed rafters.

He was thin and pallid and outlandishly dressed. His peach-coloured breeches were too tight, his white blouse too ruffled, the bobbing yellow plume on his hat too long, and the golden curls of his hair too dainty. We Hicksnittlers favoured ill-fitting grey garments woven from mudflax and cottonweed and kept our hair cropped short. His attire was one strike against him. The sword at his belt was another.

'I am Lombardo of Calador,' he said, wrinkling his nose at the stench of the place. It was important to breathe lightly at the Festering Wart. Strong men had died here by simply inhaling the foul air too deeply. Some of their bones still lay scattered in the filth on the floor. 'Many call me Lombardo the Magnificent.' We made no response and he seemed surprised that we didn't recognize his name. 'I have come to your quaint village, good peasants, seeking a man with whom I have business. His name is Jason Cosmo.'

I jumped in my seat and the others turned their heads to glare at me, holding me personally responsible for Lombardo's intrusion into their world. Observing our reactions, he approached my table. Cloying perfume assailed my nostrils even through the overpowering smells of the Festering Wart. Farmer Ames and Burlo Stumproot, my drinking partners, gagged and looked away. I held my breath and met his gaze.

'You, sirrah,' said Lombardo, jabbing a manicured finger at my face. 'Do you know where I may find the one I seek?'

'I'm Jason Cosmo,' I said. 'What do you want with me?'

'I want your head.'

'You're joking.'

'Think you so?' I looked up into his pale blue eyes, cruel as hooks. He wasn't joking.

'There must be some mistake.'

'There is no mistake, dog.' He tapped the hilt of his sword. 'Stand.'

'I'll sit, thank you.'

'I said stand, dog!' He whipped his rapier from its scabbard and pressed the point against my throat. I looked to my fellow Hicksnittlers for support and found they had all taken a sudden absorbing interest in their fingernails, despite the fact that there were nearly twenty of us to his one. Of course, we didn't have swords. I stood.

'Listen, I've paid my taxes and—'

'Silence!' he hissed. I fell silent. Lombardo raised his voice to make a general announcement. 'Good villagers! This man who dwells among you is not, in truth, a man.' He paused for dramatic effect. 'He is a demon in human form!'

The Hicksnittlers gasped with horror. Burlo and Ames quickly got up from the table and moved a safe distance away, taking their beer mugs with them.

'I always knew there was something strange about him,' said Ames. 'Always readin' them books.'

Burlo nodded. 'Yep. A normal man don't have use for books, just pigs and turnips and women. Even so, who'd have ever thought old Jason was a demon in human form?' The other men asserted that they were equally shocked at this revelation.

'I'm not a demon!' I said. The sharp steel point at my throat muffled much of my indignation.

'He lies!' said Lombardo. 'Think on it! Have your crops failed, your livestock been taken ill, your children disobeyed, your wives nagged you?' The wide-eyed villagers nodded assent to these propositions. Lombardo jabbed his rapier slightly forward, causing me to stumble back against my bench as he continued. 'Here is the cause! He poses as one of you even as he casts his vile enchantments over all you hold dear!'

'It's a terrible thing,' said Ames wisely, 'when a man casts vile enchantments over all that his neighbours hold dear.'

'True,' said Burlo. 'Of course Jason ain't a man no more. He's a demon in human form.'

This was getting out of hand. I suddenly backed away from Lombardo's sword, pushing the bench along behind me. The table was still between us and he made no move to close the gap.

'This is crazy!' I said. 'You've known me all my life! I'm a farmer like you, a Hicksnittler, a proud son of Darnk!'

'Precious little farmin' I seen you do,' said Farmer Godfrey, squinting at me from his seat across the room. 'Your turnip patch is half the size of any other man's.'

'That's because I'm also the local woodcutter, as you all know. I cut the firewood that keeps you warm through the cold Darnkite winter. I bring the lumber you use to build your proud shacks. Just as my father did before he died, and his father before him.'

'What about the books?' said Ames. 'Evil things, those books. Full of black magic.'

'They aren't! Magic isn't even legal in Darnk.'

'I know that. But I still have to wonder about those books. How do we know you haven't got a spell for calling up mottled pig pox in one of them?' The others grumbled darkly at this suggestion. Lombardo merely smirked.

'Well, if you had ever bothered to learn reading, you could see for yourself.'

'No point in it,' said Ames. 'I've got no use for reading. It's bad business through and through.'

'There is nothing sinister about reading. My dear, departed mother taught me—'

'Your mother was from parts unknown,' said Godfrey. 'She was probably a witch. That means you're at least half witch, even if you're not a demon.'

'Take that back, Godfrey, or I'll brain you.' My mother was not a witch, but the runaway daughter of Brythalian gentry who had fled an unwanted marriage and found her way to Lower Hicksnittle, where she had fallen in love with Jolan Cosmo, my father. Strong-willed, educated, and exquisitely beautiful, she had never been fully accepted by the Hicksnittlers, especially the spiteful, jealous wives who envied her looks and grace and frowned on her foreign ways. Janna Cosmo simply ignored their unkind remarks and lived her life as she pleased, which included educating me in what she considered a fitting manner. I knew more about history, geography, mathematics, and other topics than the rest of the village put together. Not that I had much practical use for my knowledge in Lower Hicksnittle, but I was grateful to my mother for her gift to me.

I started towards Godfrey but was stopped short as Lombardo turned my angry words against me. 'Fear not his threats, Goodman Godfrey,' he said loftily. 'I shall protect you from this demonic witchspawn!'

This was too much to bear. 'Don't listen to this peacock – maybe he's the demon!' I pointed an accusing finger at the swordsman.

'Good point,' said Farmer Derbo. 'It's for sure that fellow ain't from around here. He must be . . . a damned foreigner!' The crowd gasped at this stunning realization and I relaxed a little. Instinctive rural xenophobia would preserve me, for a damned foreigner was as bad as a demon in the Hicksnittler's view.

Lombardo's predatory smile undermined my confidence. 'Good squires!' he cried, promoting us several ranks in the social hierarchy. 'Do you hear how the demon betrays himself? He admits there is indeed a demon present, but seeks to deceive you into believing it is I since it was I who exposed him to you. But if I am a demon, then why would I expose him? Because I am not! Therefore, he is!' He raised his sword in triumph. The Hicksnittlers considered his argument and decided it was sound. They scrambled away from the tables and backed against the far wall, making religious signs and averting their eyes from me.

'Wait a minute!' I said. 'What kind of logic is that? Burlo! Ames! Guys! Think about it!' But it was obvious that Lombardo had won his case. Logical reasoning has never been a big part of the Darnkite national character.

'You will deceive them no longer, foul demon!' said the swordsman, taking a deliberate step forward. I was on my own. I upended the heavy wooden table and sent Lombardo sprawling. As he hit the floor I raced across the common room, through the kitchen, and out the back door.

Strong arms snaked around me as I reached the outside. It hadn't occurred to me that Lombardo had brought help. His lurking ally hurled me roughly to the muddy ground. I saw him framed in the spillage of light from the doorway, a squat, hulking man with arms like posts. He flashed a gap-toothed grin and dove atop me, knocking the breath from my lungs. We rolled and grappled, wrestling for advantage. He was exceptionally strong, but so was I, my muscles lean and hard from swinging an axe and dragging fallen trees.

Lombardo appeared and sheathed his sword with an arrogant chuckle. 'Guido will make short work of you, Cosmo. He wrestled bears before entering my service.'

I believed it. Guido forced my arm into a position it wasn't meant to assume. I slammed my knee hard between his legs, but to no visible effect. Maybe he was a eunuch. The henchman countered by sinking his teeth painfully into my shoulder while attempting to pull the lower half of my face away from the upper half. Twisting my head out of his grip, I got a knee against his chest and shoved him off me. He took a mouthful of my shoulder with him. I sprang to my feet.

Lombardo drew his sword again and danced forward, whipping the blade back and forth in the air. I backed away, trying to watch both master and henchman. Guido was back on his feet and slyly trying to sidle his way behind me.

'Why do you want to kill me?' I asked, hoping to distract them as I racked my brain for a plan.

'I am a bounty hunter,' Lombardo said. 'And with your capture I will be acknowledged as the greatest of all time. It will be nice to have my true talent properly recognized. Notice how I cleverly convinced these peasants you hide among that you are a demon, thus cutting you off from what aid they might have given you.'

'I'm impressed. But I think you've made a mistake. I've committed no crimes.' Lombardo held the weapon, and thus the initiative, but I had some choice about which way I retreated. I aimed for the tool shed across the yard where I might be able to grab a weapon of my own.

'Then someone is wasting a large reward.'

I was halfway to my goal, but if Guido eased over much further he would block me. 'Just how much of a reward are you talking about?'

'Ten million gold crowns.'

'Excuse me? I thought you said—'

'Ten million gold crowns.'

'That's insane!' You could buy a small kingdom with a mere one million crowns and still have enough change to pick up a couple of dukedoms on the side. Ten million crowns staggered the imagination.

Lombardo shrugged. 'Perhaps so. But someone is paying and I, Lombardo the Magnificent, will collect.' He lunged and nicked my chest. 'You are so smug. You pose as a stupid peasant and hide in this cesspool of a kingdom, yet go boldly by your own name – an insulting challenge to all who seek you.'

'Who's hiding? I was born here. I live here. There has to be a mistake!'

'I tire of these games!' Lombardo lunged to attack.

I was close enough. I whirled and sprinted the last few yards to the shed. Guido wasn't fast enough to intercept me and Lombardo didn't react in time. I yanked the door open, reached inside, and grabbed the first handle I felt. It was an axe. I brought it up just in time to deflect Lombardo's thrust and hit Guido in the face with the blunt end of the head. Bone crunched and he dropped to the ground. I charged Lombardo, who turned heel and ran. I pursued, screaming like a barbarian raider.

Lower Hicksnittle consisted of about a dozen wooden hovels arranged around a central square. The Festering Wart, our combination tavern and town hall, squatted on the east side of the open area. I raced around the corner and into the village square, where two horses were tethered and the villagers were just exiting by the front door. Lombardo abruptly stopped his flight and turned to face me. I skidded to a startled halt. The men of Lower Hicksnittle gaped at the sight of me, mud-soaked and bloody axe in hand, my moonlit face twisted into a grimace of rage and surprise. Lombardo dramatically extended his sword like an accusation. I knew what was coming next.

'There is your proof, good villagers! Exposed, the demon has gone mad and now seeks to murder us all, rape your wives, and devour your children! We must stop him!' The Hicksnittlers swung their heads about, gapes intact, to stare blankly at Lombardo. Letting him handle the berserker demon woodcutter was one thing; getting involved themselves was quite another. Lombardo sensed the problem before I could think of a way to exploit it. Gesturing towards his horses, he said, 'A reward of ten silver coins to each of you if you help me save your village from demonic destruction!'

That was good enough for the Hicksnittlers. They stooped and gathered stones and globs of mud which they hurled at me with indifferent accuracy. I danced and dodged as they pelted me, then suddenly charged the smirking Lombardo, taking him by complete surprise and knocking the rapier from his grasp with a sweep of my axe. He stumbled back and fell to the ground, his arms upraised. My neighbours ceased their barrage and watched with morbid fascination as I lifted my axe to finish him.

'Preserve me, good villagers!' he cried pitifully.

I reconsidered. The women and children had come out of their huts to investigate the commotion and were staring at me from every direction, wide-eyed. I couldn't hack a helpless man to bits with the whole fearful village watching. In fact, I lacked the stomach to hack a helpless man to bits under any circumstances.

On the other hand, he was dangerous. I couldn't just let him go. I looked around and saw the answer. Flinging the axe aside I reached down and yanked the quaking bounty hunter to his feet.

'What are you going to do?' he asked.

'Give you a bath.' I hefted him into the air and carried him, kicking and squirming, to the town well, which was no more than a bucket on a rope beside a deep hole in the ground.

'Cosmo, no!' Ignoring his plea, I tossed him in head first. His cry of outrage ended with a distant splash. For a moment I wondered if throwing a man headfirst down a well was morally any better than hacking him to bits. Probably not, but it was much cleaner and he had a chance, however slim, of surviving the fall and being rescued later.

The villagers eyed me warily. Some still held rocks. I chose my words carefully. 'I'm really not a demon,' I said innocently. They looked unconvinced. 'May great Grubslink, God of Impoverished Peasants, strike me down if I am.'

Even my dull-witted neighbours knew that a true demon would not invoke the name of one of The Gods. Granted, Grubslink was fairly low class as gods go, but he was a god nonetheless. More importantly, he was *our* god.

The Hicksnittlers murmured among themselves. Ames finally spoke up. 'Maybe you're not a demon, Jason, but you're still trouble. I don't know what you've gotten mixed up in, but mark my words, there'll be more like that Lombardo character to come looking for you. We don't need a bunch of damned foreigners coming here to endanger our families and mess up our village. You've already ruined the water supply. It would be best if you just left now and took your trouble with you.' The others nodded their agreement.

In a true display of Darnkite loyalty, my neighbours were throwing me out of town at the first hint of danger. But as I considered their words, I realized they were right. Until I knew the truth behind Lombardo's talk of a ten million crown bounty I had no assurance that other bounty hunters would not come looking for me. By remaining here it was very possible that I would put all of Lower Hicksnittle at risk. I had no right to do that.

'Very well,' I said. 'I will go.' The Hicksnittlers breathed a collective sigh of relief. I took the reins of Lombardo's horse and led it to my hut, where I gathered my own axe, some food, my spare shirt, and a few worn books in a leather sack. In the morning I would leave the only home I had ever known.

2

In the dingy land of dunghills that is Darnk, there is but one clean spot – Whiteswab, a pristine little town three days' ride south of Lower Hicksnittle. The actual distance between the two settlements is slight, but there is no road connecting them, a condition satisfying to the inhabitants of both places. Consequently, I had to pick my way along a narrow, overgrown trail surrounded by thorns, brush, and brambles while flies buzzed around my head and gnats attempted to fly up my nose. It was not a pleasant journey. I arrived at Whiteswab near dusk of the third day.

Whiteswab stays clean because the city fathers strictly enforce ordinances against littering, noise, profanity, untucked shirts, and a host of other practices. The penalty for most infractions is swift death by hanging. Whiteswabbers think themselves better than other Darnkites because they bathe daily rather than biannually, as is the normal custom. Other Darnkites think Whiteswabbers are uptight and waste too much water.

In Whiteswab I hoped to learn more about this supposed ten million crown price on my head. Unhospitable as it was, the town was a way station for the trickle of travellers making the trip between Darnk's eastern capital of Ordure and the kingdom's other city of Offal. If the answers were to be found in Darnk, they would be found here.

I was halted at the edge of town by a smiling Sanitary Police officer. He wore a white tunic and was armed with a clipboard and an iron mace.

'Where are you from?' he said insolently. He had to know there was only one possible point of origin for a traveller approaching from the north, but I went along with the charade.

'Lower Hicksnittle.'

His smile grew strained right on cue. 'What business do you have here?'

'I'm just passing through.' Everyone was just passing through Whiteswab. Who would want to stay in such a place?

'Why don't you go around? We don't want your kind here.'

'I want to get a room for the night and a stable for my horse.'

The guard scoffed. 'A stable for both of you, you mean. Got any money?'

My purse was filled with Lombardo's silver. I jingled the bag, then flipped the officer a coin. He bit it to test its authenticity and pocketed it, shaking his head. 'A Hicksnittler with silver – that's a rare sight. Probably got by thievery, but no matter.' He grinned evilly. 'Still, you'll have to bathe before I let you pass.'

Two large bald men with smiley-face tattoos on their heads emerged from the guardhouse, yanked me from the saddle, and tossed me into a small pond by the road. Grinning, they leapt in after me with steel brushes and cakes of lye soap. In a few minutes I was as clean as anyone in Whiteswab. The guard sold me freshly pressed pants and a shirt of cheerful yellow while the bath boys burned my old attire, gleefully stomping the vermin that ran out of it to escape the flames. When I had dressed and combed my hair, use of the comb costing me another silver coin, the guard opened a gate in the white picket fence that surrounded the town.

Whiteswab had perhaps four hundred inhabitants. Their shops and houses, all whitewashed wooden buildings, were arranged in neat rows along freshly swept cobblestoned streets lined with precisely trimmed hedges and plots of bright flowers. Every pedestrian was properly dressed and pleasantly smiling. I left Lombardo's horse at the public stable, took a room at the Whisk Broom Inn, and headed for the main tavern, the Spruce and Span.

14

I scanned the crowd as I entered. The common room bustled with efficient activity as pretty serving maids in demure green dresses brought steaming platters of roast veal, venison, and other viands to the tables along with large mugs of tomato juice and mineral water. Alcohol was outlawed in Whiteswab. There were some twenty patrons present, dining and drinking sullenly despite their legally mandated smiles. I knew they were all wishing for a good jack of stale rutabaga beer like I was. A pair of Sanitary Police sipped buttermilk at the bar and kept an eye on the proceedings.

I spotted a prospective informant drinking alone at a table on the far wall. Olive-skinned and small-framed, he had long hair and a neatly trimmed beard, both the colour of coal. His eyes were hidden by odd mirrored spectacles which reflected the light of the lanterns hanging from the ceiling. He wore a gold leather jerkin over a suit of purple. A high-collared scarlet cloak clung to his shoulders. He looked like a man who had been many places and knew many things. I approached his table.

'May I join you, stranger?' I said with a friendly smile. He tilted his head so that the glasses slid down his nose and studied me with dark-green eyes. The intensity of his scrutiny made me uncomfortable and I wanted to glance away, but couldn't. He lifted his bushy eyebrows and frowned thoughtfully, as if seeing something he didn't understand, then shrugged and gestured for me to sit.

I beckoned the nearest serving maid as I settled into my chair. 'What are you having? I'll buy you another.'

He smiled and swirled the light amber liquid in his thin crystal wine glass. 'I brought my own. Cyrillan Goddess.'

That was the rarest and most expensive wine produced in the Eleven Kingdoms, legendary for its intoxicating powers and supposedly made by magic from grapes of divine origin which grew only in the sun-drenched, southernmost kingdom of Cyrilla. I glanced nervously at the two Sanitary Police officers and ordered a large carrot juice.

'I'm Burlo Stumproot,' I said, just to be safe.

'I'm Mercury Boltblaster, of Caratha.'

Caratha was known as the City at the Centre of the World. Geographically speaking, this was true. Our world of Arden was a great disk floating in an infinite void of space; Caratha, built beside the fair waters of the Indigo Sea, was at the centre of the disk. But the appellation was also accurate whether one referred to the city as a political, commercial, military or cultural centre. The world revolved around Caratha in more ways than one, and a Carathan should be able to tell me much.

'What brings you to Darnk?' I asked.

'I'm avoiding powerful enemies whom I hope won't follow me here to the armpit of the world. I've been pursued through the rest of the Eleven Kingdoms; I figured I might as well finish out the tour.'

'I see.'

'Did you know that only seven of the Eleven Kingdoms are actually kingdoms?'

'No, I didn't realize that.'

'It's true. Zastria is a republic, Stive a theocracy, Xornos an oligarchy, and Ganth is ruled by a military dictator. Why then, do we call them the Eleven Kingdoms?'

'I suppose it would be inconvenient to speak of the Seven Kingdoms and Four Other Assorted Nation Forms.'

'I suppose it would.'

Enough small talk. It was time to get some information. 'Perhaps a man so widely travelled as you has heard something of the great reward for this Jason Cosmo,' I said, trying to sound casual.

'What of it?' he said, sipping his wine.

I was momentarily stunned, not expecting such a casual response to my casual question. I'd hoped the name would mean nothing to him, proving Lombardo to be deranged. 'News here is often incomplete,' I said quickly. 'Who is this Cosmo? Who posted the bounty?'

'They say he's sought by a consortium of merchants who have pooled their resources to offer the reward. Their agents wait in every significant city, authorized to grant a letter of credit for ten million crowns to whomsoever brings him in, dead or alive. It's set off the largest manhunt in history.'

16

The serving girl brought my juice and I took a deep draft while I thought that over. Obviously, I was not the Jason Cosmo this consortium wanted, but with ten million crowns at stake I could expect frequent trouble from greedy bounty hunters confusing me with my mysterious namesake. It might be expedient to change my name, though I'd have to come up with a better alias than Burlo Stumproot. 'They want him badly,' I observed. 'What has he done?'

'I don't know,' said Mercury. 'I hear he's a fearsome warrior who eats babies for breakfast, drinks blood like wine, and has a harem of she-demon lovers. Tall tales, no doubt. He's either the most terrible rogue ever to walk the earth or he doesn't exist at all.'

'How could he not exist?'

'It doesn't take much effort. Suppose this whole business is an elaborate charade designed to distract attention from some dark plotting. Post a reward, spread rumours, and human nature does the rest. The legend grows. That's what I think – I mean, you never even heard the name Jason Cosmo until this past year, did you?'

'Ah . . . no.'

'A strong hint that the man is a fable. But an attractive fable. The best in the bounty-hunting profession hunt this phantom.'

'Like who?' I felt a leaden ball of dread forming in the pit of my stomach.

'Like BlackMoon and the Red Huntsman. They are both rumoured to be in Brythalia now. They'll sweep Darnk next, I suppose, though this is the last place I'd expect to find anyone of importance – including myself.'

I nearly choked on my juice. I had heard of BlackMoon and the Red Huntsman. Arch-rivals, they had reputations for utter ruthlessness. Each would do anything to bring in his man before the other. BlackMoon, according to the stories, could see in the dark and hear a whisper a mile away, while the Red Huntsman used a pack of huge wolves for hunting dogs. If Lombardo had found me, they would. They were not the sort of men I could easily toss down a well. I was definitely going to change my name.

'But enough of that,' said Mercury. 'Are you a farmer here-abouts?'

'Yes. Turnips.'

'I see.' He smiled sarcastically. 'And how is this year's crop looking?'

I started to reply, but noticed my companion was no longer paying attention. He was staring intently at the entrance with his mouth drawn taut. He pushed his spectacles back in place and I turned to see what had caught his eye.

Three soldiers wearing black tunics had entered the tavern. They weren't Sanitary Police, and didn't look like regular army. I wasn't sure Darnk even had a regular army. The emblem on their bucklers was of crossed black lightning bolts, a sign I didn't recognize. They fanned out as they crossed the room, hands on the hilts of their swords. The Sanitary Police at the bar went for their maces, but froze at a sharp glance from one of the trio, not knowing what authority the newcomers represented.

Mercury sprang to his feet and spread his arms wide.

'Take him!' barked the leader. 'And his contact too!'

I realized he meant me and tried to get up, but Mercury's outstretched arm prevented me. The soldiers drew their broadswords and charged across the room. A serving girl screamed as she was knocked to the floor, spilling a tray of full mugs. Patrons whipped their heads around in confusion. The Sanitary Police lifted their maces, but still weren't sure who to attack.

'Shield your eyes!' hissed Mercury. I obeyed as the room was filled with a flash of intense white light from my companion's face. Shouts of dismay went up as everyone else in the room was struck blind. My own vision was filled with hazy coloured spots, as if I had just looked directly at the noonday sun.

'What happened?' I asked, speaking loudly to be heard over the outraged shouts of the patrons. The owner was shushing urgently, not wanting to lose his business licence on a noise violation.

'Sunshades,' said a blurry image of Mercury. 'The sunlight which the lenses absorb by day can be released in several different ways at my command. But the effect is only tempo-rary. You should recover in a few minutes.' He tucked the sunshades under his cloak.

'Are you a wizard?' I asked, utterly amazed by what I had just seen. I had never witnessed an act of magic, never met anyone who practised that art. Darnk had rather unprogressive views on things arcane.

'Good guess, Burlo. What gave it away?' Mercury's clothing seemed to have turned uniformſy black. This worried me, but I didn't mention it, hoping my eyes would clear up soon. He grabbed my arm. 'We'd better go – they'll want you too.'

'Who will? What's going on?'

'I'll show you.' We crossed to the door in quick strides, threading our way carefully between the blinded soldiers, who swung their swords wildly in an effort to strike us. We stepped outside together and were met by seven swordsmen dressed like the ones inside, their weapons gleaming in the light of the street lanterns. The leader was a swarthy, heavy-set man with gold braid on his shoulder.

'I think we went the wrong way,' I said, blinking.

'Not at all.'

The leader laughed arrogantly. 'Mercury Boltblaster, it looks like I've got you this time – and a League lackey to boot. Isogoras will be pleased.' Two more soldiers emerged from the tavern behind us, having entered from the back to seal the trap. We were surrounded.

'This is Dylan of Ganth,' said Mercury, as if describing an odd specimen in a zoo. 'He's an idiot hired by Isogoras the Xornite to capture me, a task hopelessly beyond his compe-tence.'

'Who's Isogoras the Xornite?'

'A member of the Dark Magic Society, of course.'

A chill ran down my spine at his mention of the dreaded Society. The Dark Magic Society was an ancient, secret order of evil wizards who plotted to conquer all the Eleven Kingdoms, unleash the demons of the Assorted Hells to walk the world of men, and probably raise taxes as well. Granted, we didn't see much direct evidence of the Society's activities in Darnk, but we knew they were out there, eternally scheming. What had I blundered into?

A heavy net with barbed weights enveloped us from above and two more men leaped down from the roof of the Spruce and Span to shove us to the ground. 'Your insults are empty bluster now, wizard!' said Dylan.

'The sad thing,' said Mercury, 'is that he probably thinks this is clever, just like he thought all his other plans were so clever.'

'Clever enough to net you!' Dylan was getting red in the face.

'This is the the most weak-minded excuse for a capture I've ever encountered,' said Mercury.

'Shut up, wizard! Shut up! I've had enough of your needling!' Dylan aimed a sharp kick at the kneeling wizard, but it failed to connect as the net flew off of us and wrapped itself tightly around the mercenary, the momentum throwing him to the street.

'Kill the bastard!' screamed Dylan, flopping on the pavement. 'Kill them both!'

Dylan's men closed ranks as Mercury and I got to our feet. We stood back to back and waited for one of the Black Bolts to make a move. Ten against two were not promising odds. I assumed Mercury would use more magical power to extricate us from the situation, preferably by turning all the Black Bolts into frogs. I understood wizards to be good at that sort of thing.

'I can't afford to use more magic right now,' whispered Mercury. 'It might attract unwanted attention.'

'We have plenty of unwanted attention anyway.'

'Trust me. We'll just have to hold them off until the local authorities arrive.'

'They won't help. We're disturbing the peace. They hang you for that here.'

'They do?'

My eyesight was back to normal, but I didn't like what I was seeing. The mercenaries were toying with us, shifting position to keep us guessing where the attack would come from. Dylan continued to roll about and scream insults at Mercury.

'Yes. They do. Of course, they'd probably burn you, you being a wizard.'

'They still burn wizards here?' He seemed amazed.

'Yes.'

'How quaint. That changes things, of course.' He weaved past the nearest man's guard and dropped him with an up-thrust hand that shattered the soldier's nose and knocked him senseless. Spinning in place, the wizard brought down a second mercenary with a rib-crushing kick, ducked under a flashing blade, and broke a third man's swordarm while snatching the sword from his grasp. It was an incredible display of speed and skill.

As Mercury disembowelled a fourth man and half-severed the arm of a fifth, a trio of Black Bolts came at me. I scrambled away from them and found myself backed against the wall of the Spruce and Span, dodging the deadly swings of three swords. 'You've got to do better than that!' said the wizard. A fallen soldier's sword and shield flew into my hands.

'Wasn't that magic?' I said, clumsily blocking a blow.

Mercury ran a soldier through and engaged another as he said, 'Yes. You looked like you needed help.'

'Use more!'

'Sorry.'

A Black Bolt grazed my arm, drawing blood. I swung my sword, threw myself off balance, and barely recovered in time to avoid being beheaded.

'I don't know how to use these things!'

'Learn fast.'

I would never have learned fast enough to save myself. A squad of Sanitary Police charged into the fray, swinging their heavy maces and forcing my attackers back. I dropped the sword and shield and tried to look peaceful.

'Let's go!' said Mercury, finishing his opponent and grabbing my arm. He pulled me around the corner into an alley, where we found fourteen saddled black horses.

'I figured Dylan's men would leave their mounts nearby,' said Mercury. He quickly selected the two strongest look-ing.

'My belongings are still—'

'Forget them.' The Sanitary Police were coming our way.
I saw the wisdom of his suggestion. We mounted and rode
out the other end of the alley at a full gallop, jumping the
picket fence and heading west into the forest. I was full of
questions, but it seemed best to hold them until we made
good our escape.

3

We rode hard for twenty minutes down the dark forest road,
finally slowing our pace when we realized there was no
immediate pursuit. The Sanitary Police and the Black Bolts
were evidently too busy with each other to worry about
us.

'I think we're clear,' I said, looking back.

'Excellent,' said Mercury. 'Now you can tell me who you
really are.'

'What do you mean?' I asked, afraid the wizard was reading
my mind. 'I'm Burlo Stumproot, humble and confused turnip
farmer.'

'Nonsense. I'll grant your peasant disguise is a good one, but
you must be from the League.'

'What league is that?'

'The League of Benevolent Magic, of course, though we both
know your vaunted benevolence is but a sham.'

'I don't even know what you're talking about.' Actually I
had heard of the League of Benevolent Magic, an organization
of good wizards dedicated to combating the evil Society and
working to make the world a better place through the power
of magic, but I knew very little about them. All magic was
considered bad in Darnk and had been ever since the wizard
Gorgibund the Ghastly had laid waste to the whole kingdom
after being insulted by King Septic I two hundred years ago.
Until that time, Darnk had been a scenic, if rough-hewn, little
kingdom popular with wealthy vacationers from the south.
But the land had never recovered from Gorgibund's devasta-
tion and its permanent ugliness was a constant reminder of

the awful destructive power wizards could wield. So was the massacre of Blacks Bolts I had witnessed in Whiteswab. I would have to speak carefully.

Mercury eyed me suspiciously. 'Are you saying you're not from the League?'

'I'm not even a magician.'

'Interesting. I took you for a League recruiter in peasant guise. However, if you were a League lackey, you would already be lecturing me about my duty to use my magical powers for the benefit of all mankind. Therefore you are not from the League – but your name certainly isn't Burlo Stumproot, is it?'

'Well . . . no.'

'So who are you?'

I swallowed hard and decided to take a chance on the truth. Something about this wizard, despite his sarcastic manner and demonstrated deadliness, made him seem trustworthy. 'My name is Jason Cosmo.'

'Jason Cosmo?' He was suddenly bewildered.

'Yes.'

'I didn't think you existed.'

'I don't. I mean, I'm not the Jason Cosmo the bounty is for. I'm just a woodcutter from Lower Hicksnittle.'

'Well, you must be a supernatural woodcutter. Your aura is the oddest I've ever seen.'

'My aura?'

'Aura. Auric script. The invisible glowing gold letters superimposed on a person's face which, to those who can read them, reveal his magical power level, emotional state, and other qualities of character.' He recited the words like a dictionary definition, as if he were a professor lecturing a class at a college of magic. 'I read yours in the tavern. Tried to read it, that is. It isn't even written in the standard Auric Alphabet. It's just a lot of fine print and gobbledygook.'

'That's news to me.'

'What I'm wondering is why the Dark Magic Society would offer ten million crowns for a Darnkite woodcutter with a messed up aura.'

'The Society? You said a consortium—'

'That's the gossip. I know better. What could Erimandras want with you?'

'Who is Erimandras?'

'The new Overmaster of the Society. He came to power in the last few years and the Society has been unusually active since then. I don't know much about him, except that he's said to be brilliant, powerful and utterly ruthless. Of course, most Overmasters of the Society have fit that description. See what you're up against?'

'I'm the wrong Jason Cosmo.'

'Your aura suggests otherwise. Why did you seek me out?'

'It was coincidence. A bounty hunter named Lombardo attacked me in my village. I went to Whiteswab to try and learn why.'

'Now you know.' He frowned in concentration. I grew nervous.

'You aren't going to take me in for the bounty, are you?'

He laughed. 'No. You've seen how I get along with the Society and their minions.' He frowned again. 'You're lucky you live in such a backwater kingdom. Still, BlackMoon or the Huntsman will get here eventually. They've been systematically combing every square yard of the Eleven Kingdoms looking for you.'

'I see.' I still wanted to believe I was a victim of mistaken identity, but I knew with groundless certainty that the wizard was right. I was the one the Society wanted. I felt the truth of that statement in the core of my being.

'Our situations are similar,' said Mercury. 'Except that the Society has sent a band of incompetents after me while you are stalked by the greatest hunters in the world. Also, I'm an experienced wizard who has travelled far and wide and trained with the finest masters of fencing and unarmed combat in the world whereas you are but an illiterate—'

'I can read.'

'Whereas you are but a barely literate—'

'And write. Quite well.'

'Whereas you are an unusually literate Darnkite peasant who can't handle a sword and has probably never ventured this far from home in your life.'

24

'I'll concede that. Of course, I'm pretty good with an axe.'

'Do you have an axe?'

'Not anymore.'

'Offhand, I'd say you're a dead man if they ever find you.'

'I'd agree.'

'With me, you might have a chance, but that would just make it more convenient for them to get us both at once. It would be foolish of me to take on your problems, considering I'm limited in my use of magic.'

'What do you mean by limited?'

'Take tonight. I could have obliterated the Black Bolts – or the whole town – with a single spell. But spellcasting requires that I draw on the ambient magical energy field of this world. Each act of magic creates a disturbance in that field, like the ripples in a pond when you throw a stone in. If I make too big a splash, the Society can pinpoint my location and send overwhelming force against me. I have to exercise restraint and rely on my other skills for survival.'

'They seem adequate.'

'They usually are. But so far I've been of minor concern to the Society. They've only sent the Xornite after me. With a truly concerted effort, they could force me into a join or die situation.'

'What will you do then?'

'Die, but that's not the point. I'd like to avoid that dilemma and you may be the key.'

'Me? How?'

'For the Society to want you badly enough to put up ten million crowns, your capture is vital to one of their plots, or else you're a grave threat to their existence. I suspect the latter, since they prefer to economize on plots when they can.'

'How can I possibly threaten the Society?'

'Your aura. Obviously it contains information dangerous to them. If I could learn what it says, perhaps I can use the information against them.'

'Why would my aura—'

'I don't know. Listen to what I'm saying. I'll protect you until we learn what your aura says. Then, if the information is useful, I'll use it to get the Society off both our backs. Your alternative is inevitable capture probably followed by a slow, gruesome death by torture. What do you say?'

'I accept your offer.'

'You're a smart man, Cosmo.'

'How are we going to read my aura? You already tried.'

'I know an aura specialist in Raelna,' he said, with a faint wistfulness. 'If anyone can read it, she can.'

'She?'

'Whatever the case in Darnk, it is not unheard of for women to practise the magic profession in the more advanced kingdoms.'

'Here in Darnk, it's unheard of for anyone to practise the magic profession,' I pointed out.

'True. This place is backward in many ways. Economic stagnation, limited cultural activities, military weakness, diplomatic ineptitude—'

'I get the point.'

'Sorry.' He held out his hand and we shook. 'The bargain is sealed,' he said formally. 'You are now under the protection of Mercury Boltblaster. You can call me Merc.'

'You can call me Jason.'

'I'd rather not.'

'Fine. So why is the Dark Magic Society after you?'

'It's a long story. The Society has had but one goal since it rose from the ashes of the Empire of Fear a thousand years ago – world domination. Their chief opponents have always been the members of the League of Benevolent Magic. In the old days the Society and the League had kings and generals at their beck and call. They could start wars on a whim if it furthered their purposes. Things happened on a much grander scale than they do today.'

'Why the decline? And what does this have to do with you?'

'I'm getting to that. The two groups simply wore themselves out with their constant battling. They expended tremendous amounts of manpower, energy and wealth trying to best one another and succeeded only in producing a stalemate which lasted for centuries. Now the conflict is mainly limited to the wizards; kings and generals start their own wars. That's how it concerns me. I'm a wizard of arcane master rank and—'

'What does that mean?'

'It means I'm a master of magic. One of the best. There are less than a hundred of us in all the Eleven Kingdoms. Naturally, both the League and the Society would like to have as many master wizards on their side as possible, but I refuse to serve either.'

'Why?'

'Because I don't care about their struggle. I grant that the Society is evil, but I don't think the League is much better. They're less bloodthirsty, but just as ruthless. They rely on the same kinds of tactics, they have the same goals of power and influence – they just won't admit it the way the Society does. I don't want anything to do with either group. Unfortunately, they won't take no for an answer. The League keeps sending its lackeys to lecture me; the Society has Isogoras the Xornite on my trail.'

'And the Black Bolts.'

'They were hired by Isogoras. You have to understand that Isogoras and I are enemies from way back. He's terrified of me. He won't face me personally, so he gets others to do the job for him.'

'I see.'

'Tell me more about yourself, Cosmo. It might give me a clue to your sudden popularity.'

'Until a few days ago I was just an ordinary Darnkite peasant. My parents died when I was fifteen. In the seven years since, I've supported myself farming turnips and cutting wood.'

'No wife? No family?'

'No. Nothing like that. Are you married?'

Merc looked as if I had suddenly choked him. He scowled bitterly for a moment and then shook his head almost imperceptibly. We rode in silence after that. I had evidently yanked on a very raw nerve.

After ten minutes or so, I noticed the road ahead was shrouded in a faintly shining mist. In fact, looking around, I saw that the mist filled the forest on all sides and covered the way we had just come. I heard an eerie mechanical hum.

'Something strange is happening,' I pointed out.

'Indeed.' Mercury peered ahead intently, perhaps using some magical vision I lacked. 'There's a light.'

I could see it. It was a soft amber glow penetrating the fog at what seemed to be a great distance. We rode towards it cautiously, the hum growing ever louder. The mist dissipated in our immediate vicinity as we progressed while always remaining thick just a few yards away. I gradually perceived the outlines of a small cottage. As we drew nearer I heard the rhythmic wooden creaking of a rocking chair. We halted before the porch and saw that the chair was occupied by an old man in faded denim overalls. His grey beard was gathered in his lap, his bald head creased with wrinkles, his blind eyes covered by a milky film. Beside him was a small machine that looked like a bucket with gears and a bellows on top. It was pumping out clouds of the shining mist. The amber light came from a small lantern hanging on a rusty nail in the wall. The old man spoke.

'Greetings, Jason Cosmo. Greetings, Mercury Boltblaster. I am He Who Sits On The Porch and I know many things.'

'Like what?' asked Merc, visibly unimpressed.

The old man smiled. 'I see what others don't. My function is to share that knowledge with selected heroes, to guide them in their endeavours.'

He was obviously a being of great power and we were obviously in the wrong place. 'We're sorry to have disturbed you,' I said. 'We lost our way in the mist and—'

'Nonsense, boy! You're not lost.' He stopped rocking and leaned forward. 'I have revealed myself to you for a purpose.'

'There must be a mistake,' said Merc. 'We're not heroes.'

'Of course not,' said the old man. 'You're just a woodcutter and a wizard out for an evening ride, not two men on the run from the Dark Magic Society, the most thoroughly wicked gang of thugs and would-be world conquerors in history.' He resumed his rocking.

'That sounds accurate,' I said, nodding.

'But it doesn't make us heroes,' added Merc quickly.

'I know about you and your bad attitude,' said He Who Sits On The Porch to the wizard. 'But you would be wise to listen to me. Great events are in motion and the two of you have an integral role to play.'

'You've got to be kidding,' sneered Merc.

'Silence! My time here is limited and I have much to relate before the Demon Lords are able to penetrate my obscuring fog and discover my presence.'

'What have the Demon Lords got to do with us?' asked Merc, suddenly interested.

'That got your attention, didn't it? The Demon Lords, they who rule the various regions of the Assorted Hells, have placed their infernal legions on full alert and are carefully watching events on the mortal plane. They fear an invasion of their domain.'

'Then why watch our world? None but The Gods have the power to invade the Hells.'

'It is not The Gods they fear, but one of their own. Enough of that! It suffices to know that the Demon Lords watch and it is Jason Cosmo they seek.'

'Me? Why?'

'The invasion feared by the Demon Lords can only come about if you fall into the hands of the Society. If the Demon Lords locate and eliminate you first, they can prevent the war they fear.'

'I thought the Society served the Demon Lords,' I said.

'In the past they have cooperated with the Lords Below, but the Society serves only itself. At the present time, the purposes of the Overmaster Erimandras conflict with the purposes of the Hellmasters. I know you are filled with questions, but they must wait. The Gods desire to help you, but their options are limited. I have been sent to tell you, however, that you are now a hero.'

'I feel more like a target.'

'You don't understand. Each person has a station in life and must obey the rules of his given role. A woodcutter behaves as a woodcutter, a fisherman as a fisherman, and so forth. This is divine law. But as a woodcutter you have little chance for surviving your current circumstances. The Gods have therefore removed your name from the Roll of Woodcutters and entered you in the Roll of Heroes. As a hero you have a greater probability of survival. You are allowed to make daring escapes, overcome great odds, survive certain death – useful perks like that. I've been sent to inform you of this change so you can behave accordingly.'

'This all seems a little arbitrary,' I insisted. 'I'm no theologian, but I didn't think The Gods could—'

'They can. My time is nearly up. Jason Cosmo, you and your companion must reach the land of Raelna, where your aura may be deciphered. Allies await you there and the nature of your task will be made clearer.'

'Task? What task?'

'I must go now. Proceed quietly and do not call attention to yourself. Above all, be heroic.' His blind eyes seemed to bore directly into mine as he spoke his next words. 'A great many people are depending on you.'

4

The fog swirled thickly around the cottage, obscuring the light of the amber lantern, wrapping itself so tightly that I couldn't see Mercury or even the horn of my saddle.

In a few moments the mist parted and we found ourselves on a grassy slope looking west to a small, unsightly city. Afternoon sunlight fell dully on the swift, muddy river which flowed past its drab stone walls. A caravan of wagons from the south road was passing into the city through the main gates, which faced us. I felt refreshed, as after a good night's rest.

'That's Offal,' said Mercury, putting on his sunshades. 'A two day ride from where we were last night – assuming only one night passed while we were under the old man's spell. He seems to have given us a nice lead on the Black Bolts. We'll get supplies here and head for Brythalia.' He was acting as if our arrival here was normal. To him, maybe it was. Not to me. I had plenty of questions.

'How did we get here?'

Merc shrugged. 'Who knows? It doesn't matter. That old man was a messenger of The Gods, meaning he has powers beyond mortal comprehension. No point, therefore, in trying to comprehend them.' He started his horse forward.

'What did the old man mean about the Society not serving the Demon Lords? I thought that was their whole purpose – to bring the Demon Lords back to power, like they were in the time of the Empire of Fear.'

Merc assumed his lecture voice. 'The Demon Lords hate each other and compete for supremacy. You can't speak of them as a united group the way you can speak of The Gods. The Society forms temporary alliances with the various Lords as it suits them, but it does not serve them nor seek to restore their former glory. Actually, there would not have been an Empire of Fear if the great Asmodraxas had not mastered his fellow Lords. His power alone brought the Age of Despair but he has long since fallen and vanished from the ken . . .' His voice trailed off.

'What is it?'

'That's what the old man meant! The Demon Lords fear the return of Asmodraxas!'

'You just said he vanished.'

'I'm certain you've heard the legend of the Mighty Champion?'

'Well, sure. Every child knows that he led the Great Rebellion which brought down the Empire and began the Age of Hope in which we now live.'

The priests taught that this was the fifth age since Arden's creation. Each age lasted a thousand years, from the pristine Age of Nature which followed the Creation, to the idyllic Age of Peace during which humanity enjoyed a perfect, albeit boring, society. This was followed by the arrival of the Demon Lords from Somewhere Else and the cataclysmic Age of War. After a thousand years of stalemate, The Gods and the Demon Lords called a truce and agreed to withdraw from worldly events under the terms of the Great Eternal Pan-Cosmic Holy/Unholy Non-Intervention Pact. The Gods honoured the agreement, the demons did not. The result was the misery and agony of the Age of Despair. The Demon Lords walked Arden freely and established an Empire of Fear. Finally, The Gods could take no more and sent a

Mighty Champion to end the reign of evil and bring a new age of freedom, renewal and hope.

'The Champion learned the secret of Asmodraxas's power and used it to banish him from universe, locked in a prison he can never escape. Only then could the Great Rebellion succeed.'

'What was the secret?'

'The Superwand, a magical talisman created at the Dawn of Time by a powerful race of fluffy pink rabbits older even than The Gods. Asmodraxas stole it from the rabbits and used it to further his schemes of universal conquest. The Mighty Champion stole it from Asmodraxas and hid it so that it could never be found. But suppose the Society rediscovers it. They could free Asmodraxas, who would then try to reclaim his former position.'

'Why would they do that?'

'The Society wants to restore the Dark Empire, but none of the current Demon Lords can bring that about. Asmodraxas can. He is the one Lord they *would* serve and worship. If they can free him, they will.'

'How would they find this Superwand if it's hidden so well?' I said. Mercury gazed at me silently, thoughtfully. 'Wait. You don't think that I – that my aura – that I've got the secret?'

'That's *exactly* what I think. It makes perfect sense. For some unknown reason the secret shows up in your aura, the Society gets wind of it, and the hunt is on.'

We said no more on the subject, retreating into our individual thoughts. As we rode down the hill, the last of the wagons rolled into the city. A few minutes later, the main gates swung shut and the handful of guards visible on the wall seemed to collapse like puppets whose strings had been cut. Though I didn't know much about military matters, I was sure that wasn't normal procedure.

It was the custom in many walled towns to close the gates at sundown, but that was still hours away. Darnk was neither a prime target of invasion – two nations once fought a bitter war to avoid having to take possession of it – nor a major centre of bandit activity and this degree of security was a bit much.

We reined in our horses and studied the twin gates. Each was fifteen feet high and plated with iron. The twenty-foot wall itself was built of light grey stone blocks and formed a square set against the banks of the Longwash River. It was surmounted by battlements and sported a squat watch tower at each corner. We heard no activity within. There was, in fact, no sound but the snuffling of our horses, as if we had come by mistake to a city of the dead.

'Maybe it's time for their afternoon nap,' I suggested.

'Maybe we'd better keep riding,' said Merc. He turned his horse and started south.

'Wait! Shouldn't we investigate?'

'Why?' said Merc, without turning around. 'We have problems of our own. No need to meddle in someone else's. Haste is now essential.'

'People might be in danger. We ought to at least alert the proper authorities.'

'This is the sub-capital of the kingdom. I'm sure the proper authorities are well aware of whatever is happening in there.'

'We should get word to the king,' I protested.

Merc stopped and turned his horse. 'Cosmo, Ordure is four days travel to the east. That's back toward the Black Bolts and the Sanitary Police, whom we would like to avoid. By the time we reach the royal court, assuming we do and assuming Fecal IV doesn't throw you in his dungeon and collect the bounty, the situation here will have surely run its course. So what's the point of getting involved?'

'It's the right thing to do. The old man told me to act like a hero. I think a hero would investigate.'

'They made you a hero to help you survive, not so you could go looking for trouble. We have no obligations to the people of Offal.'

'You seem to have no obligations to anyone beyond yourself!'

'You have captured the essence of my philosophy perfectly. Both our interests are best served by reaching Raelna as quickly as possible. I'm sure you'll have many opportunities to play hero before we get there.'

'I'm not playing at anything. Something is wrong in there

and I'm concerned. That's all.'

'Ah, do you have friends or relatives in Offal?'

'No.'

'Then what is your problem?'

'My problem is I'm not going one mile further until we find out what is happening in this city!' I was surprised at my own forcefulness, but I knew I was right.

'Be serious.'

'I am.'

We stared at each other for a long moment. It was like looking a big bug in the face since I couldn't see his eyes through the sunshades. For all I knew he was changing his mind about helping me and was about to disintegrate me instead. But I held my ground. If fellow Darnkites were in trouble I at least had to find out what the problem was. Still, my heart pounded.

Merc finally sighed in exasperation and rode back toward me. 'Okay, we'll go in and take a quick look. I don't think any good will come of this, but we can't sit here and debate all day.'

'Great. How do we get in?'

Merc dismounted and pulled a grappling hook and a coil of rope from beneath his cloak. He swung the hook and threw it at the wall, where it caught on the parapet and held. 'After you.'

'Where did that come from?'

'From beneath my cloak.'

'I saw that, but you didn't have it before. There's no room.'

'This is a magic cloak. Very roomy. I have a tent in there too.'

'Oh. By the way, wasn't your whole outfit just solid black? It's light gray now.' It was, in fact, the same shade of gray as the city wall.

Merc shrugged. 'Must be a trick of the light.'

'Are you sure?'

'Look, my clothing is magic too. It's from Raelna, which has a thriving magical textile industry. My outfit can be any colour or fashion I desire, mends itself, and always stays clean.'

'You're kidding!'

'Do you want to talk about clothes or climb the wall?'

I dismounted, tested the rope, and began to climb. It only took me a few seconds to reach the top, where I found the fallen bodies of four city guards. There were no signs of violence upon them. Merc joined me on the wall and knelt to examine one of the soldiers. He peeled his eyelids open, felt for a pulse, and bent his ear close to the man's mouth to listen for breathing.

'Is he alive?' I asked.

Merc nodded. 'It's dormadose. A magical gas which induces a restful sleep of a day's duration.'

'I didn't see any gas.'

'It's invisible, but smells faintly of raspberry. I don't like this at all. It reminds me of—' He lapsed into deep thought.

I sniffed the air and did indeed detect a faint raspberry scent amid the smells of garbage and decay, though whether it was due to the power of suggestion I wasn't sure.

'Let's take a closer look,' said Merc suddenly. I didn't believe my ears. He led the way down the stairs built into the back of the wall, suddenly much more interested in this mystery than I was.

From the gates, the main street of Offal ran straight about a hundred yards and widened into a large square paved with yellow flagstones. The square, strewn with rotting refuse, featured a public fountain and a collection of stinking market stalls, where craftsmen and traders hawked their wares, at least on normal days. Six caravan wagons were drawn up there, filled with crates and barrels, but untended. The draft animals were still in harness, though asleep like every other person and animal in sight.

Several narrow secondary streets and alleys, also cluttered with garbage, radiated outwards from the square, winding into shadow between various shops and apartment houses, none higher than two stories. The main avenue continued west to the blockish keep, which towered above the rest of the city, being some eighty feet above the ground at its highest point. There lived Governor Paulish Birksnore, the king's deputy in charge of this half of Darnk. Four more wagons were parked at intervals along the street, the last just outside the entrance to the keep.

We walked down to the square, stepping gingerly over the comatose bodies which littered the ground, and approached the wagons. Merc climbed aboard the last one in line and rummaged through the crates, all of which were empty, until he found a blue metal canister six inches in diameter and a foot high. Its top featured a conical nozzle and a little metal lever.

'This is a pressure canister, only available in the more advanced kingdoms,' said Merc grimly. 'The gas is kept inside, under pressure. When the nozzle is opened, it sprays the gas out over an area of several hundred yards. One of these fired from each wagon would be enough to put the whole city to sleep. Especially on a windless day like today.'

'But what about the caravanners? Wouldn't they be affected too?'

'Not if they wore protective masks or took an antidote beforehand.'

'So where are they?'

In reply to my question, an arrow thunked into a crate beside Merc, who dove out of the wagon, and did a handspring which ended in a crouch. The archer, having appeared on a rooftop across the square, notched another arrow into place and fired again as we crawled under the wagon for cover.

'Damn!' said Merc. 'I was careless! We were under observation from the moment we entered the city. We're probably surrounded by now.'

'How do you figure that?'

Five more arrows struck the wagon above us and the flagstone near by. They came from five different angles and directions. Merc spread his hands in a 'see what I mean' gesture.

'So what do we do?'

'Think fast.'

Half a dozen burly men were approaching from the direction of the palace, armed with swords, clubs and maces. After seeing Merc handle the Black Bolts, I didn't doubt we could take them – but the archers were another matter. If we got into a brawl, they'd simply pick us off at leisure.

'My shades aren't fully recharged yet,' said Merc. 'All I can do is give a couple of them a sunburn.'

'Could you make this wagon roll on its own?' I asked.

'Yes.' Merc's face lit up and he tucked his shades back under his cloak. 'Yes indeed!'

The peg attaching the tongue to the wagon flew out at Merc's mental command, freeing us from the dead weight of the slumbering draft horses. Merc and I clung to the underside of the wagon, wedging our fingers between the cracks in the floor planks. It rolled backwards, gathering speed as it headed for the main gate. Arrows struck the sides and top, but we were safe underneath. The approaching thugs broke into a run.

'Can you go any faster?' I asked. 'They're gaining on us!'

'The least of our worries!' said Merc. Another troop of brigands was charging toward us from the direction of the gates. An archer was among them, and he knelt to aim his arrows under the wagon, directly at our dragging bodies. Merc made the wagon swerve back and forth to deny him a clear shot. As our speed increased, this manoeuvering threatened to sling us out into the street.

A burning arrow hit the wagon and caused the empty wooden crates to burst into roaring flame. I felt my fingers blister as the planks I gripped grew hot.

'They mean business,' said Merc.

'Can you open the gates?' At the speed we had now reached, I didn't want to crash.

'One thing at a time!' The brigands ahead of us scattered as the flaming wagon bore down on them, then pursued us along with the others. Merc drove the wagon almost to the gates, then swung a hard right and brought it to a sudden halt. Inertia slammed us both to the ground. We were at the base of the stairway. Keeping low, we scrambled up the steps until we encountered several pairs of boots in our field of vision. We looked up into three drawn bows as the crowd pursuing us gathered around the burning wagon at the base of the wall.

'Suggestions?' I said.

'We surrender,' said Merc. 'For now.'

Two caravanners seized us and marched us along the wall toward the palace. The archers were right behind us so we didn't try anything foolish as we were led up a winding staircase and into the governor's top floor office. It was lit by an open skylight, with additional light from the balcony overlooking the city. The rotund governor, wearing a thread-bare green robe, was sprawled on the rug asleep. In his chair sat another man, his feet propped on the governor's desk. Behind him stood a living mountain.

I had never seen anyone so large – ten feet tall and over a yard wide at the chest. His neck, arms, thighs, and hands were of similar proportions. He wore only a black loincloth, reveal-ing the vast, muscular expanses of his mottled grey skin. His square face was pocked and scarred, made uglier by his filmy yellow eyes, beetled brow, sneering purple lips and jagged brown teeth. Most grotesque of all was his greasy blond hair, which hung to his shoulders and was knotted around a human rib.

The man at the governor's desk had dark olive skin and close-cropped black hair. A long white scar ran down his left cheek. He wore bright-yellow boots, pantaloons with vertical purple-and-white stripes, a wide red sash, and a loose black shirt open at the chest. Gold bracelets, rings, and ear-rings decorated the appropriate parts of his body.

'What is it?' he demanded.

An archer saluted with his fist. 'Interlopers, commander. They scaled the wall and investigated the wagons. We believe they are wizards.'

'Why?' said the commander.

'They made a wagon roll around on its own.'

The commander laughed and looked us over with disdain. 'A truly fearsome power. Wizards indeed! These are spies sent by the corrupt tyrant of this backwater kingdom to interfere with our glorious revolutionary activities. Yes, I know their ilk.' He stood and, clasping his hands behind his back, strutted toward us. 'I am Zaran Zimzabar, Supreme Commander of the People's Army of the New Glorious Order – PANGO. It is our mission to liberate the oppressed classes from all outmoded forms of society and government. I represent a new world order of universal brotherhood.'

'You're a lunatic,' said Merc. He turned to me and con-tinued in the same pedantic manner he had used when describing Dylan. 'This is just who I suspected we'd find here. Zaran here is a notorious terrorist responsible for dozens of assassinations, hijackings, kidnappings and massacres. He kills women, children, nobles, peasants and barnyard animals without remorse, all in the name of his twisted ideology. He's mentally sick.'

'I see,' I said uneasily. While I could believe everything Merc was saying, it seemed unwise for him to be saying it in our current situation.

'You have heard of me then?' said Zaran, evidently pleased at Merc's denunciation. He stopped before the wizard.

'Some of your past victims were friends of mine,' said Merc. 'What brings you to Darnk? Run out of babies to butcher in the civilized realms?'

'My mission knows no boundaries,' said Zaran, strutting anew. 'Eventually the demands of history will bring all lands under my sway. I have come here to claim this ill-protected pimple of corruption called Offal in the name of the New Glorious Order. It shall be renamed Zaranopolis and its people freed from their bondage to foul monarchy so that they may serve PANGO. This place shall be a haven for my cause, a training ground for my cadres, a base from which to strike numerous blows for liberation!' He leaned against the desk and crossed his arms. 'But, meanwhile, what am I to do with you?' Zaran nodded toward the figure behind him. 'Yezgar here is the son of a woman raped by an ogre. He enjoys killing. He would enjoy killing you. Can you give me a reason to let you live?'

'Give us just a second,' I said quickly, before Mercury could insult our captor again. Good reasons for our continued existence filled my mind like exploding kernels of popcorn.

Before I could share them two glass balls dropped into the room from the skylight above and shattered on the floor, filling the air with hazy fumes that made me choke and cough and my eyes burn. Through my tears, I saw the attacker jump down into the room.

She looked like a goddess of war. As tall as me, her every firm curve was outlined in silver sheen by an armoured bodysuit of metallic cloth. Most of her tan face was hidden by a winged helmet, but what I could see was grim and lovely, dominated by red lips drawn taut. She wielded a gleaming broadsword in her right hand, a small hand axe in her left, and had an array of other knives and blades strapped to her arms, thighs and calves.

'You are finished, Zaran Zimzabar!' she said. 'Natalia Slash has found you at last!'

5

My eyes burned like hellfire and I could barely breathe. Zaran, Merc and Zaran's men were also incapacitated. Not so Yezgar. The half-ogre sprang across the chamber with a bellowing roar and swung a massive fist at Natalia Slash. She deftly sidestepped it and hurled her hand axe into the monster's chest. Undaunted, he swung again, this time connecting and knocking Natalia across the room and into the stone wall, which cracked under the impact. She crumpled to the floor but was quickly back on her feet, sword at the ready.

I jumped out of the way as Yezgar charged her again. One of the thugs wasn't as quick and got trampled, dying with a bloody splash. As Yezgar drew near, Natalia sank her sword into his gut, yanked it out, and skipped around behind him. Yezgar crashed into the wall and went through it into the next chamber under a cascade of stone. Natalia turned toward the rest of us. 'Now you perish, Zimzabar!'

'Kill her!' commanded Zaran. His remaining men, however, rushed from the room in search of fresh air. The terrorist leader drew a curved knife from his sash. 'You'll not stop me, fools! I am the Living Scourge!'

Combat seemed to involve a great deal of posturing, needling and assertion of identity by the combatants. I had seen this in Lombardo, Dylan, Merc, and now Natalia and Zaran. Maybe they did it to bolster their own confidence or just to break the monotony of a life or death struggle. In any event, I hadn't yet picked up the habit. While Zaran waved his knife and ranted, I acted, running and tackling him. Attacking an armed man when I had no weapons may seem brave, but seeing Yezgar returning I decided I'd rather handle Zaran.

Natalia turned to confront the half-ogre again, who seemed unfazed by the wounds inflicted on him so far. The hand axe was still embedded in his chest and he carried a large chunk of stone in each hand.

Merc now entered the fray, picking up the dead man's mace and attacking Yezgar from behind with a strong swing to the kidneys. This distracted the monster enough for Natalia to dance in and sink her sword up to the hilt in his midriff. That got his attention and he slammed one of the stone blocks against her head, shoving her to the floor before she could withdraw her weapon. This time she didn't recover so quickly and the ogre struck her full in the back with the second block while she was on her hands and knees. She lay prone and motionless before him.

I was doing a good job of manhandling Zaran, but now realized my mistake in engaging him. Yezgar, having beaten his immediate foe, now turned his attention to me, the fool who had attacked his master.

'Run, Cosmo!' said Merc. 'Get out of here!'

I pushed Zaran away from me and looked for a way out. The terrorist's men had regrouped and were pouring in through the door we had entered. Yezgar smiled and gave a throaty growl as he pounced at me.

I vaulted over the desk and through the narrow door beyond. It led to an equally narrow passage running back to the governor's private quarters. I briefly hoped Yezgar would be balked by the lack of the space, but was disappointed by the sight and sound of him plunging after me, the stone walls on either side giving way before him like tall grass before an elephant. He bellowed loudly, his volume doubled by the echo. The sound gave me added speed.

I entered the governor's bedroom. It was as opulent as one could expect in Darnk, with a large feather bed, gilded furniture, a frayed tapestry, and a worn rug on the floor. A shapely young woman lay sprawled on the bed. Through my teary eyes, I noted deeply tanned skin, honey blond hair, and gossamer red silk as I rushed by. Such was her beauty that, even with Yezgar at my heels, I was distracted enough that I tripped over a second girl curled up on the floor. She was the identical twin of the girl on the bed, but clad in blue. From the looks of it, Governor Birksnore was stocking a harem. That wasn't the social norm in Darnk, but I had bigger worries at the moment.

Yezgar burst into the room as I clambered to my feet and tried the heavy wooden bedroom door. It was barred from the other side. Naturally, the governor wouldn't want his playthings roaming away. Now I was angry. I was going to die because of the governor's lustful appetites. There was nowhere to run.

Yezgar grasped me by both shoulders with a single hand and lifted me off the floor, his thick fingers pressing against the side of my neck. He crooked his arm so that our faces were at a level and I could feel his hot, stinking breath which smelled of regurgitated carrion.

'Yezgar,' I said. 'Perhaps we could discuss this before you do anything rash.'

He snapped his arm to full extension and let go, propelling me through the bedroom door and across the sitting room beyond. I landed on the floor with a backside full of splinters and a soundly ringing head.

Before I could note further damage, Yezgar had me again, this time scooping me from the floor and flinging me directly upwards. I was lucky. I didn't hit the stone ceiling, instead crashing through the glass of the skylight and sailing a good twenty feet above the top of the keep. I had a broad, tear-gassed view of the rolling grey hills of the surrounding countryside, the jagged rocks and whitewater rapids of the Longwash at the keep's base, and a purple dragon with gold wings hovering high above me. I began my descent and the exhilarating sensation in the pit of my stomach was displaced by a tense, hollow feeling of naked terror at the thought of where I would land.

I came down atop a large, potted cactus on the balcony adjoining the sitting room, crushing the hapless plant and absorbing most of its spines. I was wedged into place, unable to move. Yezgar spotted me and pounced, lifting the pot and slamming it to the tiles.

In that instant, sitting there amid the sandy soil, crushed plant matter and broken clay with my eyes burning, my body aching, and a homicidal half-ogre towering over me, unbothered by the axe and sword protruding from his torso, I wished sincerely that Merc and I had ignored Offal and gone on to Brythalia.

Yezgar stooped to molest me further, but suddenly tottered as a gilded couch from the sitting room hit him in the back, to be followed by several stuffed chairs, a desk, a table and a cloud of gaudy bric-à-brac. I feared he would fall on and crush me, but his height and centre of gravity carried him over me and over the edge of the balcony, along with the iron guardrail. I felt the spray as his huge form hit the water with a thunderous splash. Glancing down, I saw him go under, bob up into sight again, then vanish beneath the rushing waters for good.

Mercury was standing in the middle of the unfurnished sitting room, a satisfied grin on his face. His cape and clothing were now midnight blue.

'Got him,' he said.

'Why didn't you do that in the first place?' I asked.

'That manoeuvre would hardly have worked in the office. There's no balcony high above deadly rapids there.'

'There's a balcony high above the hard, unyielding city street.'

'True, but it's not the same. Style is important. Are you okay?' He helped me to my feet.

'Other than the cuts, bruises and collection of splinters, glass fragments and cactus spines embedded in my skin, I'm fine.'

'You were lucky. You should be dead. The benefits of hero status have already preserved you from your own folly.'

'My folly? You were the one who said take a closer look.'

'I wouldn't have had the chance if you hadn't insisted we investigate in the first place. Next time you'll listen to me.'

'What about Zaran and his men? We still—'

'I threw him off the other balcony since he didn't rate style,' said Merc with a shrug. 'After that, his men fled. Those that still could.'

'And the warrior woman?'

'Natalia?' He frowned. 'I suggest we be on our way before she recovers.'

'Recovers! She should be dead!'

'Look who's talking. That armour of hers is made of the enchanted metal miraculum. It protects her from most physical harm.'

'You talk like you know her.'

'We've met. She's an adventuress who sells her services to the highest bidder. She was probably hired by Prince Ronaldo of Caratha to kill Zaran. He's committed major atrocities in Caratha.'

'So why should we worry?'

'May I suggest ten million crowns is a damn high bid for anyone's services?'

'Good point.'

'I think our horses are still where we left them. Ready to go?'

'The girls in the bedroom!' I said suddenly.

'What about them?'

'I think they're being held here against their will.'

'So?'

'That's outrageous! We've got to take them with us.' I led the way into the bedroom.

'Why? I know it's part of the heroic tradition to run around with half-clad women, but you're new at this. Ease yourself into the role.'

'Look at them, Merc. So young, so innocent, so lovely.'

'Young and lovely, yes. I wouldn't make a wager on innocent. We can't take them with us. We're in a hurry.'

I knelt beside the girl on the floor and lifted her up. She could hardly be twenty, if that old. 'Only as far as Brythalia,' I said. 'Then they can go their own way.'

'That would be doing them a favour,' said Merc. 'Two unescorted, attractive girls loose in the rough and ready realm of Brythalia. Better to leave them here.'

'Then we'll take them all the way to Raelna. That's a more lawful kingdom, isn't it?'

'Yes, but—'

'Can you wake them?' I asked.

'Probably,' said Merc hesitantly.

'Do it.'

'Cosmo—'

'It's only right.'

'Look where that's gotten you so far.'

'Just do it, Merc.'

The wizard knelt beside me and placed his hand over the girl's face. He mumbled a few unintelligible magic words and her big blue eyes fluttered open.

'Are you okay?' I asked.

'Yes,' she murmured. She seemed disoriented.

'What's your name?'

'Sapphrina Corundum.' She knitted her brow in confusion. 'Who are you?'

'My name is Jason Cosmo.'

Her face contorted in sudden horror and she screamed. Before I could react, she jerked out of my grasp to scramble across the floor until her back was to the wall. 'Jason Cosmo! The Gods preserve me!'

'That's the way to keep a low profile,' muttered Merc as we stood.

'Stay back, you fiend!' She cast about desperately for a route of escape, but Merc and I were between her and the exits.

'Fiend?' I said. 'Me?'

She laughed bitterly. Straightening up and covering herself as much as her immodest dress allowed, she said, with strained conviction, 'You won't ravish me, villain!'

I turned to Merc. 'Just what kind of rumours about me are circulating?'

'Most people assume you've committed pretty horrible crimes to be worth so much. As a rule of thumb, if you can imagine it, someone thinks you've done it.'

'Am I going to have this effect on everyone we meet?'

'Only if you tell them who you are. Well, she obviously doesn't want to come with us, so perhaps we should be going.'

'Wait.' I addressed the bold but frightened girl, who had followed our exchange with interest. 'Listen, Sapphrina, I'm not what you think. If you want to get out of here, this is your chance. If I've jumped to the wrong conclusion about your situation, we'll be on our way.' I flashed my most reassuring smile.

She gave me another appraisal, warmer than the first, and said, with a soft, hopeful voice, 'Are you sure you aren't going to ravish me?'

'Positive.'

She relaxed a little more, but remained wary. 'You jumped to the right conclusion. My sister and I are prisoners of that pig Birksnore. We've been planning to escape, but hadn't quite worked out the details yet.'

'You can come with us,' I said, ignoring Merc's exasperated expression. 'This is your chance for freedom.'

'You came here to rescue us?'

'Not exactly,' said Merc. 'But as long as we're here, we might as well correct all the injustices in the world.'

'Ignore him,' I said, shooting Merc a dark glance. 'I noticed your plight while fleeing a rampaging ogre.'

'Could we speed this up?' said Merc.

'What's the hurry?'

'Natalia, remember?'

Sapphrina rushed to the bed with a rustle of silk and shook her sister. 'Rubis! Wake up!'

Merc brushed her aside and repeated his magic formula. Rubis awoke, saw Merc and bolted upright, covering herself. 'Sapphrina! Who—?'

'It's all right,' said her sister. 'This is Jason Cosmo, who—'

'Jason Cosmo!' Rubis screamed even more loudly than her sister and leaped hysterically from the bed. 'Run, Sapphrina! Run!'

'This is ridiculous,' muttered Merc, rolling his eyes heavenward.

Sapphrina caught and shook her sister. 'Rubis! It's okay! They're here to rescue us . . . I think.' The twins looked at me expectantly.

I smiled. 'That's right.'

'Look,' said Rubis, calming down. 'He doesn't have fangs or cloven hooves or anything like they say. And I thought he was older.' She bit her lower lip. 'Actually, he's kind of cute.'

46

'I noticed,' said Sapphrina.

I blushed.

'But are the rest of the stories true, I wonder?' said Rubis, narrowing her eyes.

'I hope so,' said Sapphrina.

I blushed more furiously.

'Listen,' said Merc. 'We're in a rush so if you'll get dressed we can find provisions and extra horses and be on our way. Natalia will be up soon.'

Even as he spoke, the war goddess strode out of the passage to the governor's office. She had a cruel pout on her face and a long dagger in each hand. 'In a hurry, Boltblaster? I didn't recognize you at first because of the beard. I've been hoping I'd find you.'

Merc raised his hands in a placating gesture. 'You're not still mad about that little misunderstanding in Xornos, are you?'

Natalia sneered. 'Are you referring to the incident when you left me buried under several tons of Ganthian wheat flour in the cargo hold of a sinking ship?'

'That's the one,' said Merc. 'But you obviously got out alive, so why hold a grudge? It's unprofessional.'

'I can live with that,' said Natalia coolly. 'Can you?'

6

'Natalia, be reasonable,' said Merc.

In reply, the adventuress hurled one of the knives with a flick of her wrist. As Mercury snatched the blade out of the air with his right hand, she threw the second dagger. He caught it in his left hand with equal deftness.

Natalia Slash laughed. 'Return them.'

'What's the point?' said Merc.

'Do it.'

The wizard threw both daggers at once. The woman caught and resheathed them with graceful ease. 'You could have let Yezgar finish me, Boltblaster. You didn't. I appreciate that so I'm going to forget about our last encounter. No ill will.'

'Fine with me,' said Merc, visibly relieved. I relaxed as well. The twin sisters just looked confused.

'Do you have my sword?'

'Yezgar took it with him when he fell into the river.'

'That blade has been in the family for over two hundred years.'

'Sorry.'

'I'll find it. Where's Zaran? I didn't see him among the litter of bodies you left in the office.'

'You should find his remains in the street below the balcony.'

Natalia shook her head. 'He knows how to take a fall. No matter, he can't have gone far. He'll regroup his men somewhere nearby and I'll sweep them all up at once.' She flexed her armoured hands. 'Still running from the Society?'

Merc shrugged. 'Yes, but I enjoy the chance to travel.'

'And who is your new companion?' Her steely grey eyes met mine. Merc shot me a desperate warning glance, but I didn't need the hint.

'I'm Burlo Stumproot, madam.'

Sapphrina and Rubis both started to speak, but quickly caught on. Merc moved to my side and clapped me on the back. 'Burlo is my squire as it were. He handles provisions, hotel accommodations and the like. The mundane things.'

'I see,' said Natalia, her eyes still locked with mine, probing and measuring me. I gave her a thin smile. She pursed her lips and nodded slightly before glancing away. 'It may interest you to know that Zaran is being financed by the Society these days. They find him useful. I expect to capture him before he contacts his masters, but you may want to leave the area soon anyway.'

Merc bowed slightly. 'I thank you for the warning.'

'It's only fair,' said Natalia. 'Once I get Zaran, I have an assignment from the Theocrat of Stive – the swamp trolls are marauding in force again. After that I have a contract to fulfill for Isogoras the Xornite. I leave its nature to your imagination. Farewell.' She speared me with her gaze once more before striding from the room.

'I get the impression she knows who I am,' I said weakly.

'She does,' said Mercury. 'That was obvious.'

'How could she?'

'Perhaps all the recent screaming had something to do with it.' He glared at the twins. 'She won't be a problem until she carries out her current contracts but I guarantee she'll round up Zaran and the swamp trolls in record time. That only gives us a few weeks to reach Raelna.'

'If she's working for Isogoras—'

'Then it means he's finally realized the Black Bolts will never bring me in. Hiring Natalia is probably the first intelligent thing he's done in years.'

'You don't have a very high opinion of this Xornite.'

'And I never have. We were both apprenticed to the master wizard Pencader. Isogoras took an interest in the forbidden art of demonology. When Pencader discovered this and rebuked him, he opened a gate to the Hells in an effort to murder our master. I intervened and Isogoras lost control of the spell, falling through his own gate. No doubt he learned more about demons than he wanted to know.'

'No doubt.'

'Unfortunately he survived, though badly scarred, and eventually returned to Earth to join the Society. Now he's been given the task of recruiting me, which must gall him greatly.'

'Why?'

'He'd rather kill me,' Merc laughed. 'But it's Natalia we have to worry about. As I was just saying, I think we can reach Raelna before she comes after us, but to do so we need to travel light and fast.' He nodded towards the girls.

'They're coming with us,' I said.

'Then you take care of them. I'm just responsible for you and me.'

'Fine. Look, how can Natalia get to Stive and back before we get to Raelna? Isn't it even further west than—'

From outside sounded the roar of the purple dragon I had seen earlier, as it wheeled past the keep with Natalia on its back.

'That's Golan of the Heights, Natalia's dragon steed. Do you have any idea how many miles a flying dragon can cover in just one day? Think about it.' Merc left to hunt provisions.

'What's his problem?' asked Sapphrina, slipping out of her wispy garment without a trace of embarrassment. I turned my back just in time to prevent my eyes from bulging clear of their sockets. I could feel my ears glowing a hot red. What I had just seen was too much for my Darnkite sensibilities.

'He's got a sour disposition,' I said, trying to get my breathing back under control. 'So, how did you two end up here?'

'Bad luck,' said Rubis as her discarded garment landed on my shoulder. 'We were at this party in Caratha, the wine was drugged, we were captured by slavers and bought by Birksnore at a private sale in Rumular.'

'Sold?' I knew about slavery but it wasn't practised in Darnk, where the people could hardly afford to support themselves, much less chattels. The idea of one person owning another had a certain wrongness to it in my mind anyway.

'It was awful,' said Sapphrina. 'They only asked eight thousand crowns for us.'

'And Brythalian crowns at that,' added Rubis. 'Which exchanges to only six and a half thousand Carathan.' The Carathan crown was the standard for international commerce.

'We're worth at least twenty thousand,' said Sapphrina. 'After all, we're healthy, good looking, intelligent and of nearly noble birth.'

'And very talented,' said Rubis.

'And Birksnore has no class at all,' continued Sapphrina. 'Do you know what he wanted us for? Not what you would imagine. That disgusting man wanted us to—'

'Are you Carathans?' I asked, hastily cutting her off.

'Zastrians,' said Rubis. 'Have you heard of the Corundum Trading Company?'

'No.'

'It's the largest merchant enterprise in Zastria. Father owns it. You can turn around now.'

They were clad in tunics and hose, Rubis in red, Sapphrina in blue. The outfits weren't much more seemly than what they had been wearing. Their hems were daringly high and their necklines daringly low. The garments didn't even cover their shoulders and must have been held up by magic.

'We look awful, don't we?' said Rubis.

I realized I was staring and tried to find a safe place for my eyes to rest. 'No, not at all.'

'Those slavers stole our jewellery,' said Sapphrina, looking in the mirror to adjust her hair. 'And my hair! Ick!'

'It's lovely. Spun gold.'

'You're sweet,' said Sapphrina, throwing her arms around me and kissing my cheek. I flushed a brighter shade of scarlet. Women neither looked nor behaved like this in Lower Hicksnittle. It would take getting used to.

'What *are* we going to do with that pig Birksnore?' asked Rubis as she combed her hair.

'You should write a letter of complaint to the king,' I said. 'Keeping slaves isn't allowed in Darnk and I'm sure the king will give the matter prompt attention.'

Rubis gaped at me in dismay. 'You're joking, aren't you?'

'Of course he is,' said Sapphrina, pinching my cheek. 'Write a letter to the king! That's rich! No, we should hang him from the top of the tower by his testicles.'

They both laughed wickedly at that idea, though I didn't find it particularly amusing. In fact, it made me blush again.

'Wait!' said Rubis amid her laughter. 'I have a better suggestion.'

Without knowing what it was, I knew I didn't want to hear it. 'If you ladies will excuse me,' I said. 'I think I will go and help Merc.

We departed Offal two hours later, leaving the city to its slumber. Merc and I had located food, spare clothing, blankets and horses for the girls. At his insistence I borrowed a sword, dagger and chainmail shirt from the keep's armoury. We also tended our wounds, though Merc's consisted solely of a tiny scratch on his left arm.

Governor Birksnore was spared the grotesque punishments imagined by the girls, though they did manage to talk Merc and me into helping them transport his unconscious body to the market square, where we left him bound and naked. He would be thoroughly humiliated when the city woke the next day – and would have no idea how much worse his fate could have been.

The road we took paralleled the river, running initially south, but gradually bending west to the Brythalian border. The territory between the kingdoms, an area of rough scrub and stubby trees, was unclaimed and largely uninhabited. Brythalia had no interest in expanding its territory northward toward Darnk, and Darnk already had more rough scrub and stubby trees than it needed. It would take us several days to cross this no man's land.

I found riding with a punctured posterior painful, but talking with the vivacious twins took my mind off my discomfort. They rode on either side of me, plying me with questions, while Merc rode just ahead, looking dour and doing his best to ignore us.

'Is is true you are Death's first cousin?' asked Rubis with grave seriousness.

'No. Where did you hear that?'

'Here and there. Since the bounty was announced there has been endless speculation about who you are and what you've done, because no one knows for certain.'

'What *have* you done?' asked Sapphrina.

'I'm just a woodcutter,' I said. 'I do a little turnip farming too.'

'I would have taken you for a warrior at least.'

'No. I'm no warrior.' I told my story from the beginning. They listened attentively, with few interruptions. 'And here we are,' I concluded. 'Now tell me more about yourselves.'

'What would you like to know?' they chorused.

'Everything.'

'I'll bet,' said Rubis. Sapphrina merely smiled.

Alternating every few sentences, they skimmed through their life stories. Their mother had died giving birth to them. Their father, Corun Corundum, was not only a wealthy merchant, but a member of the Zastrian Senate. They grew up among the rich and powerful and had travelled extensively. Their father had thrown them out two years ago when they had refused to go through with unappealing marriages of alliance which he had arranged for them.

'He thought cutting off our allowances would make us give in to him,' said Sapphrina, 'not realizing that we had saved and invested enough over the years to live quite comfortably without him.'

'We *are* his daughters after all.'

'So when he told us to walk, we did.'

'And had more fun than ever.'

'At least until we got kidnapped.'

'And sold to Birksnore for a ridiculously low price.'

'We'd only been there for a week when you rescued us,' said Sapphrina. 'And we're very grateful.'

'Very, very grateful,' said Rubis.

By the time we stopped to make camp for the night I had ceased to be shocked or embarrassed by their suggestive comments, for it was apparent to me that their flirtatious manner was more show than substance. They were not quite the naughty nymphs they pretended to be, but were actually two intelligent, capable, courageous young women. I decided that I liked them very much.

Mercury, however, was still annoyed by their presence. 'They're going to slow us down,' he groused as I helped him set up the small tent he had produced within the folds of his cloak. We had decided to pass the night in a small copse atop a low hill.

'They haven't so far,' I said, glancing down the slope to the river bank where the girls were watering the horses.

'We've only been riding for a few hours. Tomorrow we'll be in the saddle all day. And the next day. And the next. And so on for weeks. They won't be able to maintain the kind of pace we've got to set.'

'They might surprise you. They've got more experience in the saddle than I do.'

'I don't doubt it, but it's not just that. The Black Bolts are going to pick up our trail in Offal. In a couple of days they may even catch up with us. If that happens, your friends are going to be in the way. They might get us all killed.'

'We handled the Bolts before. Sort of.'

'And what happens if Natalia attacks us? Or the Red Huntsman? Or even Isogoras? The girls are our weak link and any enemy is going to realize that and go for them.'

'So what are you saying? We should abandon them?'

'No. But I want you to realize the risks we're running by bringing them along. We need to be rid of them as soon as possible.'

'Before we get to Raelna?'

'If possible.'

'You said Brythalia was no place for young women alone.'

'Neither is Hell.'

The sisters shared the tent while Merc and I took turns on watch, but the night was uneventful. We were up and riding before dawn, and covered over twenty miles of rugged terrain that day, but Mercury was not satisfied. We covered almost thirty miles the next day and we were all stiff, sore and filthy with sweat and grime when we stopped for the night, still at least a hundred miles from Brythalia.

'I hope you've got some soap under that cape of yours, wizard,' said Sapphrina.

'Why?' said Merc.

'Because I haven't bathed since we left Offal and I smell like that city's namesake.'

'You'll smell worse before we get where we're going.'

'The soap, wizard. Why should you ride all day and look immaculate while the rest of us look like the horses have been riding us?'

'I'm the only one with self-cleaning clothes,' said Merc, producing a bar of black soap.

'Black soap?' said Rubis.

'It's the Ebony brand,' said Merc. 'It works like any other colour – and it floats, so you won't lose it in the river.'

'Thank you.' Sapphrina took the soap and they trotted to the edge of the water and quickly shed their clothing. I pretended not to notice their activity and bent to help Merc erect the tent. Suddenly he stiffened and a worried frown crossed his face.

'We've got a problem,' he said slowly.

'What is it?'

'We've been observed.'

I started and looked to and fro. 'Where?'

He shook his head. 'It was magical observation. Scrying. I sensed it due to my heightened magical awareness.'

'Someone used a crystal ball on us?'

'Something like that.'

'The Society?'

'No. The impression I got was of a medium much more powerful than any crystal ball mortal magic can master. It can only be the Mirror of Ouga-Oyg.'

'And what, may I ask, is the Mirror of Ouga-Oyg?'

'Ouga-Oyg of the Thousand and Thirty-Two Eyes is one of the Demon Lords. He is nicknamed the Peeper from the Pit because he has a great magic mirror with which he can spy on events almost anywhere in Arden. That is what I felt.'

'Then the Demon Lords know where we are.'

'Where we are, but not necessarily who we are. The impression was fleeting. Likely Ouga-Oyg was merely scanning the countryside. He may not have even noticed us, but it troubles me that he would be looking in this area.'

'Why?'

'Because this is where we are. Our interview with He Who Sits On The Porch was obscured by magic mist, and he transported us many miles from the spot afterwards, but the Demon Lords must have noticed and taken an interest in this part of the world. We must guard our words, thoughts and actions carefully. If Ouga-Oyg turns the full power of his mirror upon us he will be able to read them all.'

'I'm getting paranoid.'

'Good. It will keep you alive.'

'Hey, Jason!' called Sapphrina from the river. 'Aren't you going to come and scrub our backs?'

'You could use a bath!' added Rubis. 'And we'd be delighted to help!'

'Go ahead,' said Merc, with an uncharacteristic smile. 'You smell like the backside of a buffalo.'

I joined the girls in the river and we emerged twenty minutes later – after much splashing, scrubbing and racy banter – much cleaner than we went in. Merc's bar of soap was now half its original size.

As we ate our meal of fruit and cheese, Merc explained to Sapphrina and Rubis the new danger of Ouga-Oyg's mirror and the precautions which were now necessary, then volunteered for the first watch.

Merc shook me awake four hours later for my turn on duty. The night air had gone chilly and the moon was obscured behind a bank of clouds which glowed like luminous frozen smoke.

'It's been quiet,' whispered Merc. He nodded at the clouds. 'We'll probably have rain tomorrow.'

'Yes,' I agreed. 'That should obscure our trail.'

'And slow us up. And get us wet.' He shrugged. 'Beginning tomorrow I think we'll put the girls on watch too so we can get more sleep.'

'Good idea.'

Merc rolled himself into a blanket and was quickly asleep. I stood and stretched and ambled slowly around the perimeter of our camp to get my blood flowing. I checked on the horses then headed for the river bank. The water slid through the night like a great dark serpent, hissing and murmuring hypnotically. An occasional moonbeam broke through the cloud cover and danced across the river in glints of silver before winking out as if it had never been there.

I sat beside the river for a long while reflecting on all that had happened to me in the past few days, on sorcerers, bounties, mercenaries, and the struggles of gods and demons. I almost wished I was back in Lower Hicksnittle. Almost.

I heard a light footstep behind me and realized I had not been a very alert watchman while lost in my reverie. I half-turned to see one of the twins standing behind me. I couldn't tell which one it was.

'I'm Sapphrina,' she said, sitting down beside me. 'I was looking for you.'

'Why?'

'I really haven't thanked you properly for freeing us.'

'That's not necessary.'

'I think it is. You didn't have to bring us with you. I know you've added to your own danger by helping us.' She clasped my hand and looked me earnestly in the eye. 'I appreciate that.'

I was silent a moment before saying, 'I don't think I could have done otherwise.'

'I know,' she said, smiling. 'That's what I appreciate. Your motives are so . . . honourable. You didn't even blink when Rubis told you who we are, how wealthy we are. You haven't any advances toward us – which is bruising to our egos I might add – and I think you're a very rare and noble kind of man.'

I shook my head in denial. 'I'm just an ordinary—'

'You're not,' she said. 'That's my point. In the other kingdoms we make jokes about the poor, stupid, cowardly, backward Darnkites—'

'Most of them are probably accurate.'

'—but in all the lands I've visited, I don't think I've met anyone as brave and decent as you.'

'You've probably just been looking in the wrong places.'

'Yes,' she said. 'I should have looked in Darnk.' She leaned over and gave me a lingering kiss, then quietly got up and walked back to the tent.

Despite the danger and the hardship, I could get used to being a hero.

7

We reached the settlement of Grimmel on the Brythalian frontier after five straight days of riding through heavy rains. My companions and I were drenched, chilled, mud-splattered and exhausted. Our horses were nearly spent from the effort of trudging through the thick mud. We had been forced to abandon the relatively level track beside the river for higher ground when the Longwash spilled over its banks and flooded the surrounding territory. We wanted nothing more than to kick off our boots and prop up our feet by the hearth of a homey inn.

Unfortunately, no such place was to be found in Grimmel, which was little more than a logging camp. The forest region of northern Brythalia boasted oak, ash, birch and maples mingled with spruce, fir and pine. The Brythalian forest was said to be the overgrown remnant of the nursery in which The Gods first developed the various kinds of trees. This was highly unlikely considering the destruction wrought during the Age of War and the fact that none of the trees in the area were more than a few hundred years old, but every nation needs its folklore.

In any event, Grimmel was a crude and sullen collection of several bunkhouses, a mess hall, a guardhouse, and a few other structures used for storage, all clustered atop a barren mound of earth and stone beside the swollen Longwash, from which protruded the pilings of the flooded docks. The twangy rasp of saws and the loud chop of axes from the surrounding woods suggested that most of the men who lived here were at work, but perhaps a dozen loggers and brown-shirted Brythalian soldiers were milling about the camp itself. They greeted Sapphrina and Rubis with appreciative looks and occasional catcalls as we rode into town. Merc and I rated only surly glares.

When we reached the open area between the buildings, the men surrounded us, spreading out in a loose circle around our horses. Some held sticks, knives or axes. The soldiers placed their hands on the hilts of their swords. So did I. Most of the workers in these camps were criminals consigned to hard labour by the Brythalian courts. They were ruthless, unprincipled men. Their military overseers were not much better since the courts also provided many of the recruits for the Brythalian army. I noticed that no one was in chains here. The guards and the guarded were united in their intentions regarding us.

'I would advise you girls to stick close to Cosmo and me,' whispered Merc, 'lest you get dragged behind a woodpile and never come back.'

I gave the girls a weak smile that was meant to be reassuring. 'We're outnumbered,' I said to Merc. 'Should we make the first move?'

'Don't do anything. I may be able to defuse this situation.'

Merc cast his gaze slowly over our would-be assailants. He was wearing his sunshades, so no one could be certain just who he was looking at in any given instant. Suddenly he raised his hand and pointed it at the largest, ugliest man present, a burly logger holding a thick tree branch like a club. Five thin beams of blue light emanated from Merc's fingers and converged on the man's bare chest, which promptly exploded in a spray of gore and shattered bone. He fell over backwards in the muck with blue smoke curling from the ragged hole in his chest.

'I am Shadrizar the Sadistic,' announced Merc in a low, menacing voice as the other loggers and soldiers backed away, stricken with fear. 'I seek a night's lodging for myself, my associate Burlo Bonecracker, and my two man-eating vampire succubi slaves.' Rubis and Sapphrina's faces glowed with an eerie green light and when they opened their mouths they appeared to be filled with sharp, curving fangs. Merc pointed at a soldier. 'You! See to it! Or I will give you to them.' He indicated the twins, who smiled their fangsome smiles. The soldier blanched and hurried away. The rest of the crowd was not long in following.

Merc laughed. 'That is what you call creative spellcasting. A simple blue bolt of death and a minor illusion and we have averted the senseless slaughter of an outright mêlée.' He regarded the twins. 'And I don't think any of the locals will be disturbing you two tonight.'

'Wasn't that risky?' I asked. 'I thought any use of your magic would allow the Society to pinpoint us.'

'Those were minor spells and quickly cast. This little incident will serve to confirm for Dylan that we passed this way, but I think little else will come of it – except some welcome co-operation. Ah! Here is the camp commander now, no doubt hastening to offer us the hospitality of his own private quarters.'

He was. The commander bunked elsewhere for the night while we occupied his cabin. The furnishings were rough-hewn and plain, but for the first time since leaving home I slept with a roof over my head, even if I was on the floor. The girls, naturally, got the bed. We all took a turn on watch. Even with Merc's display of sorcerous power we weren't taking any chances.

As we rode out the next morning, much to the relief of Grimmel's inhabitants, a notice on the camp message board caught my eye.

'Merc!' I cried. 'That has my name on it!' I urged my horse over to the board and ripped the poster down. My name was written across it in bold script. Below it, in equally prominent print, was the sum of ten million crowns. The smaller writing stipulated that this bounty would be paid when I was brought dead or alive, but body intact, to any major city and turned over to a designated agent of the bounty's unnamed sponsors. This was the first tangible proof of the bounty offer I had encountered and seeing it all laid out in black and white chilled my blood.

'Cosmo,' said Merc in dismay, 'this is not the way to maintain a low profile.'

I stared at him uncomprehendingly for a moment, then noticed that every logger and soldier within earshot was staring at me, jaws agape. Then they dropped whatever they were holding, turned heel, and ran screaming into the forest.

'I'm sorry, Merc. I was just surprised to see this.' I crumpled up the notice and dropped it to the ground.

'Get used to seeing it. Those notices are tacked on every wall and tree from here to Cyrilla.'

'That's not a comforting thought.'

'I've got a less comforting one. Word of your presence – and your description – are going to spread through these logging camps like an outbreak of the Orphalian flu. If the Red Huntsman is still prowling around Brythalia it won't be long before he hears the news and picks up our trail. I was hoping to avoid that.'

'I'm sorry, Merc.'

'Let's hope we all don't get a lot sorrier.'

We found all of the other logging camps abandoned upon our arrival. After two days of travel the forests gave way to broad farming estates worked by serf labour. On the third day we followed the river road west towards Rumular, passing through the lands of several nobles, each sporting a sprawling manor house or small castle. We were, by and large, unmolested, a most unsettling development. Each of the many dukes, earls, counts and barons of Brythalia is semi-independent of the crown and absolute master on his own estate. Consequently, each noble typically charges outrageous tolls and other fees for passage through his territory. Yet we had been asked to pay not one copper dross, despite having encountered over a dozen roadblocks. In each case the soldiers manning the barrier had raised it as we approached, fearfully eyed our progress, and lowered the barrier behind us with audible sighs of relief.

As evening drew near, we entered the small village of Goatgloss to the accompaniment of much banging of shutters and bolting of doors. As we passed along the dirt lane that bisected the village I heard from within the thatched cottages the fearful wailing of mothers and daughters, the tears of small children, and the muttered curses and prayers of husbands and fathers. Dogs tucked their tails between their legs and scurried away whimpering at our approach. Cats arched their backs and hissed their feline defiance. Horses rolled their eyes and neighed nervously. No goats were in sight.

'Not exactly a warm, friendly welcome we're getting,' I observed.

'This is not a good sign,' said Merc. 'Your reputation has preceded us since Grimmel. If we're lucky the Huntsman and BlackMoon are in southern Brythalia.'

We dismounted before the Dancing Donkey Inn, a square, two-storey, wooden structure adjoined by a kitchenhouse and a stable. A weathered picture of a donkey doing backflips hung above the door.

'Let's go in,' said Merc.

The proprietor, a rotund man with drooping jowls and several chins met us at the door, wringing his hands nervously and bowing as best he could.

'Welcome, welcome good sirs, to my humble establishment,' he wheezed. 'How may I be of service?'

61

'We need a hot meal and rooms for the night,' said Merc, flipping him a gold coin. 'Also, our horses need tending.'

'At once!' said the owner as the coin hit the floor and rolled beneath a table. 'You may have any room you desire, as all of my other guests have just fled out the back door. Roasted beef, steamed mushrooms, fresh baked bread, Orphalian cheese and my finest wine will be on the table momentarily. And your horses will be – ah, what do your horses eat?'

'Hay,' I said. 'Or oats. What would you expect?'

'Not human flesh?' he asked, licking his lips.

'No. Just the usual fare.'

He looked relieved. 'Please, please be seated kind masters and your meal will be served. I will see that your horses are carefully groomed and given our best feed. Your rooms will be prepared, your—'

'Thank you,' said Merc. 'I am certain you will see to it.'

'Oh, yes! Yes! Absolutely!' The nervous innkeeper bustled into the back room, shouting instructions.

'Good service here,' said Merc as we took our places at a rectangular, wine-stained table. Merc sat at one end of the table, I at the other. The girls sat near my end, one at each side.

'I hope the food is as good,' I said. 'The rations you store in your cape taste odd.'

Mercury shrugged. 'Ionization caused by the transition to and from the pocket dimension within the folds of my cape. You get used to it.'

'I haven't.'

A trembling young serving girl appeared bearing a steaming platter of roast, gravy and mushrooms. She never took her wide eyes off of me as she approached the table.

'This looks delicious,' I said, smiling hungrily. The dark-haired girl gasped, set the tray on the table with a thump, and scurried away like a startled rabbit. 'Why is everyone so frightened of me?' I asked. 'Women particularly?'

'They've probably heard how you raped and pillaged along the Free Coast, ravished all two hundred and forty-five members of the harem of King Oriones of Cyrilla, massacred an entire Zastrian town with your bare hands, violated the Seven Sacred Sylphs of Serragonia, debauched with the daughters of demons amid the holy Vesper Hills, and kidnapped the concubines of the Thirteen Oligarchs of Xornos,' said Sapphrina. 'That's why I was frightened of you.'

'I told you your image was somewhat fearsome,' said Merc. 'That's why I wanted to travel incognito. Your name creates too big a stir.'

'I never expected it to be like this. You'd think I was a Demon Lord myself.'

'Some think you are,' said Rubis.

'We've got to duck all this attention soon,' said Mercury, 'before we have to fend off the full might of the Society.'

A red-headed serving girl rushed in with a tray of wine goblets and distributed them quickly. She spilled mine in my lap, whimpered in terror, and bolted from the room.

'How will we do that?' I asked as the twins dabbed at the spill with their napkins.

'We'll have to avoid Rumular. Nor can we risk the main road any longer. We'll have to turn southwards now and head directly for the Raelnan border. It is also time to make a decision regarding the girls.'

'What do you mean?' said Rubis.

'We're not leaving you,' said Sapphrina.

'Be reasonable, ladies. You are not part of our quest, except by accident. Your real objective is to return to Caratha. I think the best means of achieving that is for you to book passage on a river boat which will take you all the way down the Longwash to that fair city.'

'Land or water, this is still Brythalia,' said Sapphrina. 'Unescorted, we'll soon be in chains again.'

'Why don't we all take a boat?' asked Rubis. 'It would be the quickest way for you to reach Raelna, wizard, and I'd much prefer a deck to a saddle.'

'We're too exposed on a boat, too vulnerable,' said Mercury. 'If you insist on coming with us, you'll have to stick with the saddle – and you'll have to take your chances. My primary concern is keeping Cosmo and myself alive.'

'Fine,' said Sapphrina.

'Are you sure about this?' I asked.

The sisters exchanged a quick glance. 'We know the dangers of riding with you,' said Sapphrina, 'and we accept them.'

'This is the greatest adventure of all,' said Rubis.

Sapphrina looked me straight in the eye. 'And we're not going to miss it.'

As the inkeeper had said, we had our pick of rooms. We spent the night in peace and rose early the next morning. We cooked our own breakfast, as Goatgloss had been abandoned during the night, and set out as the sun rose. It was a sunny day with a slight breeze and a mild blue sky. We headed south, leaving the Longwash behind.

By mid-morning we were riding along a dry and dusty lane between freshly ploughed fields and green pastures filled with cattle. A sprawling manor house was visible to the east and the road skirted a small cow pond just ahead. Beyond it was a stand of oak.

'Get ready for trouble,' said Mercury suddenly, the first words he had spoken all day.

'What is it?' I said, looking all about.

'I sense danger.'

A powerful horn blast split the air from the east, followed by an excited chorus of howls. Looking to the manor, I saw half a dozen shaggy grey wolves the size of ponies racing around the corner and bounding across the field towards us. They were followed by a massive rider on a roan stallion. He wore a mask and trappings of red leather and held a great black horn in his hand. He sounded a second blast and the wolves increased their hellish pace.

'I see what you mean. The Red Huntsman, I suppose?'

'Good guess,' said Merc, spurring his horse to a gallop. The rest of us followed, our frightened mounts needing little encouragement once they caught wind of the wolves.

By the time we reached the pond, it was obvious our pursuers would soon overtake us. The wolves were only sixty yards or so behind us and the Huntsman was right behind them. I glanced back and saw that he was notching an arrow to his bow. At this point, Sapphrina's horse stumbled and fell. Her scream was cut short as she tumbled down a low bank and into the water.

I wheeled my horse about and called to her. 'Come on! Get up!'

She got to her feet in the shallow water and tried to clamber up the embankment to reach my outstretched hand, but the mud was slick and she lost her footing, sitting down hard in the muck.

The lead wolf was almost upon us. I drew my sword, but in so doing lost control of my horse, which treacherously dumped me and galloped on. I somehow landed on my feet and braced for the attack. I still wasn't a competent swordsman, but Merc had given me a few pointers. Of course, those were tips on fighting other swordsmen, not slavering, red-eyed giant wolves.

The Huntsman loosed his arrow at Merc, who had turned his own horse and come back to help. Rubis wisely kept riding for the trees. The wizard deflected the missile at the last instant with a wave of his hand. It landed harmlessly in the middle of the pond.

The wolf leaped over Sapphrina's downed horse and flew at me, jaw open wide. I swung my sword two-handed and rapped it on the side of the muzzle with the flat of the blade. I had actually hoped to decapitate the beast. I didn't get a second chance. I was crushed to the ground, the wolf snapping at my face.

The second wolf dove into the water after Sapphrina. All I heard was the splash. No scream. Two more wolves ran at Merc, and the last pair continued on after Rubis.

Mercury leaped clear as the wolves savaged his horse, biting through its neck and flank. As it fell, the beasts turned their attention to the wizard, who had dropped into a ready stance, sword drawn. I was using all my strength to keep the wolf atop me from biting my head off. I held on tightly to the sides of its furry neck and kept my arms extended. Hot wolf spit showered my face.

The Huntsman drew up short and notched another arrow. Merc gestured and the bowstring broke. With a shrug, the bounty hunter cast the bow aside and crossed his arms to watch the wolves do his work for him.

It occurred to me that if I could get my legs in the right position I might be able to kick the wolf off of me. I was wrong.

Beams of intense red light emanated from Merc's sunshades and struck one of the wolves in the face. Its head burst into flame. With a horrible cry of pain it forgot about Merc and began racing about in panic as the flames spread across its body. The other wolf charged the wizard with a snarl. Merc danced to one side and sliced open the animal's shoulder with his sword. Enraged, the wolf turned to snap at the wizard, again missing its mark. This time Merc stabbed through to its heart.

As he did so, the Huntsman released a whirling bola, which wrapped itself tightly around his neck before he could react. Surprised, Mercury dropped his sword and went down, his shades flying off to land in the dust. The Red Huntsman dismounted to finish him.

I concocted a new strategy. By wriggling along on my back, I led the wolf to the edge of the embankment. We slid down it into the shallow water, landing atop the wolf which had gone after Sapphrina. I saw no sign of the girl herself. A couple of well-placed paws served to embed me in the muck. Now I had two wolves atop me. It was progress of sorts.

The Red Huntsman stood over Mercury, his sword raised to be plunged into the wizard's heart. Merc rolled out of range and regained his feet, but the Huntsman mounted a furious attack, pressing him hard and keeping him on the defensive.

Through sheer brute strength, I managed to break one wolf's neck and get the other into a position where I could hold its head underwater until it drowned. Not that it was as easy as it sounds. I staggered from the pond torn, bloody and muddy. My clothing, even my chainmail, was ruined. I started forward to help Merc.

I was blocked by the Huntsman's stallion. The horse came at me with flying hooves and chomping teeth. I thought about trying to punch it out, but those snapping teeth made me reconsider. I gave way, backing into the pond and standing in the shallows with the dead wolves. The horse stood on the shore and eyed me like I was a big red apple it wanted to take

66

a few bites from. Sure, I had just killed two giant wolves with my bare hands, but that didn't mean I was eager to tackle a trained warhorse. Merc was on his own unless I could figure out a way past the beast.

He wasn't doing well. Too stunned for magic, and hampered by the constriction of his throat, Merc was unable to move fast enough to avoid the Huntsman's blade. The bounty hunter had cut him twice. I couldn't imagine this scene getting any worse.

Then I heard the thunder of hooves from the north and saw nine black horses approaching. The riders were clad in the familiar uniforms of the Black Bolts. Dylan of Ganth had found us. He could have picked a more convenient time.

8

If I couldn't leave the water, I could at least project my strength into the fray. The Red Huntsman momentarily had his back to me, so I hefted up one of the vanquished wolves at my feet and hurled it at its master. The dead animal knocked the Huntsman to the ground. This gave Merc enough time to magically unravel the bola from his throat and send it whirling into the skull of the Huntsman's warhorse. The animal neighed in pain, rolled its eyes and staggered as if about to collapse. I helped it along by hitting it with the other wolf I had killed. The horse fell onto its side and lay motionless.

I scrambled out of the lake and scooped up my fallen sword. Merc's weapon flew to his hand and together we faced the Huntsman, who had regained his feet.

'It's a whole new battle, Huntsman,' said Merc, ignoring my lack of proficiency at swordplay and the approach of the Black Bolts in making his assessment.

The Huntsman made no move to attack. 'I have no quarrel with you, Mercury Boltblaster,' he said. His deep voice was muffled by his mask. 'Cosmo is my prey. Stand aside and leave him to me. You have problems of your own.' He gestured toward the oncoming Black Bolts. 'Though they would be no problem to me.'

For one frightening moment, Mercury seemed to hesitate, as if seriously considering the Huntsman's implied offer of aid against the Black Bolts in return for abandoning me. Then the wizard snorted derisively. 'Those buffoons would be no problem to a blind cripple armed with a teaspoon.'

'So be it.'

Dylan and his men drew up short of where we stood and glared at us with hostile curiosity. I noticed most of the Black Bolts wore dusty bandages somewhere on their bodies – reminders of their last encounter with Mercury. They were eager to do the wizard great bodily harm but also looked terrified at the prospect of suffering more harm themselves.

'I am the Red Huntsman,' said the Red Huntsman. 'This man is mine.' He pointed his sword at me. 'The wizard you may have.'

Dylan smiled. 'The wizard is all we want.'

'But can you handle me?' said Merc.

The Black Bolts began to mutter curses. Dylan raised his hand to silence them and addressed the Huntsman. 'We would appreciate any assistance you could offer in apprehending the wizard.'

'How great would this appreciation be?'

'Ten per cent of our fee.'

'Sixty.'

'Done.'

'Then make it eighty.'

Dylan scowled. 'Very well,' he said testily.

'Hold the other one for me,' said the Huntsman, turning to confront Merc. At Dylan's signal, four Bolts dismounted and drew their swords eagerly.

'Who is he?' asked Dylan.

'Jason Cosmo,' said the Huntsman as he closed with Merc. The mercenaries suddenly looked less eager. They mounted up again, and Dylan had to signal twice before all his men reluctantly dismounted and surrounded me. Evidently, they had not yet connected Mercury with the Jason Cosmo rumours they must have encountered all across northern Brythalia. Or perhaps they had thought the rumours a dodge by Merc to throw them off the scent. In any event they didn't seem to recognize me from that night in Whiteswab or their fear would not have been so great.

Playing on that fear was my only hope. It was time to join the trend of boastful talk in combat. I slashed the air with my sword and forced a contemptuous laugh. 'I suppose slaying those giant wolves with my bare hands was enough of a warm-up for you clowns. Who's first?'

No one volunteered. I started forward, praying the mercenaries were scared enough to give way. Those nearest me did back up a step or two. I decided not to press my luck.

'I'm waiting,' I said, halting my progress and trying to look fearsome. My bleeding wounds and tattered armour helped.

'We'd rather handle Boltblaster, sir,' said one of the soldiers to Dylan.

'You cowards!' raged the Black Bolt commander. 'Take him! He's only one man!'

'So is Boltblaster,' muttered another mercenary. They didn't move. I had achieved a temporary standoff. How long it would last depended on the outcome of Merc's duel with the Red Huntsman.

It was an uneven fight. Mercury was fast, but the Huntsman was both quick and strong. His blade traced silver ribbons in the air and Merc had to dodge and skip to avoid it. Warding off the Huntsman's attacks gave him no chance to mount one of his own. If it continued like this, the bounty hunter would eventually wear him down.

'Surrender now and I'll go easy on you,' said Merc.

'You are mine.'

'I thought it was Cosmo you wanted.'

'I will attend to him when I finish you.'

The Black Bolts sighed with relief at that news. All they had to do was hold me at bay while the Huntsman finished Merc. The bounty hunter had already cut the wizard thrice in this exchange and taken only one small wound in return. I was getting worried.

Then I got just the diversion I needed to turn the tide. Sapphrina rose unexpectedly from the water at the edge of the lake, her soaked blue tunic clinging selectively to her body and exposing enough of her curvaceous legs and ample bosom to catch any man's eye. Her golden hair hung wetly around her face, giving her the allure of a siren. In a husky, forceful voice she demanded, 'Who dares disturb the dread Goddess of the Lake?'

To me it was obvious she had swum into the lake to escape the wolf and had returned to help Merc and me from our predicament. The Black Bolts, however, had no way of knowing that she was not truly an angry deity from the depths of this perhaps sacred cattle pond. They fell back in confused amazement, invoking their own gods for protection. One even dropped to his knees in supplication.

I pressed my advantage, screaming like a wounded dragon and leaping forward to transfix the nearest mercenary on my sword. I yanked the weapon free and lopped off the head of a second man before they were all out of range except for the kneeling one. I killed him as he tried to stand.

I had slain a third of their number in seconds, confirming the Black Bolts' fear of me. The survivors hurried to mount up and get away, heedless of their mission or Dylan's curses. I got another one as he hopped beside his mount, having tangled his foot in the stirrup through haste.

The Huntsman saw what was happening and said, 'The wench is no goddess, fools! Hold him!'

It was too late. Their panic was complete. As his four remaining men galloped away to the east, Dylan dismounted to face me.

'I don't fear you,' he spat. 'Or your muck goddess.'

'You should,' I said, standing my ground and hoping he wouldn't actually attack me. It would all be over then. Sweat drenched my palms and my hand was stiff from clenching my sword as tightly as a drowning man does a passing log.

'Come and taste steel,' said Dylan, his voice cracking.

He was bluffing in the face of my bluff. I decided to call him on it. 'Dylan, I think you're a coward seeking to redeem yourself for past failures by pretending to face me while you wait for the Huntsman to finish Merc and save you from the certain death I will give you.'

That hit home. Dylan's eyes went wide with fear and he hastened to mount up and follow his men. I turned to attack the Huntsman, not pausing to consider that he was a far more dangerous foe than Dylan. I wasn't thinking now, just reacting to the sight of Mercury in danger.

I rushed the Huntsman from the flank, only to have him casually disarm me with an intricate flash of his blade. He barely glanced at me, returning his full attention to Merc before my sword even hit the ground.

The brief instant it took him to unarm me, however, gave Mercury an opening at last. He lunged. That, unfortunately, was just what the Huntsman expected Merc to do and he deflected the attack at the last instant. Merc's weapon spun away as mine had, leaving him defenceless.

'Yield, wizard, and live. I want Cosmo.'

'He is under my protection,' said Mercury.

'Then you perish.'

'Wrong!' said Merc. 'Spiritual lightning!' Bolts of blue lightning leaped from his fingertips like a more powerful version of the blue bolt of death he had used in Grimmel. The crackling streams of energy struck the Huntsman, driving him to his knees as they electrocuted his soul. 'You made the mistake of talking when you should have finished me. Now we fight on my terms.'

'Your spiritual lightning won't stop me,' The Huntsman proclaimed, rising anew. Smoke curled from the holes in his mask. Mercury redoubled the attack and knocked him to the ground again. Again the Huntsman rose. 'My . . . will . . . is . . . strong,' he insisted, though he was obviously in great pain.

'My spells are many,' said Merc. He extended his arms and spoke rapidly and forcefully in an arcane tongue while making odd and intricate gestures with his hands. The ground beneath the Red Huntsman boiled like soup in a kettle, churning up thick black and brown soil, hidden stones and disoriented earthworms. Trying to keep his footing, the Huntsman pitched forward as the ground dissolved beneath him. He stumbled as the seething of the soil grew wilder, obscuring his sinking, flailing form in a towering spray of earth.

'Boltblaster! No! Curse you, wizard!' screamed the Huntsman before his voice was totally muffled. The disturbance gradually subsided until the patch of ground looked like any other freshly plowed spot. The Red Huntsman was gone, buried alive.

Mercury stumbled and I rushed forward to catch him.

'I shouldn't have done that,' he said.

'Why? Are your wounds troubling you?'

'No, wizards heal quickly. It's automatic.'

'The energy of casting the spell – was it too much for you?'

'No, I'll be fine when I catch my breath. I'm just out of practice. I haven't done any casting so powerful in quite a while.' He stepped away from me.

'Then what's the problem?'

He waved his hand and the sunshades flew into place on his face. 'Do you remember why I don't use my more powerful magic? The Society might get a fix on my position. The Huntsman thought I would surrender rather than risk that. His mistake. But we had best get away from here quickly.'

Sapphrina came to my side and I put my arm around her. 'Good thinking, O Goddess of the Lake.'

'Thanks.' She leaned closer and her lips almost met mine, then she stiffened. 'Where's Rubis?'

I recalled the sight of two huge wolves pursuing her into the trees. My thought must have showed in my face, for Sapphrina took on a look of horror. 'No,' she said, shaking her head in fearful denial, 'No!'

We all ran for the trees, our wounds and fatigue forgotten amid urgent concern for our missing companion. I reached the copse first and found the torn remains of Rubis's horse. Beside it were the lifeless bodies of the two wolves, with no visible wounds upon them. There was no sign of the girl herself.

Sapphrina blanched at the sight of the dead animals. 'Where is she?' she said, a note of hysteria in her voice. 'Rubis!'

'Up here!' called her sister from above. She was perched in the lower branches of an oak, clinging tightly to the trunk of the tree, her body quaking, her face stained with tears of fright. I noticed deep claw marks gouged into the bark lower down. The back of her tunic was missing, torn away. Rubis clambered to the ground and embraced her sister with tearful relief.

'What happened?' I asked.

'They downed my horse and chased me up this tree – then fell over dead,' said Rubis.

Merc knelt and examined the bodies. He plucked a tiny silver dart from one wolf's neck and held it up for me to see. It bore the emblem of a black crescent moon.

'BlackMoon is here,' he said. He sniffed the dart. 'It's coated with Wolfaway, a poison particularly toxic to wolves.'

'What do you mean BlackMoon is here?' I asked.

'He's hiding among these trees right now, watching us and listening to every word we say.' I drew my sword and snapped my head to and fro. 'Forget that,' said Merc, laying a restraining hand on my arm. 'If he wanted to kill us we'd all be dead. BlackMoon is subtle, an artist of the hunt. He won't come for you until he thinks the circumstances are aesthetically perfect. I think he killed these wolves to frustrate the now-dead Huntsman and give fair warning that he's on your trail.'

I glanced at Rubis. 'Whatever his motives, I'm glad he was here.'

Before we could make further comment a shadow seemed to pass over the sun and the air grew thick and oppressive around us. I felt as if a million eyes were watching me, their foul gaze probing beneath my skin, violating the inner core of my being. It was a sensation like that of bathing in a pool of maggots and I could see by their expressions that the others felt it too.

'The Mirror of Ouga-Oyg,' whispered Merc. 'He has us in his sights.'

Dark clouds from nowhere were gathering directly overhead, though the rest of the sky remained clear. The temperature abruptly dropped and a stiff breeze knifed through the trees.

'Are your wounds serious?' asked Merc.

'No. They just look that way. Ladies?'

'We're fine,' said Sapphrina, still cradling her shaking twin.

'Then let's go,' said Merc. 'I don't want to be here when that hellish little thundercloud breaks.' He whistled and four of the

73

horses of the fallen Black Bolts trotted over to us. We mounted up and rode rapidly southwards.

An hour passed without incident. But, looking back from time to time, I saw the cloud front over the pond pursuing us as relentlessly as the Huntsman's wolves.

'What is it?' I asked Merc.

'Something unpleasant, I'm sure.'

'What happens when it catches us?' asked Sapphrina.

'We can't let that happen,' said Merc. 'We can't afford to stop riding for even a moment because, truthfully, I have no idea what will happen when that cloud catches us. I just know we won't like it.'

We rode hard for the rest of the day, feeling Ouga-Oyg's foul gaze upon us every instant. Already sore from the battle with the Huntsman and the Black Bolts, my muscles burned with silent agony. By dusk we had covered nearly forty miles and our horses were at the verge of death. We dared not push them – or ourselves – any further. Yet we dared not stop.

'Halt!' said Merc, as his horse stumbled and fell. The nimble wizard landed on his feet. The girls and I reined our grateful horses in and dismounted. We had bottomed the last of the rolling northern hills an hour ago and now stood at a crossroads on a broad flat plain. Oddly, there was no settlement here, though we saw the lights of a small town several miles to the east. The only construction nearby was a low stone wall around a well from which the girls drew water while Merc and I conferred.

'The west road loops south of Rumular and joins the main thoroughfare to Rae City. The south road is a little used byway that runs seventy-five miles straight to Raelna.' Merc glanced at the advancing cloud, still some ten miles behind us. It stood out in the gathering gloom as a blot of blackness darker than darkness. 'I'm certain that cloud is from the Demon Lords. We cannot allow it to catch us during the night, for demonic power is strongest in the dark. If we can reach Raelna, we may escape it. Raelna is a land favoured by The Gods. Ouga-Oyg's Mirror has no power to spy in that kingdom and it is through the Mirror that the Hellmasters guide the cloud.'

'We can't go any further. The horses are spent.'

'I know. And so are you and the girls. I'm not because wizards do not tire in the same way other people do, but even I am greatly fatigued.'

'So what do we do? Make a stand here?'

'Hell no. We go on. Ride all night.'

'How? Can you banish our fatigue with magic?'

'In a manner of speaking.' He reached under his cloak and withdrew a black leather pouch. Within it was a wad of dried leaves.

'Leaves?'

'Mulka leaves. The Malravian berserkers chew these leaves to make themselves mighty in battle. The juice acts as a powerful stimulant which blocks all pain and fatigue for up to several hours. I carry a supply for emergencies such as this.'

'Mulka is forbidden,' said Sapphrina. 'At least in Zastria. Like poppychew and hemphash root.'

'Yes,' agreed Merc. 'And with good reason. Aside from inducing phantom lightshows and other visions, mulka can kill. It can make your heart beat so fast it bursts in your chest. It can make us so euphoric we forget why we took it. The risk is great, but it's the only escape I see. I don't want that cloud to overtake us in the dark.'

'It will kill the horses,' said Rubis.

'Probably. But we need them. Even with the mulka we can't make it on foot. We need to decide our course quickly. Ouga-Oyg hears every word we're saying.'

'Let's do it,' I said. 'It's our only hope.' The girls nodded grimly.

'Okay.' Merc gave each of us a portion of the mulka leaves and fed some to each of the horses. The animals flared their nostrils and whinnied wildly.

I put my leaves in my mouth and chewed, swallowing the juice. The taste was bitter, like coffee brewed from sawdust, but the effects were almost immediate. I felt new energy coursing through my limbs like a warm liquid fire. My senses grew sharper, sight and hearing and smell and touch honed to razor keenness. This made the malignancy of Ouga-Oyg's attention twice as palpable. It didn't bother me. I didn't care if all the demons of all the Hells were gazing upon me. I felt no fear as I gulped down great lungfuls of air and my heart hammered thunderously within my breast.

'Let's go,' said Merc.

I seemed to float into the saddle. My mount surged forward with the grace of a swan and the power of a charging bear. We flew along the south road like we were racing through a dream, the landscape whipping past in an endless blur. Sapphrina rode beside me with rapture on her face. Rubis was just ahead of me, shouting wild and joyful gibberish. Merc was in the very forefront, his cape flowing out behind him like a sail.

I had no awareness of the passage of time or miles as we rode our endless ride across that broad, dark plain. When dawn finally caught us, the cloud wasn't far behind. We slowed our pace to a jerky stagger as the sun rose and the effects of the mulka began to wear off. We were passing through a narrow band of light forest less than five miles from the Raelnan border. The land was starting to rise again, curving gently upwards into a ridge of low, sloping hills.

The cloud was a mere hundred yards behind us, radiating violence and malice that beat at our ever-deadening senses like hard iron mallets. When it finally caught us the sky darkened in a matter of seconds, blotting out the new sun.

'This is it!' said Merc.

Our horses halted suddenly and reared back as a curtain of flame sprang up from the road and quickly encircled us.

'We can ride through it!' I said hoarsely.

'No!' screamed Merc. 'It's demon fire! It will destroy you instantly!'

The horses bucked and neighed with terror as they gathered in the centre of the circle. We had to fight to stay in the saddle.

'If that's demon fire, where's the demon?'

The answer boomed down from above. 'Here I am, little man!' The demon was like a man twenty feet tall, pitch black and muscular, hovering over us with the aid of huge red bat wings. Smoke and fire flowed from its nostrils and it bore a flaming scythe.

'You certainly look the part,' I said. The twins screamed once in unison, then fell silent, trembling.

'I am Babbadabbas of the Deepest Pit! I will bring you all as broken prizes to my masters below! I will flay your living flesh from your bones, little men, and take my pleasure on the flesh of your women! I am your doom!'

'Well, I'm glad you've made your objectives clear,' said Mercury. I drew my sword. We were ready to fight this hellish terror with all our might.

Babbadabbas laughed. 'Your weapons are useless!'

'Does he speak in nothing but exclamations?' I asked.

'Annoying, isn't it?' said Merc. 'But he does have a point. A sword is useless in this instance.'

'You have a better idea?'

'Chew a little mulka and you think you're invincible. Observe.'

Merc looked up at the demon and a flashing ray of pure white light lanced from his sunshades. Babbadabbas roared with rage as his flesh smoked and burned.

'He can't stand the pure light of the sun,' said Merc, launching into another of his crisis lectures. 'That's why he clouded the sky over before appearing. Unfortunately, I just used up the remaining charge on my shades and merely scorched him.'

'Was that a good idea? He looks angry.'

'Indeed I am, mortal! You shall suffer for that affront, Mercury Boltblaster!' The demon hefted his burning weapon. 'Your little trick has availed you naught! Now feel the sting of my wrath!'

Babbadabbas swung his flaming scythe downwards, tracing a blazing arc through the air.

9

We all dove from our saddles and hit the ground as the demon's weapon sliced through the space we had just occupied. The four horses fainted from sheer terror, then shuddered and died. Laughing, Babbadabbas alighted in our midst. He scooped up Rubis with his huge free hand, holding her aloft like a squirming doll. She screamed and beat at his hand, but was unable to break his grip.

'This is grand sport!' boomed the demon, stamping at me with his foot. I leaped out of the way, almost hitting the wall of deadly demon fire.

'The game is over,' said Merc, standing defiantly before the looming creature from the Deepest Pit.

'Indeed it is!' agreed Babbadabbas. 'You are mine!'

'I don't think you understand,' said Merc. He raised his hands. A sudden powerful updraft sucked the air from our immediate area into the sky, punching through the supernatural cloud cover and letting the bright morning sun shine full upon us.

'Noooooooo!' screamed Babbadabbas as his flesh sizzled and his body rapidly shrank. He dropped Rubis when he reached normal human size and continued to shrink until he vanished from sight at our feet.

I stood with my sword at ready and a dumbfounded look on my face. 'That was certainly easy. What were you so worried about?'

'We were lucky,' said Mercury. 'Had he caught us during the night, the encounter would have gone quite differently, but this particular demon was vulnerable to sunlight. The Lords of Hell made a tactical error, one they won't repeat. But we'll be in Raelna before they can attack again. I – get down!' Merc knocked Rubis to the ground. I did the same to Sapphrina, landing atop her.

A stinking green cloud exploded into being above us. It

dissipated to reveal twenty disembodied human eyes floating in the air. They were all looking down at us.

'Damn!' said Mercury. He stood and pointed his index fingers at the eyes, projecting narrow streams of fire. The eyes scattered in all directions, darting to avoid the flames. Merc was unable to hit any of them, but did ignite most of the trees and shrubs in the vicinity.

'I thought you were just saying the Demon Lords wouldn't attack again before—'

'Do you know what those are?' demanded Merc, still firing.

'Flying eyeballs?'

'Wizards call them prying eyes. They're the eyes of dead murderers, animated by necromancers and used for surveillance by the Society. We've switched one watcher for another.'

'The Xornite?'

'The Xornite. He can track our every move until we get rid of those things, which won't be easy.'

'Wonderful. Can you make us all fireproof?'

'No.'

'Then let's get away from here before we're toasted.'

Merc revived the dead horses, which were now animated solely by his sorcery, and we were quickly on our way, the eyes floating in our wake. The border was only another five miles, but by the time we reached it my head felt like a pulsing brick, my mouth like it was full of gritty sand and ashes, and my limbs like they were made of lead. The mulka had worn off and I was on the verge of collapse. The twins were in same condition, red-eyed and flirting with the ragged edge of unconsciousness. Our horses stumbled along with drooping heads and dull eyes. Merc seemed to be no worse for the night's wild ride.

The border was indicated by stone marker posts placed at twenty foot intervals along the length of the frontier. Each nation constantly sought to expand by moving posts a few yards into the territory of the other. Though both kingdoms maintained regular patrols to prevent such encroachments, the border was quite irregular and organic, bulging north and south for miles like the trail of a giant serpent.

The road ahead was blocked off with wooden sawhorses and our way barred by a pair of Brythalian regulars in brown tunics. A foot patrol of ten or so soldiers walked the line west of the road, paralleled on the other side by a like number of Raelnan troops in red uniforms. We slowed to an easy trot as the guards looked curiously in our direction.

Well they might. In addition to our drugged looks, I was bare-chested, unshaven, and caked with blood and grime. Rubis was unsuccessfully trying to hold her torn garment in place with one hand, and finally gave up, giving the leering soldier an eyeful of her magnificent chest. Sapphrina was still crusted with pond mud. Only Merc looked civilized, in a magically immaculate red cloak and purple tunic. Behind us loomed a billowing column of smoke from the forest fire he had set and twenty dead eyes hovered in the air above us, watching everything.

'They'll ask for our permits,' said Merc softly. 'We don't have any, so let me do the talking.'

'Fine by me,' I said with a shrug, though it came out as 'Fume b'muf.' My tongue suddenly felt too big for my mouth.

'Do you think you could sway in the saddle? Try to look beat up.'

'Ner prob'm.'

The guards crossed their spears as we drew near.

'State your name and purpose,' demanded one.

'Thank the heaven's we've reached you!' said Merc loudly. 'I am Mercutio Blasterbolt, agent of Baron Tieced of Troth. We were beset by bandits just a few miles back.' He nodded at me. 'Thanks to my valiant man Burlo we escaped, but he sustained serious injuries.'

I slumped to the left, almost falling from the saddle, and gave a groan of agony. 'R wen sif, massr?' I said.

Merc grasped my arm and pulled me back up. 'Yes, dear Burlo. We have reached the border and the king's brave soldiers. The baron's daughters are safe.'

The foot patrol hurried up to the road and its leader stepped forward. The Raelnan patrol meanwhile gathered on the other side of the barricade to watch.

'I'm Captain Volf, said the leader. 'What's going on here?'

Merc gave him a haughty look. 'Captain, I demand you apprehend the bandits who attacked us just now. It is unthinkable that the agent and daughters of Baron Tieced of Troth be molested my such ruffians.'

'Bandits, you say? How many?'

'Fully half a dozen. They leaped from a ditch and ambushed us. Why, if not for brave Burlo here, who knows what they might have done to the baron's daughters?'

Sapphrina and Rubis sighed on cue. Captain Volf looked doubtful.

'Baron Tieced of Troth? Never heard of him.'

'Well, of course not. This is western Brythalia and he has a minor holding in the far reaches of eastern Brythalia.'

'So what are you doing here?'

'Are you going after them or not?' demanded Merc. 'The scoundrels are getting away!'

'Answer my question,' said the captain.

'I am escorting the girls to visit their maternal grandmother in Raelna, not that it need concern you.'

'So. You wish to cross the border. Do you have permits?'

'No, we lost them in the struggle.'

'I thought as much.' His men fanned out and lowered their spears. 'What's the real story?'

'What are you talking about?' said Merc.

'Do you have any idea how many times a week someone comes through here claiming to be the agent of a minor lord in eastern Brythalia who has lost his permit in a struggle with bandits?'

'Rather frequently, I gather.'

'Quite. You're no Brythalian and neither are those girls. Now get down from those horses – you're all under arrest.'

'Very good, Captain Volf,' said Mercury. 'I commend you for seeing through our cover story. I must trust you with the truth.'

'Let me guess. You're travelling incognito on a secret mission for the king.'

'How did you know?'

'Get off the horses. Now.'

'Would you like to hear about the floating eyeballs?'

Volf glanced up at the prying eyes, as if noticing them for the first time. He frowned. 'They are beside the point.'

Merc sighed. 'The truth of it is that I am the wizard Mercury Boltblaster, these girls are the daughters of a Zastrian merchant, and this fellow is Jason Cosmo. We were just attacked by a demon and urgently need to get to Rae City.' He paused, then added, 'The fate of the world may be at stake.'

Captain Volf laughed. Evidently word of my progress across Brythalia had not yet reached this isolated checkpoint. 'Now that's creative! Nonetheless, you lack permits and you are under arrest.'

'I think not.'

As soon as Mercury had announced his true name, the Raelnan troops perked up. Now they knocked the barricades aside and charged the Brythalian contingent from behind. At the same time, we urged our horses through the fray and across the border. Once we were over, the Raelnans broke off the fight and withdrew to their own side as well. Eight Brythalians lay dead and the survivors awaited Captain Volf's command to counterattack.

He raised his sword, then reconsidered and sheathed it. 'No need for further bloodshed,' he said. 'I will report this incident and a formal diplomatic complaint will be lodged. This will make an excellent pretext for this year's invasion. I might even get a promotion. But if you ever return to Brythalia, you are mine.'

The soldiers escorted us to their camp just over a low rise, where roughly a hundred troops were stationed. I understood Captain Volf's decision to drop the incident. What I didn't understand was the camp commander's deferential attitude towards Mercury. A balding, paunchy colonel with a chest full of ribbons, he saluted the wizard smartly as he emerged from his tent.

'Welcome back to Raelna, Lord Mercury. Colonel Nathaniel Brimcottar at your service.'

Mercury returned the salute. 'At ease, colonel. My companions need medical attention, baths, a hot meal and fresh clothing before we say anything more. Also post archers to shoot down some of these eyes.'

'At once, my lord.'

That was the last thing I heard before blacking out and falling from the saddle.

I awoke lying on a cot in a spacious canvas tent, Merc seated on a camp stool beside me. I felt well rested but stiff and very hungry.

'How long was I out?'

'Three days,' said Merc.

'Three days!'

'You were lucky. Some people never recover from a mulka coma, but you seem to have more stamina than a horse.'

'And Sapphrina? Rubis?'

'Fine. They're sleeping now, but it's normal sleep. Their comas were even milder than yours. Nonetheless you all gave us some nervous moments. Fortunately, Raelnan army healers are the best in the world. We've been transporting you by wagon, but now that you're awake you can ride again. The exercise will aid your recovery.'

'Breakfast would aid my recovery more.'

'Dinner, you mean. It will be here momentarily. We've made camp for the night. Colonel Brimcottar has kindly given us a twenty man escort to Rae City, including some damn fine archers. They've already brought down half the prying eyes.'

'No attacks by Isogoras?'

'He hasn't worked up the nerve yet. He's probably waiting for Natalia to return and do his dirty work. Hopefully she's been sucked down a slime pit in the Great Mucky Swamp.' He shrugged. 'Now that you're awake we can leave the wagons behind and reach Rae City in two more days.'

'Fine. Tell me, what is this "Lord Mercury" business? Are you an aristocrat?'

'Hardly. It's an honorary title, but it does have its advantages. Ah! Here is your supper.'

The two day ride to Rae City was the most pleasant part of our travels thus far. Raelna was a prosperous agricultural nation, blessed with fair weather and fertile soil. Colourful flowers and clover-filled pastures lined its well-tended roadways.

Mercury told me something of the history and nature of Raelna as we rode. A thousand years ago, just after the fall of the Empire of Fear, the sun goddess Rae transformed what was then a wasteland into a beautiful and bountiful kingdom which she gave to her son, Blaze Shurben, and his followers. Blaze founded Rae City in honour of his mother and established a kingdom devoted to justice, mercy and goodness. Though the high moral standards of the kingdom and its rulers had slipped somewhat in the following millenium, Rae was still considered the patron goddess of the kingdom.

Raelna's current ruler, Queen Raella, was attempting to restore the kingdom to its previous glory. She had instituted a programme of controversial liberal reforms: giving land to the peasants, outlawing slavery, banning torture, ending imprisonment for debt and other such radical notions. Needless to say, she was much loved by the common folk, though unpopular with the noble class. I sensed there was more to the story than that, but didn't press it.

As we drew nearer to Rae city, Merc shifted his clothing to pure black and his mood became as dark as his cloak. I didn't understand why. The Raelnan capital was awe-inspiring, a circular cluster of low, colourful towers on the kingdom's central plain. Its terraced buildings shone red, blue, purple and gold in the sunlight. The city was fifty times larger than Offal and infinitely more appealing.

We passed unchallenged through one of seven city gates and proceeded directly through clean streets to the Solar Palace, the seat of royal power. Dominating the city, it was a mountain of gold-streaked white stone, vast expanses of glass, and numerous mirrors and prisms which sprayed sunlight across the city in intricate rainbow patterns.

We left our horses in the stables and a detachment of guards in formal uniforms escorted us through the lower levels of the palace. We left the last of the prying eyes behind – outside. According to Mercury the protective wards surrounding the palace kept them at bay.

The guards turned us over to a mob of servants who whisked each of us into a separate chamber. The servants bathed, powdered and perfumed me, then dressed me in hose, knickers, doublet and waistcoat. Amazingly, everything was a perfect fit. When I rejoined the others, I saw the same to be true of the elegant silk gowns Sapphrina and Rubis wore. Mercury had retained his usual attire, though it had taken on a more formal look. Clothing magic was indeed an advanced art in this kingdom.

The palace guards took custody of us once more and brought us quickly to the throne room. A chorus of bells, chimes and horns announced our arrival as the great silver doors swung open and we entered a rainbow wonderland.

The spacious chamber was a series of terraces connected by wide and carpeted steps. Bright and fragrant flowers surrounded hundreds of coloured fountains, pools and waterfalls. Prisms hanging from the glass dome ceiling cast slowly moving slivers of colour across everything in the room. Parrots flew about freely, some even perching on the heads and shoulders of the courtiers. I noticed the men were dressed as I was and hoped I didn't look as ludicrous as they did.

The central feature of the room was the throne itself. Carved from a single huge crystal, it glittered like a resting star atop a high dais. There sat the queen, looking small and distant amid the splendour.

As the music died, two heralds spoke in unison. 'Her Most Enchanting Majesty, Raelna Shurbenholt, Queen of Raelna, Princess of the Silver Sands, and Daughter of the Sun welcomes the Lord Mercury Boltblaster and his companions!'

I felt I ought to bow or otherwise acknowledge the welcome, but Merc was briskly surmounting the steps to the queen, so the girls and I followed.

The queen seemed much more majestic close up than she did from below. Wearing a simple black gown – a stark contrast to all the colour surrounding her – she was short, with a delicate, girlish figure. Her features were fine and pale, combining the fresh vitality of youth with an elfin quality of otherness and haunting beauty. The lightness of her skin suggested she didn't spend much time in this sunny throne chamber. Her reddish-blond hair hung loose about her shoulders and she wore no crown. Indeed, she wore no jewellery at all save a shimmering diamond necklace, which was enough. But her most compelling feature was her eyes. Blue and mysterious, ancient and wise, they belied her youth. They were the timeless eyes of a goddess and they were firmly fixed on Mercury Boltblaster.

I looked to the wizard and understood much. On these two faces were written a tale of frustrated love and unguessed pain. Mercury's voice cracked slightly as he said softly, 'Greetings to you, my queen.'

A tear rolled down Raella's cheek and they gazed deeply into each other's eyes for a long moment while the rest of us shuffled awkwardly. Finally, the queen spoke with self-mocking regalness, asking, 'What brings you back to my kingdom, dear sir?'

'I need your help in reading this gentleman's aura.'

'Your aura specialist is the queen?' I blurted.

'Indeed, sir,' said Raella sweetly, sparing me a fleeting glance before returning her gaze to Mercury. 'What is the trouble?'

'You'll have to see for yourself,' said Merc. He paused and smiled. 'If it's what I suspect, we've got a huge problem. You see, this is Jason Cosmo.'

'Is he indeed?' This time the queen looked me over long and well.

'I am, Your Majesty,' I admitted awkwardly.

'Then the full resources of my kingdom are at your disposal,' said Queen Raella. I would have taken that for a ritual expression of hospitality were it not for the expression of utter shock on Mercury's face.

10

'Have you gone totally insane, Raella?'

Mercury confronted the queen angrily as we entered her private study. After yesterday's formal audience I slept off weeks of difficult travel in the softest bed I had ever known. This morning a squadron of handsome soldiers had taken the delighted twins off for a grand tour of the city while Raella led

Merc and me here to examine my aura. The queen and the wizard had evidently begun their argument last night, for tension crackled in the air this morning, even before Merc's outburst when he saw the three men awaiting us in the study.

Raella met Mercury's anger with aplomb. 'They are my guests and only wish to speak to you – and Master Cosmo.'

Mercury glared at the waiting trio. 'I have no wish to speak to them.'

'Please hear us out, Lord Boltblaster,' said a wizened little grey man with wispy white hair. He wore a plain grey robe and clutched a gnarled wooden staff. His voice quivered with age, but didn't lack force. 'And you as well, Master Cosmo. We have come far at great risk to meet you, arriving only last night.'

'I'm flattered. Who are you?'

'The League,' said Merc icily, crossing his arms.

'We represent the High Council of the League of Benevolent Magic,' confirmed the man. 'Actually, we comprise the whole of the High Council since the loss of several members to assassins of the Dark Magic Society. I am Timeon. The others are Votarius and Ormazander.'

Votarius wore red-and-blue robes decorated with white stars. He was middle-aged, just starting to grey, with a thin, hawkish face and intense brown eyes. Ormazander was of the race of blue-skinned humans from the far south, beyond Cyrilla. He wore a feathered cap and numerous bead necklaces. His silk robes were green and yellow. All three League representatives were studying me carefully.

'Let us sit,' said Timeon. When we were seated, he continued. 'We have been searching for you, Jason Cosmo, since the Society began their massive manhunt a year ago, hoping to reach you before they did. We are grateful to Lord Boltblaster for bringing you here.'

'Which I would not have done had I known you vultures were waiting to pounce on him,' snapped Merc. Raella gave him a sharp look and he said no more.

'What do you want with me?' I asked.

'You are a very special man,' said Ormazander, giving me an odd look, as if puzzled that I should ask such a question.

'So I'm told. He Who Sits On The Porch said something to the same effect.'

'He Who Sits On The Porch?' said Votarius, with a strange kind of eagerness. 'You saw him?' He turned to Ormazander. 'It's incredible! Even the wisest priests assured me he was only a myth.'

'He seemed real enough to me,' I ventured.

'He Who Sits On The Porch is a messenger of The Gods who counsels only the élite of heroes,' said Timeon, with obvious respect in his voice. 'His appearances have been so rare that his very existence is doubted in many circles. Votarius wrote a dissertation on the subject and will no doubt wish to question you about your encounter – later. For now, suffice to say his appearance only confirms the words of the Luminous Oracle of Mount Suradel, who told us you are our only hope.'

I knew the Luminous Oracle to be the most honoured and accurate prophet of all. His predictions always came true. Such, at least, was his reputation.

'The mumblings of oracles are notoriously vague and subject to many interpretations,' said Merc.

'Votarius, would you read the transcript of the Luminous Oracle's pronouncement?' said Timeon.

The younger wizard unrolled a parchment scroll. 'These are the words of the infallible Luminous Oracle of Mount Suradel: "The man called Jason Cosmo is the key to victory or defeat. Preserve him from the Dark Magic Society if you would preserve all that is good in the world." End of quote.'

'You're way off,' said Merc.

I sensed another ugly confrontation brewing and decided to hold my tongue. I wasn't sure just what was going on here, but I knew I was out of my depth.

'You are a blind, selfish, stubborn fool!' raged Votarius, jabbing an accusing finger at Merc. 'The threat of the Society is plain for all to see, yet you deny it!'

'And the League is harmless as a lamb, I suppose?'

'We estimate that half the master wizards in the Eleven Kingdoms serve the Society, either openly or covertly,' said Votarius. 'The League has but four arcane masters.'

'I count but three,' said Merc.

'I have joined them,' said Raella softly, not meeting his eyes.

Mercury looked at her in disbelief, moved his mouth soundlessly a few times, then suddenly lost his vigour and animation, bowing his head with a beaten sigh.

Votarius continued ominously. 'Two out of three wizards of lesser rank serve the Society. Four out of every five new apprentices in the profession serve the Society. Meanwhile, independents and League members are killed regularly. This means the Society will soon have a monopoly on the practice of magic. All magical power and knowledge will be turned to their aims of subversion and world domination.'

'As opposed to your goals of making the world a safe and happy place in which to live,' muttered Merc. 'I have heard all this before. Why do you repeat it now?'

'For the benefit of your companion,' said Timeon earnestly. 'We wish to make clear to him the nature of the threat which hangs over all our heads. Jason Cosmo, the League of Benevolent Magic exists for one purpose, that of preventing the Society from gaining dominion over the nations and peoples of the world. We have opposed them for centuries, exposing their plots, rooting out the corruption they spread. We have held them in check. Many have bravely given their lives to this purpose. Yet now, as our numbers dwindle, the Society is the strongest it has ever been – and it is poised on the brink of total victory.'

'What do you mean?' I asked absently. Mercury had sunk into his gloom and Raella had withdrawn from the conversation as well, averting her pained face. I could see the fresh teardrops glistening on her cheek. Just looking at the two of them made a lump form in my throat, yet the League wizards seemed oblivious to the pain around them.

Votarius took up the pitch, eyes glittering with righteous fervour. 'He means the Society has achieved a position of power in almost every kingdom. Court ministers, generals, nobles, priests, great merchants – perhaps even a few ruling monarchs are under their sway. The Society can profoundly influence events throughout the Kingdoms. Our sources indicate they are in the final stages of a timetable for domination

– ready to achieve total victory within ten years. Only you can save us.'

'Me? Why me?'

The trio frowned and bent their heads together for a quick, whispered conference, looking in my direction several times with hopelessly puzzled expressions.

'What do you know of the Age of Despair?' asked Ormazander at last.

'Only what's common knowledge,' I said. 'The Gods abandoned the world and the demons set up a Dark Empire.'

'And how did that Empire come to an end?' he prompted.

'The Gods finally sent a Mighty Champion to cast it down. Everyone knows that.'

'And what was that champion's name?' he said, leaning forward eagerly.

'I don't know. In the stories I've heard he was always just the Mighty Champion.'

Ormazander lifted from the table beside him a thick leather book with pages of yellowed vellum. 'This is *The Book of Uncommon Knowledge*, a compendium of little-known facts recorded by scribes down through the ages. Herein you can learn the eye colours of The Gods, how many drops of water it takes to fill the oceans, and the lyrics of the first song ever sung.'

'Sounds fascinating.'

'I turn now to the section on the Age of Despair. It says here that the true name of the Mighty Champion who liberated the earth from the Empire of Darkness was Jason Cosmo.'

'Let me see that.' He handed me the book. Incredulous, I scanned the page, confirming his claim. 'How accurate is this?'

'It is certified by the Mnemonic Monks of Everwhen Keep, the most renowned scholars in the educated world.'

'Okay, what does it mean?'

'We believe,' said Votarius, 'that you are the living reincarnation of the historical Jason Cosmo who defeated the Empire of Fear. The Society has its roots in the fallen Empire and seeks to restore it. This they are close to doing. We believe you have been chosen by The Gods to defeat them, as your earlier self, who was perhaps your ancestor, defeated the original Empire. It is your destiny.'

'The Society knows this,' said Timeon. 'They have their own dark oracles who could reveal these things to them. That is why they seek you. They want to destroy you before you destroy them.'

'Yet there are limits to their knowledge,' said Ormazander. 'They were unable to divine your location and thus employed the tactic of offering a great reward. Now that you have surfaced they will turn all their might against you.'

'You are the last hope of the free world,' said Votarius, with the passion of a zealot. 'You can vanquish the Society, turn the tide to victory for the forces of truth and justice.'

'Hold on a minute!' I cried, holding up my hands. 'I think you're getting a little carried away. You sound like you expect me to single-handedly defeat the Society when your League has been fighting them for centuries to no avail!'

'That's the general idea,' said Votarius. He was dead serious.

I laughed. 'You're crazy! Even if the Mighty Champion did bear my name, that doesn't make me him. This is all getting a bit too apocalyptic for me.'

The three wizards were taken aback at my outburst.

'Perhaps he is correct, sirs,' said Raella, suddenly all queen again. 'These speculations are premature. Once I have read his aura we will better understand Master Cosmo's significance to the Society and to ourselves.'

Votarius's bright eyes suddenly shone brighter, with a weird purple light. 'The aura!' he cried, in a voice not his own. 'The secret is in the aura! Spiritual lightning!' He stood and the blue bolts from his fingers struck me, hurling me across the room. I felt as if my insides, my skin, the very blood in my veins had been changed to flaming liquid pain. This was what the Huntsman had experienced at Mercury's hands. It wasn't pleasant. I screamed.

'His eyes!' cried Raella. 'Possessor!'

Timeon and Ormazander were slow to react, but Mercury dove across the room and tackled Votarius. They crashed into a small table, shattering a crystal vase. The bolts quit hitting me as Votarius turned them on Merc at contact range.

Raella stood over me and conjured up a protective shield of rose coloured light. Mercury produced a knife from beneath his cloak and slashed Votarius's right hand, which ceased to conduct the spell.

'Don't kill him!' cried Ormazander, levitating the knife from Merc's hand to his own.

'You fool!' said Merc. Votarius put his left hand across his face and pumped magic energy into Merc's head. He broke free and rolled across the floor, clutching himself and trembling violently. Votarius leaped up and came at me. I was still unable to stand.

Timeon tried to intercept his possessed colleague with his staff, now glowing with green light, but Votarius batted it aside and knocked the older man down. Ormazander came at him with the knife and was likewise cast aside with ease.

'Cosmo must die!' proclaimed Votarius.

Raella's shield protected me, but not the queen herself. A shower of pink sparks flew from her hands and surrounded her attacker's head, but he ignored them and plunged onward, backhanding the queen to the floor. As she fell, her shield vanished. Votarius lifted me by the throat with his bloody right hand, the demon giving him supernatural strength. He held out his left hand and Merc's knife flew into his grasp.

'Now perish in the name of the Demon Lords!' he hissed. His face was contorted with hatred, dripping with sweat. His glowing eyes, twin beacons of bedevilment, burned with a sick madness.

He stabbed at my gut, but I caught his arm with my still free hands. Squeezing my throat, he fought to drive the knife onwards, into my body. He was stronger than I, and the blade moved slowly closer.

Then he collapsed, releasing my throat and falling on his face at my feet. Two holes the size of fists were burned in his back. Across the room, Mercury removed his sunshades.

'An item of many uses. I'm glad you gave me these, Raella.'

The queen rushed to him. 'Are you well, my love?'

'More or less,' he said weakly. 'And you?'

She had a purplish bruise on her face where Votarius had struck her. 'I live.'

'I'm going to throw up,' I announced.

'You just feel that way,' said Merc. 'It will pass.'

'Did you have to kill him?' asked Ormazander accusingly.

'Yes,' said Mercury.

'We were three to his one. We could have driven out the possessing devil and saved our comrade.'

'Yes, we were making real progress in that direction, weren't we?'

'You are a murderer,' said Ormazander.

'The situation here is far more complex than you League numbskulls could ever comprehend. You've had your say, now do us a favour and get out of my sight!' The battle with Votarius had restored Merc's vigour and morale.

'Come,' said Timeon, placing a restraining hand on his companion. 'He did what had to be done.'

'I didn't think it possible for a possessor to reach anyone within this palace,' said Raella.

'It isn't,' said Merc. 'He was possessed already.'

'Liar!' said Ormazander.

'He is correct,' said Timeon. 'The possessor must have lain dormant in him for a long time, waiting for a chance to strike.'

'A sleeper,' said Raella. 'That means none of us can be fully trusted.'

'I've known that all along,' said Merc, glaring at Ormazander and Timeon.

Timeon and Ormazander bent to lift their fallen comrade's body. As they touched it a small ball of purple light flew out of the corpse's mouth, zipped around the room, and disappeared down an air duct.

'The possessor is free!' said Raella. 'Find it!'

The League members hastily departed, dragging the body.

'They are as blind as ever,' said Merc.

'Now, Mercury—' began Raella.

'Did you hear them? They see everything in terms of their own conflict with the Society. They take even an explicit statement from the Luminous Oracle that Cosmo must be protected and interpret it to mean that he is a great saviour sent by The Gods to grant them victory over the Society in spite of their own ineptitude. They're lunatics!'

'You forget that I am one of those lunatics.'

'I'm certainly trying to. Why, Raella?'

'They are brave and dedicated to ideals even you once held to.'

'Ideals are just words. Especially for the League. The Society, at least, is honest about its nature.'

'Mercury, I think you should go before we both say things we will regret. I have work to do.'

'So be it.' Merc stalked from the room, leaving me alone with Her Majesty, the Queen of Raelna.

11

'I apologize for this unpleasantness,' said Raella. 'Mercury's hostility toward the League often transcends the bounds of reason.'

'Why it that, Your Majesty?'

'He still bears them ill will for old wounds. I see the justice in his complaints, but I think this has gone on too long. There comes a point when personal considerations must be set aside for the common good.'

'I'm not sure I follow you.'

She laughed. 'How could you? I'm referring to events a decade old, but if you're to be caught up between the League, Mercury and myself there are certain things you ought to know. Mercury, for example, was not always the man you see now. You didn't know him before he lost his idealism, his faith in the good.' She took on a distant look.

'I sense the onset of a tragic tale.'

The queen ignored me, already lost in the past. A hidden violin sounded faintly as she spoke, magically triggered by her emotional state. 'He came to my father's court when I just a silly little princess. The great mage Pencader served my father, King Raegon, as court magician and also tutored

94

me. Mercury was his handsome young apprentice. Inevitably, we fell in love.' She sighed. 'He said I was the living image of the goddess Rae herself.'

'That's very sweet,' I said.

'Unfortunately, it is also very true. According to tradition the Shurbenholts are semi-divine, being descended from Blaze Shurben, the Son of Rae and first king of Raelna. As such, we may only wed royalty. I was promised at birth to Prince Halogen of Orphalia. That marriage would unite the two thrones, cementing Raelna's traditional alliance with its northern neighbour.'

'I think I can guess what comes next.'

'When word of our love reached my father, he banished Mercury from the kingdom on pain of death. My heart was broken. Three lonely years passed and my wedding day arrived. With Pencader's secret aid Mercury returned and spirited me away in the midst of the ceremony. We eluded my father's forces and fled to Caratha to seek sanctuary at the court of Prince Ronaldo. Halogen followed with an élite force and would have captured us, but word arrived that my father had died, making me queen. Once I assumed the throne, no one could make me marry against my will – but neither was I free to marry as I desired. The only way for me to wed Mercury would be to renounce my heritage, and that I could not do.'

'I'll bite. Why not? If you truly love him . . .'

'I have a duty to my kingdom, to my people. I am in a position to improve their lives, to make Raelna the just and beautiful kingdom it was meant to be. I love Mercury with all my heart, as I could never love another, but my duty must come first. Were I to step aside, power would pass to a council of reactionary nobles and the people would suffer.'

'I see the problem.'

'I wanted Mercury by my side anyway, but powerful interests had other ideas. The nobility urged me to marry Halogen in order to preserve peace. The League also desired the marriage, believing a combined kingdom would be better able to resist the cabals of the Society. Mercury was at that time a candidate for League membership. High-ranking members pressured him to forget me. Mercury refused to bow to their will and Pencader backed him. Then Pencader was expelled from the League and later died under mysterious circumstances. Mercury believes he was murdered on the orders of the High Council.'

'That would explain his dislike for the League all right.'

'With Pencader gone, the League and the nobles launched a campaign of lies, threats and extortion to drive us apart. Eventually they convinced each of us that the other truly desired an end to our relationship. Mercury departed to become the bitter wanderer you know. I threw myself into my rule, consolidating my power and beginning my reforms. Each of us believed we had been abandoned by the other, and it was only three years ago that we began to discover the truth.'

'How awful.'

'Our *rapprochement* has been slow and difficult. He still blames the League for our troubles. I have not forgotten what happened, but feel the threat of the Society is more important than holding a grudge. Halogen still believes that I and my kingdom are rightfully his. His father, King Lanthanide, kept the peace between our nations but recently died. Halogen will soon come to claim me with an army at his back and many nobles still feel I should marry him and avert a costly war. Do you see more clearly now the complex web of relationships you must navigate?'

'Indeed I do, Your Majesty.'

'Please call me Raella, Jason.'

'Thank you, Your – Raella. I understand what you've told me. What I don't understand is why the League thinks I'm some kind of saviour.'

'That is largely wishful thinking. You are probably unaware how many signs and omens in the past year have indicated your great importance in the struggle against evil. The High Council interpreted these to mean you were sent by The Gods to destroy the Society because the League is currently losing its centuries-long struggle.'

'Why?'

'The Society's new Overmaster, Erimandras, is a brilliant, subtle, ruthless leader and a magical genius. He has revitalized the Society and taken the offensive throughout the Eleven

96

Kingdoms. A saviour of darkness, so to speak. The League suffers a leadership crisis and loss of will stemming from what they did to Mercury and me. The High Council craves a strong leader. They hoped it would be you as a reborn champion from the past.'

'I'm sorry to disappoint you.'

'Don't be. We were foolish to look to legends for our strength, but defeat upon defeat has quenched the fires of hope within many. Having lost faith in themselves, they are ready to lay down and die.'

'You obviously aren't, Raelna. Why, can't you lead them?'

'Leading my kingdom comes first. I cannot effectively lead the League.' She paused, then said softly, 'But Mercury could.'

'Merc?'

'He has the skill, the daring, and the will to fight. If his analysis of Society's plans regarding Asmodraxas is correct, then the League needs to adjust its strategy. Unfortunately, they won't listen to him and vice versa.' She smiled. 'But if your aura holds the location of the Superwand it could change everything. Enough of this chatter. Let's find out.'

She directed me to stand before a black tapestry on the wall. 'The contrast helps the clarity of your aura,' she explained. She gazed intently at me. 'Interesting,' she said after a moment. 'It isn't in the Standard Auric Alphabet, but the style looks familiar. Stay put.'

The queen pulled *Opthamalio's Guide to Unusual Auras* from the bookshelf and leafed quickly through it, occasionally glancing at my aura as she searched its pages. 'Aha!' she said suddenly. 'Your aura is done in the Old Archaic Style of High Primitive Celestial Proto-Auric.'

'What's that?'

'Very obscure,' she said, as she walked to her desk and withdrew a pair of wire-rimmed crystal spectacles from a drawer. When she put them on, her blue eyes appeared to be as large as hen's eggs. 'Magnification glasses, for the fine script,' she explained.

The queen stared at my face and read my aura aloud, frequently consulting the *Guide* for pronunciation. I didn't understand a thing she said, but the words did sound very old and obscure. At the desk, an animated quill pen wrote a translation of my aura on a sheet of parchment.

Raella removed the spectacles when she finished reading my auric script and looked at the transcript. Her eyes got almost as big as they had been with the spectacles, and her mouth fell open in astonishment.

'Is it the secret of the Superwand?' I asked, dreading the answer.

'It's a message,' she said softly, gazing at me in wonderment. 'To you.'

'From whom?'

'Read it for yourself.'

She handed me the sheet of parchment and I read my own aura. It said:

Dear Jason,

The Dark Magic Society is eager to locate you and willing to devote great resources to that purpose. It is urgent that you not fall into their hands. The future of all people depends on this. Quite frankly, if the Society gets you, no one will have much of a future.

We have done what we can to protect you. We've watched over you from birth and have done much to confuse and divert your enemies. If we may say so, we've done a pretty thorough job of looking out for you. For example, your ancestors were wealthy and powerful monarchs in their own right. Had that trend continued, such prominence would have made you easy to locate. So we reduced your forefathers to grinding poverty and led them to obscurity in the land of Darnk, thus wrapping you in a protective blanket of anonymity. You can't beat planning like that.

Still, we are limited in what we can do by the terms of the Great Eternal Pan-Cosmic Holy/Unholy Non-Intervention Pact, (as modified and revised by the Pantheonic Committee on Modification and Revision) which governs the extent of our direct involvement in worldly affairs. Nonetheless, we've tried to send help your way. We've issued a flood of omens, signs, oracles and prophetic warnings to encourage our earthly servitors to render you any needed assistance. Once your enemies find you, we will make a hero of you. That will be a big help in your efforts to stay alive.

We urge you to go to the Shrine of Greenleaf at the juncture of the Hidden River and the Arbenflow in the midst of the Incredibly Dark Forest. There you will find the means to ensure your survival as well as more complete information about what is going on. The Keeper of the Shrine is awaiting your arrival.

We would like to tell you these things in a dream or by divine messenger, but the Demon Lords have means of monitoring such communications and would quickly locate you if we did. We've imprinted this message in your aura in the hope that each man is intuitively aware of the content of his own aura and that you will therefore get at least the gist of what we're saying.

We hope this works.

We apologize for any inconvenience all this may cause you, but those are the breaks. Good luck. We're all pulling for you up here.

Sincerely,

The Gods

I put the letter down. 'I did sense part of the message! Enough that mention of the Society made me uneasy.' I looked at the letter again. 'But it doesn't really explain much. If I don't have the secret of freeing Asmodraxas, then why does the Society want me?'

'It does seem quite probable that you are directly descended from the Mighty Champion even if you are not the Champion incarnate. Perhaps they believe you know the location of the Superwand by virtue of your ancestry.'

'What's this Shrine of Greenleaf?'

'I have never heard of it.'

'Great. The Society wants me because they think I know the location of a magic Superwand they need in order to free the greatest of all demons. The Demon Lords want me dead in order to thwart the Society. The League expects me to save the world and The Gods won't explain all this to me until I visit a non-existent shrine in the heart of the Incredibly Dark Forest, which no man enters without suffering death or at least great bodily harm and mental anguish.' I shook my head in dismay. 'Did I leave anything out?'

Before Raella could reply, the study door burst open and a babbling crowd of lords, generals and court officials stumbled into the room, shouting about war, doom, blood and disaster. I could make out nothing amid the hubbub, nor could the queen.

'Silence!' she commanded. The uproar ceased. 'Thank you. General Hawkinstern, what is the matter?'

The supreme commander of Raelna's armies stood at stiff attention and spoke briskly. 'Invasion. News just in. Multiple fronts. Brythalians from the east. Orphalians across the Longwash. No accurate battle reports as yet.'

'Well, get them!' snapped Raella. 'I want complete estimates of enemy troop strength, an analysis of their strategy, an update on the disposition of my forces, and a list of response options. Convene the High Command immediately. I will be there in a moment.'

Her officers scrambled from the room to carry out her instructions. Raella faced me sadly. 'The moment I feared has arrived.'

Mercury swept into the study and embraced the queen. 'This is not one of your better days is it?'

'No,' said Raella, glancing at me.

'What did your aura reveal?' Merc asked me.

I started to reply, but was cut short by the return of the babbling generals and court officials.

'I thought my commands were clear,' said Raella, silencing them.

'New development,' said General Hawkinstern. 'Rae City under attack.'

'By what force?' demanded Raella.

'Demons, Majesty. Winged marauders.'

Mercury looked at me. 'That must be some aura you've got.'

12

The tower at the pinnacle of the Solar Palace was surmounted by a dome of magically unbreakable glass and gave an unimpeded view of all Rae City and the green countryside beyond. Queen Raella observed the attack on her city from the centre of the bubble, standing calmly amid a swirl of alarmed military officers and scurrying aides. Merc and I stood out of the way to one side.

The winged marauders, perhaps three hundred in number, did not venture this high, instead wheeling and darting amid the lesser towers of the city and diving to attack anyone they spotted in the streets below. I studied one through binoculars as it swooped down to street level and gleefully impaled a fleeing pedestrian on its spear. It was an orange, scaly, man-shaped creature with a long spiked tail and membranous, fan-like wings. The shape of its face reminded me of a jackal. The rest of the horde was identical, though some were armed with large iron hooks or sacks of oblong metal balls which exploded violently when hurled to the ground.

'From the direction of their attack, I'd say the marauders gated in north of here,' observed Merc.

'What does that mean?' I asked.

'Someone had to open a gate to the Assorted Hells for these demons to reach Arden. It would take a dozen sorcerers to summon a force this large, unless you had the Horn of Hockessin or something like that.'

'What's the Horn of Hockessin?'

'A magic horn that summons demons. It was created by Hockessin the Unclean, the greatest demonics expert that ever lived. He was so powerful and wicked that even the Society feared him. In fact, the Demon Lords themselves paid him homage. Which raises the question of who is responsible for this attack.'

'Whoever has the Horn of Hockessin, right?'

'Wrong. The Demon Lords could have sent this force, the Society might have summoned it with or without the Horn, or it may have nothing to do with you at all.'

Rae City's defenders battled the marauders with amazing weaponry. On the roofs of fifty towers were batteries of auto-matic arbalests, referred to by the soldiers as ack guns. These were large, powerful crossbows which cocked and loaded themselves after each shot and could fire a stream of ten steel-tipped quarrels in as many seconds. Each ack was manned by a skilful crew of four. The gunner, seated in a reclining chair, sighted his target through the scope, worked the elevation gears, and pulled the trigger. Two more strong men wheeled the turntable on which the gun rested, always keeping it aimed in the right direction. They pushed to and fro, changing direction or making a complete circle as needed, all without looking up. Through long training or sheer instinct they knew which way to go. The fourth man rode on the platform and fed the belts of quarrels into the weapon. The crew was supported by several more men who spotted targets and brought up fresh belts of quarrels.

The ack crews were highly accurate and brought down numerous marauders – it's hard to miss a bright orange target – but were too few in number to get them all. The bomb-throwing marauders disabled several ack emplacements and others were overwhelmed by squadrons which swooped below the level of the tower tops and thus out of range, then swarmed upwards to attack the crews with their hooks and spears.

'Why isn't AMOK engaged?' demanded Raella angrily. 'The acks won't last long!'

'Unknown, Your Majesty,' said General Hawkinstern.

'Find out!'

'What's AMOK?' I asked Mercury.

'Automated Magical Object Killer system. Something Rae's technowizards dreamed up to protect the city from aerial attacks such as this. It cost millions to develop and is supposed to automatically destroy every airborne attacker in range.'

'Then why do they need the ack guns?'

'AMOK is unproven. It's an expensive technomagical gamble that doesn't seem to be paying off. I warned Rae she was throwing her money away and merely lining the coffers of her researchers.' He glanced at the queen, whose now tense face was drawn into a worried frown.

A new force entered the battle, flying out from the Solar Palace to engage the marauders. This was the Gryphon Corps, an élite force of twenty soldiers mounted on gryphons. A gryphon is a large beast with the body and hindlegs of a lion, but the the wings, head and forelegs of an eagle. In the wild, they nest on mountain tops and prey on horses, cattle and other animals, not hesitating to attack men as well. These, however, had been stolen from the nest while still in the egg and trained from hatching to serve as mounts. Nonetheless, they remained dangerous. The Gryphon Corps were brave men to ride such monsters into battle against a force of vastly superior numbers.

They acquitted themselves well, keeping in tight formation and pursuing those marauders which had flown low to evade the ack guns. It can't be easy to fire a bow from the back of a swift-flying gryphon, but the Corps did so with great skill. Still, even they were not enough to check the oncoming demonic flock.

'Say, Merc, if this AMOK system starts up, won't the Gryphon Corps be in trouble?'

'They wear charms which are supposed to identify them as friendly.'

'I hope the charms work.'

'So do they.'

The first marauders were reaching the lower terraces of the Solar Palace when the sky lit up with streaks of brilliant red light emanating from those selfsame terraces. The scarlet beams lanced through the nearest marauders, blasting them out of the air, and kept up a constant flashing against the rest of the intruders. They dropped by the dozens. Within our tower, the general staff cheered and Raella allowed herself a brief smile.

General Hawkinstern reported. 'Light pump required excessive warm-up time.'

'That could have been costly,' snapped the queen.

The beams came from ruby crystal rods, a yard in length and collared by curved mirrors. The whole apparatus was mounted on a swivel to allow it free motion. It was called a resal, short for *regulated emission of sorcerously amplified light*. There were two hundred of these resals firing from the terraces of the palace. According to Merc, the devices magically converted sunlight into destructive energy to be projected from the tips of the rods. The sunlight, however, was not directly from the sun, but was stored in liquid form in great tanks beneath the palace and pumped through insulated tubes into each individual device. This allowed AMOK to operate at night or on cloudy days. The details were too technical for me to fully understand, but I gathered that liquefaction of sunlight was the breakthrough which made the system possible and that the process was a closely guarded state secret.

'And no one is guiding these resals, you say?' I found that hard to believe as I watched the beams cut down more and more of the retreating marauders.

'Each is guided by a magic smart crystal, which tracks targets based on instructions imprinted in the crystal with an imprinting spell.'

'Whatever. I think the instructions were a little unclear, though.'

The marauders had flown down amid the towers of the city to evade the resals as they had the ack guns, but AMOK was not letting them off so easily. The resals concentrated fierce barrages on the buildings which blocked their targets, sending huge chunks of debris falling to the street. AMOK also opened fire on the Gryphon Corps as well as soldiers and citizens on the ground.

'I knew it!' exclaimed Merc. 'AMOK has run amok!'

'Stop it!' commanded Raella. 'Shut it down!'

'Your Majesty!' protested General Hawkinstern. 'Estimate over fifty percent kill ratio. Counterproductive to disengage now. Let us finish them.'

'With protection like this, we don't need the marauders at all,' said Merc.

'Shut the system down!' said Raella, more forcefully than before. The command was relayed downstairs. Long moments passed, bringing more destruction to the city. The bad news was relayed back upstairs to the queen.

'The pump is jammed!' exclaimed an excited lieutenant. 'We can't shut it off!'

AMOK had pulverized the upper floors of the towers nearest the palace and was starting on the next circle. There was already panic in the streets as citizens fled the crumbling structures and headed for the outer fringes of the city, gradually becoming a rampaging mob as fear and anger took control.

'How long until the tanks run dry?' asked a colonel.

'They hold enough to run the full system for another two hours,' said a technical advisor. 'By then, it will have levelled most of the city.'

'Shut it down!' commanded the queen. 'Find a way! Now!' Soldiers hastened to obey.

'One advantage,' noted Hawkinstern. 'Few marauders left.'

I surveyed the city with my binoculars. The general was right. Most of the surviving marauders were retreating to the north, but some were still attacking the outskirts of the city, where the AMOK resals couldn't yet reach them. I took a closer look at a band of three harrying a detachment of soldiers several blocks away, near one of Rae City's numerous parks.

It was no ordinary group of soldiers. It was the unit assigned to escort Sapphrina and Rubis. I had forgotten all about them amid the excitement of Ormazander's attempt on my life, the revelation of my aura, and the attack of the winged marauders.

The sisters were huddled against an overturned touring carraige with the soldiers, six in all, ringed about them in an effort to repulse the flying demons. This band was fortunately armed with hooks, not bombs, but were nonetheless dangerous. Even as I watched, one marauder decapitated a soldier with a single swipe of its hook, the severed head bouncing down the street like a ball.

'Merc! The twins are out there! We've got to help them!' I pointed out the scene. Mercury looked at me like I was insane.

'There's nothing we can do,' he said. 'If we go out there AMOK will cut us to ribbons.'

The marauders lifted a soldier into the air and ripped him in half. Rubis looked as though she had injured her leg and was unable to stand. Sapphrina picked up the sword of a fallen soldier and bravely stood over her sister, holding the weapon inexpertly. The marauders caught up another soldier and hacked off his limbs one by one, letting them fall on the frightened girls.

They were toying with them, slaying all their protectors and saving the twins for last. Who knew what horrible deaths they would suffer? I remembered the boasting of Babbadabbas. Demons had a sick appetite for mortal women.

'We have to save them!' I cried, dropping the expensive binoculars, which were caught by a diving staff sergeant before they hit the floor. I ran for the stairs, intending to race through the street dodging resal blasts and falling towers if necessary.

'Wait, Jason!' said Mercury. It was the first time he had called me by my given name. I paused and looked back. 'I'll come with you. There may be a way to reach them.'

'Then let's go!'

'To the queen's bedroom,' he said, leading the way. Puzzled, I followed, grabbing a jewelled battle axe from a wall display as we ran through the palace corridors.

Raella's bedchamber was opulent and spacious. The walls were decorated with gold, silver and platinum filigree studded with precious gems. The ceiling was painted with scenes of birds, clouds and celestial bodies. The birds moved, while the images of the sun, moon and stars actually glowed, giving off the light that illuminated the room. The bed, wardrobe, settee and other furniture were all of rich craftsmanship, but I didn't have time to admire them. We had come for the rug.

The plush blue carpet was shot through with threads of gold and silver and covered the floor from wall to wall, but seemed otherwise unremarkable.

'I don't see the point of this,' I said.

Mercury waved his hands and a rectangular section of the rug, ten feet by five, floated into the air, revealing the bare marble floor beneath it. Almost immediately, the remaining carpet grew to cover the exposed space.

'Magic carpet grass,' explained Merc. 'It can grow anywhere with the proper spells and tending.' His outfit changed to black fatigues and his cloak turned purple as he hopped aboard the hovering rug and sat cross-legged. The rug promptly fell back to the floor. Merc winced, waved his hands again, and the rug reluctantly staggered back into the air.

'We're going to fly?' I asked nervously. 'On that?'

'It's the only way to get there in time.'

I willed my clothing to become denim jeans and a grey workshirt and sat down beside him. The carpet felt soft but solid beneath me. I wasn't greatly reassured.

'I don't trust this thing.'

'You can't fall off unless you jump or get pushed,' he said. 'I promise not to push you.'

A hole opened beneath me and my posterior fell through as the flying carpet shot forward and over the edge of the balcony to fall straight down with alarming speed. Raella's room was on an upper level of the palace, so we dropped over a hundred feet before skimming inches above the glass surface of the skylight above the throne room. None of the AMOK resals fired on us until we dipped down to the lower terraces.

'I thought you said I couldn't fall off!'

'You haven't, have you? And I didn't say anything about not falling through. Raella must not be giving this grass all the proper nutrients. I'll have to mention it to her.'

'Do that, would you?'

Merc made the carpet dance through the air so erratically that the smart crystals were unable to track us properly. The air around us blazed with arcane power bolts, but none struck the carpet. Our wild flying, however, caused the fabric around me to rip. The hole widened and more of my body sank through it until I was bent double with my knees beside my ears, held up only by my calves and arms. We reached the far side of a circle of towers, putting their bulk between us and the resals, and streaked above the rubble-filled streets.

'Wasn't that easy?' said Mercury.

'I think I left my stomach back in the palace,' I said queasily as my legs slid through the hole. I maintained my grip on the battleaxe, the haft of which spanned the gap in the rug and served as a crossbar to hold me aloft.

'We'll pick it up later.'

'Could you give me a hand?' I said irritably.

'Sorry, I'm driving. Just hang on, we're almost there.'

A panicked mob was nearing the scene of the sisters' peril. We zipped above their heads and sped onwards. Only one soldier survived. As we approached, a marauder struck him in the chest with its spiky tail, crushing ribs and splattering blood. He fell lifeless.

The demon lunged at Sapphrina and easily batted the sword from her grasp. As it reached for her she screamed and fell beside her equally hysterical sister.

Merc had donned his sunshades and now unleashed a resal blast of his own, striking the marauder dead. A second demon flew at us, but met the same fate. The third marauder elected to retreat, but flew too high and was nailed by an alert ack gunner.

The frenzied, frightened mob was almost upon us. Merc brought the carpet almost to the street and my feet touched solid ground. Sapphrina rushed to embrace me. Merc commanded the carpet to mend and helped her aboard while I lifted Rubis in my arms and hopped onto the carpet myself. We lifted off and the running crowd passed harmlessly beneath us.

'We dare not return to the palace until AMOK shuts down,' said Mercury. 'We'll take cover in one of these other towers.'

I cradled the two crying girls and murmured soothing phrases while we flew towards a nearby conical tower formed seamlessly of pink stone. The ack gun atop it had been destroyed by demon bombs, but the tower itself was still intact. We swept through the ground floor entrance into a large open court overlooked by a circular indoor loggia. The building was an enclosed bazaar filled with small clothing and novelty shops. There was a pile of rubble in the centre of the round plaza. While some fearful patrons huddled beneath whatever cover they could find, others looted the shops over the protests of the owners and fled with their arms full of stolen merchandise to join the mob outside.

We flew up to the highest gallery, where the soldiers were stationed and had access to the roof, which had apparently caved in on them when the bombs struck. A dozen dead and wounded men lay amid broken boxes of ack quarrels, fragments of pink stone and the splintered remains of the ack itself. There was a ragged hole in the ceiling where the bombs had struck.

'Who is in command here?' said Mercury. We stepped off the carpet just as it dissolved into a tangle of hovering thread.

A young gunnery sergeant with blood dripping from his head snapped a salute. 'I am, Lord Boltblaster!'

'Why aren't your men controlling the looting below?'

'We lack the numbers to be effective, sir. Five dead, seven wounded.'

Merc nodded. 'Just checking.'

He mounted the stairs to the damaged roof and surveyed the city from that vantage point while I further calmed the girls.

'What do you see?' I called.

'AMOK has shut down,' Merc said grimly, leaning over the hole.

'That's great!' I said. His expression said otherwise. 'Isn't it?'

'No. The marauders are regrouping and a fresh wave is coming in.' The sergeant and I scrambled up to look. Another swarm of winged demons, as numerous as the first wave, was approaching from the north. The survivors of the first assault were gathering to meet them. 'Without AMOK, they'll swamp the remaining ack guns.'

'What can we do?' I asked.

'Fight back the old-fashioned way – with high sorcery.'

13

We returned to the Solar Palace and climbed once more to the pinnacle tower. The guards didn't want to let Sapphrina and Rubis enter, but I wasn't willing to leave them behind. At a word from Mercury, they relented.

'That was a mad stunt!' cried Raella when we entered the crowded bubble.

'All in a day's work,' said Mercury, squeezing her hand briefly. 'And it looks as though we'll have more work before the day is through.'

Without, the demons stormed one ack post after another with brutal precision. Fires burned in several areas of the city and panicked citizens had forced open the seven gates and were fleeing into the countryside.

Timeon and Ormazander entered the bubble, accompanied by fourteen lesser wizards – Leaguers and members of Raella's staff of court magi. General Hawkinstern led his military underlings from the room. The defence of the city was now in the hands of the wizards.

'You'll want to depart as well,' said Raella to the twins and me. 'It will be safer below.'

'Begging Your Majesty's pardon, but if what you're about to do fails, is any place in the city safe?' I asked.

'No,' she admitted.

'Then I'd rather be where the action is. The girls can go below.'

'We'll stay,' said Sapphrina, clutching me. 'Don't make us leave, Jason.' Rubis nodded less certainly. I shrugged.

'As you will,' said Raella. 'But I advise you to keep your heads down.'

I sat with the girls at the top of the stairs, one on either side of me. The magicians gathered around the queen for instructions.

'Our peril is great,' she said gravely. 'The numbers of our enemies are vast, too numerous to count.'

Timeon lifted his staff. 'Let the numbers of our enemies be known!' Glowing red numerals appeared in the air beside him. There were three hundred and sixty-six winged marauders.

'That is still a great many,' said Raella. 'And our defences are rapidly failing.'

The number dropped by five as the surviving ack batteries took their toll, but these were quickly bombed. The only non-magical defences remaining were squads of archers and crossbowmen on rooftops, but these were scattered by intense bombing from the marauders. The demons now massed to attack the Solar Palace.

The queen's eyes shone with regal passion. 'I must therefore do what has not been done in nearly a millenium and call directly on Rae, Goddess of the Sun, to preserve us, praying she will hear the plea of her chief priestess. If Rae City falls and the man Jason Cosmo is captured by the minions of the dreaded Society or the pawns of the Demon Lords – whichever these marauders may be – then beauty and truth, justice and honour, hope and peace, may be forever lost to the peoples of all kingdoms.'

'In other words,' said Mercury. 'This is very important.'

'The ancient rite of summons demands my total concentration,' said Raella. 'It is up to you to hold back the demons until I complete it.'

'I suggest we use the Cascading Calligraphy of Chaos,' said Merc. 'Is everyone familiar with that spell?' The others nodded, some of the junior magicians a little hesitantly. Mercury noticed their unease. 'Don't worry, it's as easy as ABC.'

'The difficulty,' said Timeon, 'lies not in casting the spell, but in maintaining it, which requires great stamina.'

'We've only got to keep it up until Raella petitions the goddess,' said Merc. 'After that, it won't matter – one way or the other.' He pulled a handful of little brightly coloured rods from under his cloak. They looked like some sort of writing tool, but were made of a substance I didn't recognize. Each wizard took one.

'Are these the scented variety?' asked Ormazander.

'No, and don't sniff them,' warned Merc.

Holding the rods between their fingers, the wizards joined hands to form a circle around the chamber, with Raella in the centre. They were facing inwards, their backs to approaching invaders. The glass dome slid open, exposing us to the open air. The breeze blew stiff and cool. The noonday sun stood directly above us. The demons were closing in fast.

The wizards hummed a single note in unison to aid their concentration for the coming conjuration. Whatever this spell did, I hoped it worked quickly. Rubis trembled with fear. Sapphrina seemed oddly calm.

Raella lifted her arms to the sun and spoke in an ancient language of power. Her diamond necklace glittered with brilliant blue-white fire and grew in size until it passed easily over her head to hover like a halo. Suddenly it flared golden, becoming a solid ring of light, no longer a string of jewels. The ring continued to rise and expand until it was larger than the diameter of the platform which held us and floated a good twenty feet above our heads. The sun was perfectly centred within the ring.

The marauders streaked through the air towards the tower from all directions. The wizards had now added more notes to their repertoire and were happily humming a familiar tune used to help children remember the alphabet. How much help did their concentration need? The demons were almost upon us!

As the first marauders got close enough that I could see the orange of their eyes, the wizards broke the circle and turned to face their enemies. Loudly singing the alphabet song – not, unfortunately, in perfect harmony – they began to madly trace glowing letters in the air with their magical markers. Some wrote the same letter over and over, as if performing a handwriting drill. Others autographed the air with their repeated signatures or scrawled curses and insults directed at the demons. Whatever they wrote, it took on substance. Expanding webs of red, blue, purple, yellow, green and orange surrounded the platform and enveloped the demons like a net woven of rainbows, entangling their wings and preventing the use of their weapons. The winged marauders were balked, unable to penetrate the web of colour which soon all but obscured them from view.

Several tried to get at us by flying in through the golden ring, which was not coloured over. They were reduced to ashes as they passed through it. Timeon's enemy counter recorded their demise.

Sapphrina curled against me and I felt something hard amid the softness of her chest. Before I could open my mouth, she pulled a dagger from her bodice and slashed at me with an unearthly scream. Her eyes glowed with a sickly purple light. The possessor which had escaped Votarius's body now controlled hers! I tried to wrestle the knife from her hand, but she broke my grip with superhuman strength and shoved me down the stairs. Rubis grabbed at her but was easily cuffed aside.

The wizards were busy with the marauders and Raella with calling the goddess. I was on my own. Fortunately, Sapphrina was no sorceress. I didn't have to worry about spiritual lightning this time around.

I did have to worry about my battle axe, which the girl hefted as easily as I had, discarding the dagger. I fled down the winding stairs. She followed, screaming profanities only a demon could imagine.

I rounded a turn in the stairwell, waited, clubbed her in the gut with a doubled fist as she came into sight. She lost her footing and the axe, which clattered on down the stairs. I pounced on her, twisted her right arm painfully behind her back. Oblivious to the pain, she pitched forward, causing us both to tumble down after the axe.

Our painful descent ended with us sprawled together on a landing. Ruffles and petticoats were wrapped around my face, blinding me. I struggled to disengage, but was immobilized as she scissored my head tightly between her legs.

She sat up, still pinning me. I heard the scrape of the axe as she grasped it, felt the tensing of her muscles as she lifted it to deliver the fatal blow. I reached up blindly and clutched her long hair, which had fallen loose. I yanked her face down against her own knee and felt the axe strike the stone floor on the other side of my body. I was now able to wrench free and roll clear from my intended murderess. She still had the axe in her hands.

I noted that we were in the chamber at base of the observation tower where the general staff awaited the outcome of events above. Hawkinstern and the other officers looked up from their maps and charts in surprise as I yelled, 'Get her! Hold her!'

'Unwise to get involved in lovers' quarrels,' observed Hawkinstern. 'War is safer.' The soldiers returned to their planning, ignoring my pleas.

I scrambled to my feet. Sapphrina swung, the axe missing me and sinking into the wall. She started to tug it free. I reluctantly hit her in the face with all my strength, hoping to punch her purple lights out and bring this bout to an end. Blood gushed from her nose and mouth, but she was unfazed.

The demon cared nothing about the damage done to its host. I did. I didn't want to hit her again.

She freed the axe. The only thing for me to do was keep running until I could trap her or tire her out. That seemed unlikely. I headed for the far door.

Then the possessor got a new idea.

'Look at me!' commanded Sapphrina, and something in her voice compelled me to obey, though I knew it wasn't a good idea to take any suggestions from her just now. She flashed a bloody smile. Our eyes met and everything went purple. I saw Sapphrina collapse to the floor. My head began to ache. The demon was trying to take control of me!

'Let's go kill that wench of a queen and her spineless boot-licking wizards,' said a nasty violet voice in my mind. 'And then we'll jump off the tower and make a nice splash.' Its suggestion seemed powerfully attractive. Wouldn't it be fun to remove Raella's lovely head and chop the others into little pieces?

No! I bent double and ran full tilt into the nearest wall. Now my head really hurt, but the possessor was out of it. The little purple glow was flickering on the floor, almost as stunned as I was. I grabbed a jade urn being used as a wastebasket and used it to trap the possessor's essence. The experts could deal with it later.

Sapphrina was unconscious. She would ache all over when she woke up, but hopefully wouldn't remember our fight. I knew it was really the demon I had battled, but I felt guilty anyway.

Rubis rushed into the room and I left her to tend her sister while I staggered upstairs. I emerged to see Raella throw back her head and gesture imploringly to the sun. Looking up through the ring of light, I saw the bright solar disk shift and warp until it no longer looked like the sun at all, but a beautiful woman reclining on a cushioned couch. The shimmering and scanty gold bikini she wore revealed most of her perfectly formed body. Her skin was tanned a deep coppery brown and her long hair, bound up in a ponytail, was reddish-gold. She wore sunshades like Merc's and when she pushed them up to the top of her head I saw that her face was almost identical to the queen's. Without a doubt this was Rae, Goddess of the Sun.

'What is it?' she said, and her voice was like a hot summer day at the beach.

'Goddess!' called Raella. 'Demons are destroying your city!'

'What city?' said the goddess; lifting a can of Diet Sola-Cola, evidently some elixir of The Gods, to her divine lips and taking a sip.

'Rae City!' exclaimed the queen in dismay. 'Capital of the kingdom founded in your honour – Raelna!'

'Raelna? Is that still around?' said the goddess offhandedly. 'It must have been, oh, a thousand years since I attended the dedication ceremonies. I really haven't been keeping up with events in the mortal world lately.'

Rae was not at all what I expected a goddess to be like. If this conversation became common knowledge it would have severe theological implications for her followers.

'We have survived these many centuries, O Goddess,' said Raella. 'But we are now gravely threatened and beg your aid. The man Jason Cosmo is here and the Dark Magic Society seeks to—'

'Jason Cosmo?' said the goddess, perking up. 'Where is he?'

'Here, O Divine One,' I said, waving. I suddenly found myself flying up through the ring and into the realm of the Sun Goddess. Looking back through the ring I saw Rae City and the Solar Palace far below in miniature. I could see vast expanses of the world, including the waters of the Indigo Sea and the jungles of Cyrilla far to the south, the wheat fields of Ganth to the west, the uncharted wilderness of the east, and the legendary blue ice fields of the Ultimate North. It was as if I were perched on the sun, looking down on the world from that vantage point. Which, in effect, I was. I floated amid a hot, endless glare which, thankfully, neither blinded nor burned me.

The goddess looked me over carefully. 'You're Jason Cosmo?' she asked.

'Yes, Goddess.'

She took another sip from her drink 'So what's your story?'

'What do you mean?'

She sighed, a glorious sight to behold. 'I just haven't been going to staff meetings or reading the briefings and I'm so out of touch, but I've been hearing your name in conversation with the others. Are you important for some reason?'

'Well,' I said, not sure how to begin. 'As I understand it, Dark Magic Society wants to capture or kill me so they can bring back Asmodraxas and rule the world, the Demon Lords want to capture or kill me so they can thwart Asmodraxas and the Society, and The Gods want to prevent my death or capture so that neither the Society nor the Demon Lords can win. Meanwhile, the League of Benevolent Magic thinks I'm the reincarnation of the Mighty Champion and destined to destroy the Society. I guess you could say interested parties consider me important.'

'Yes,' she said, puckering her lips and knitting her brow in thought. 'I suppose so.'

'This all made more sense when I thought my aura held the secret of freeing Asmodraxas. I've learned that it doesn't and personally I no longer have the slightest idea why I'm so important for everyone's plans. I can supposedly find out at the Shrine of Greenleaf.'

'The Shrine of Greenleaf?' she said absently. 'What's that?'

'In the incredibly Dark Forest,' I prompted.

'Never heard of it.'

That wasn't promising. On the other hand, Rae didn't strike me as the most informed of deities.

'You serve The Gods?' she asked.

'Yes. I suppose I do.'

Her eyes lit up. 'Great. Rub some of this oil on my back.' She handed me a brown bottle and leaned forward until she was lying prone on the couch. 'I can't reach,' she explained as she unhooked the strap of her top.

Bemused, I moved to her side and rubbed tanning oil into her divine skin. It was unblemished and silky smooth to the touch. Warm tingles ran through my fingers and up my arms as I worked my hands across her.

'Mmmmm,' she sighed. 'You've got a wonderful touch. Are you a masseur?'

'Just a woodcutter – and novice hero.'

'You should be a masseur. Would you like to stay here and serve me? All you'd ever have to do is what you're doing right now.'

'Goddess, I thank you for your offer, but I must return. My friends and many innocent people are dying down there.'

'Oh,' she said. 'A little to the left, please.'

Rae was the most exasperating being I had ever encountered, but I had to get through to her the urgency of the situation in Rae City. 'Goddess, that is your kingdom, filled with your worshippers, and they need your help.'

She sat up suddenly and turned to face me. 'Do you think I'm pretty?'

I hastily and reverently averted my eyes from her uncovered bosom and said, as sweetly as I could through my frustration at her constant changing of the subject, 'You are the most beautiful goddess I have ever encountered, O Rae.'

'Do you really think so?' she beamed. 'More lovely even than Lucinda Everfair?' Lucinda was the Goddess of Love and Beauty, said to be the most comely woman, mortal or divine, in all the universe.

'From what I've seen,' I said, 'there is no comparison. You are gorgeous, stunning, mind-boggling.' The last for certain!

'How sweet you are, Jason Cosmo! I have always thought Lucinda overrated. She's so pale.'

'Goddess, the city—'

'Oh, yes. What was the problem again?'

'An invading horde of demons,' I said, intentionally biting my tongue before I could say more.

'Right, of course. And you want me to deal with them?'

'If you would. Your daughter is in danger.'

She frowned. 'I don't have a daughter. At least, I don't think so.'

'She is called so, though she is actually a descendent of your son from centuries ago, Blaze Shurben.'

'Blaze!' she said. 'My darling baby! You say his line still lives?'

'The woman who summoned you is Raella Shurbenholt, Queen of Raelna, his direct heir several dozen generations removed.' I finally had her attention.

The goddess looked through the gate, zooming in on the tower. Raella still stood with upraised arms, pleading with the goddess to help her, while the wizards continued to beat back the marauders.

'See the resemblance?'

'She *is* of my blood!' said Rae angrily, leaping to her feet. 'A little pale, but I can fix that. And they *dare* to threaten her! I've been oblivious for far too long! These demons shall feel my wrath!'

This sounded more like a goddess. She grew in stature until she towered above me like a giantess and her bikini grew into a suit of golden armour. A sword of flame appeared in her right hand. 'I just hope I can remember how to use this thing,' she said.

'I sympathize,' I said.

'What am I forgetting? Oh yes, the hair.' Her hair burst into flame as well, becoming like the corona of the sun. 'Let's go,' she said, her voice now thundering with the fury of a thousand blast furnaces.

She stepped through the gate and I followed. The wizards stopped their writing and the effects of their spell instantly vanished. The rampaging demons halted in mid-air, then turned to flee. She swung her sword thrice above her head and beams of purest radiance leaped from it, blasting every single marauder to fine ash. Timeon's enemy counter dropped immediately to zero.

The wizards, suffering from intense writer's cramp after their heroic efforts, gave a ragged victory cheer. Raella fell to her knees before the goddess with tears of happiness streaming down her face.

'You know what?' said Rae. 'I think I'm in big trouble. I got carried away and forgot that the Modified Non-Intervention Pact forbids this sort of thing.'

'Nonetheless, Goddess, we thank you!' said Raella.

Rae smiled down on her. 'You are welcome, daughter. Actually, you're more like a granddaughter, I suppose. Well, it doesn't matter, you're family, so I don't mind taking the heat for helping you, though the others will be very upset with me.' She put out her hair and made the fiery sword vanish as she shrank to human scale and took Raella's hands. 'I'm not supposed to even set foot on Arden, so I must be going. I'll call you later and we'll talk. I have a lot to catch up on, I think.' She pulled the queen to her feet, gave her an affectionate hug, and kissed her brow. 'You're pretty – runs in family – but you should get some sun, darling.' Rae turned to me, the sudden spark of a divine whim lighting her face. 'Do you have a patron goddess, Jason Cosmo?'

'No,' I said, fearing that I was about to get one.

'I haven't been patron goddess to a hero in ever so long and I think it would be great fun. And in view of your clever touch, your keen eye for beauty, and your importance to the cause of The Gods – for whatever reason – I think you would be a marvellous hero to sponsor. Don't you think so?'

'I'm . . . honoured, O Rae.'

'Splendid! Raella, dear, you're my chief priestess, aren't you?'

'Yes, Goddess.'

'Excellent. You can handle the paperwork for me. I'm not quite sure what all the regulations on patronage are, but you can look them up.' She frowned. 'You know, there is a meeting of The Gods scheduled for today. I suppose I had better attend if I am to get back in the swing of things, so I'll just give you my blessing, Jason Cosmo, and be on my way.'

She pulled me to her and pressed her burning lips against mine. A surge of infinite pleasure jolted me into blissful oblivion and I sank back into the waiting arms of two wizards who lowered me gently to the floor as the goddess rose into the air on a column of light. The last thing I saw before my eyes fluttered shut was her golden form merging with the disk of the sun.

14

When I regained consciousness I found that my skin had become darkly tan, even in places where the sun should never shine. My wounds had fully healed and I felt exceptionally vibrant and energetic. The last thing I remembered was Rae ascending into the sky. After that there was just a warm, bright blank in my mind.

I rolled out of my bed in the guest quarters and had just finished dressing when Raella, Merc and Timeon entered.

'It's about time you woke up,' said Merc, dropping into a chair. 'Three days is a long time for a nap.'

'I slept for three days – again?'

'It is getting to be a habit with you. You should get out of bed once in a while, be more active.'

'How do you feel?' asked Raella, moving towards me.

'Wonderful, Your Majesty. I feel wonderful.'

'And well rested, no doubt,' observed Merc.

'You are truly a special man,' said Raella, 'for the Goddess Rae to become your sponsor.'

'Indeed,' said Timeon. 'That you stand high in divine favour can no longer be doubted. You have aptly demonstrated that it is you we must look to for our salvation.'

'You're not going to start that again, are you?' I said, rolling my eyes.

'You cannot escape your destiny,' insisted Timeon.

Merc was about to make an undoubtedly sour comment, but Raella quickly cut him off. 'Your role in unfolding events is important, as we have seen, but we certainly don't expect you to do more than is reasonable, nor to carry on your quest alone. However, before we discuss your journey, there are certain duties I must perform in my capacity as chief priestess of the Church of Rae. We must formalize your acceptance of Rae as your patroness. Sign this.' She thrust a faintly glowing sheet of parchment and a pen into my hands.

'Did I accept?'

'Her mark is quite vividly upon you.' Looking at my tanned face in the mirror, I had to concede the point. I shrugged. 'You seem hesitant,' said the queen. 'What is the matter?'

'I don't mean to give offense, Majesty, but doesn't the goddess strike you as a bit . . . ah . . . scatterbrained?'

'What of it?' said Raella sweetly, but with a hint of steel in her voice.

'I believe Jason is suggesting that Rae is not quite what he is looking for in a patron deity,' said Merc, with his characteristic tact.

'I'm really not looking for a patron at all,' I said. 'As I told the Goddess Rae, I'm deeply honoured, but—'

'But?' said Raella archly. I promptly shut my mouth. Seeing that I had no further comments at the moment, the queen continued. 'The goddess Rae is one of the most powerful beings in the universe, responsible for the life-giving, warmth-bringing sun, and she has chosen to favour you with her sponsorship. I must think that your thoughts of spurning her offer spring from ignorance. You witnessed her destruction of the demonic horde – know you not that in times of gravest peril you too may call upon her for succour? Wherever the sun shines, she will watch over you and guide you in need. All who honour and serve her, in Raelna and elsewhere, will welcome you like a brother and honour you like a king, and render you whatever service you may require if it is within their ability. And you would say no to all this? In your situation?'

'When you put it that way, how can I refuse?'

'You cannot. If it is any comfort, you will probably deal with the goddess through me most of the time. As her chief representative in Arden I am charged with interpreting her will and ministering to her followers.'

'In that case, O gracious queen, I heartily accept the sponsorship of your goddess.' I signed the document and returned it to her.

'Excellent. I welcome you to her service. May the sun ever shine on your face, but not in your eye.' She lightly touched my brow with both hands as she spoke these words. 'Just between us,' the queen whispered, leaning forward, 'she does seem a bit unfocused. But you can't except anyone to be perfect.' She smiled covertly and stepped away from me. 'Now we must discuss your expedition.'

'Yes,' said Timeon. 'It is now of utmost urgency that you go quickly to Greenleaf and learn what you can. The League will give you what assistance we have to offer.'

'I may need quite a bit if I'm going to have more days like yesterday.'

'You mean yesterday thrice removed,' said Mercury. 'But not to worry, I'm coming with you. And we can avoid a lot of problems travelling by air.'

'Fly again? I think I'd rather walk and take my chances.'

'This flight should be less harrowing than the last.'

'How could it not be?'

'We survived, didn't we?'

'True. Okay, we're flying.' I swallowed hard. 'When are we leaving?'

'Immediately. We have to move before the opposition mounts another major attack.'

'Of course.'

Timeon withdrew from his pocket a gold ring set with a clear purple amethyst and held it aloft. 'Behold the Ring of Raxx, reputed to have been worn by the Mighty Champion who ended the Age of Despair, the original Jason Cosmo. It is said to possess wonderous magical properties.'

'Ah,' I said, my imagination fired by the possibilities. 'What does it do? Make the wearer invisible? Grant wishes? Make one invincible in battle?'

Timeon coughed with embarrassment. 'Actually we don't know what it does. It has been in the keeping of the League for many years and we have studied it carefully, but have been unable to determine its capabilities. Still, if you are truly a new incarnation of the original Mighty Champion, it may reveal its powers to you.'

'And if it doesn't?'

'We can always pawn it for quick cash,' said Merc.

I took the ring and slipped it onto my right hand. I felt absolutely no sort of arcane tingle or other indication that the ring was in any way remarkable.

'May it serve you well,' said Timeon.

'I'm sure it will.' I waited, expecting more, but soon realized the ring was the extent of the League's assistance.

Mercury stood. 'Eat your breakfast, take your leave of the twins, and join me on the north plaza within the hour. I already have our supplies stored in my cloak.'

The trio of wizards departed and a servant brought in my breakfast of fruit, bread, cheese and wine. I wolfed down the food, combed my hair, and strolled across the hall to see the girls. Sapphrina lay in bed, her face still puffed and bruised. Rubis sat beside her holding an ice-pack in place against her jaw.

'Hi, Rubis.' I approached the bed. 'Good morning, Sapphrina. I'm really sorry about this.' I took her hand in mine and squeezed it gently. 'How do you feel?'

She gave me a weak but winning smile. 'Not much better than I look. Between the flying demons, the possessor and a certain dashing Darnkite I took some serious abuse the other day. Nothing broken, but my jaw was dislocated. The healer repaired it yesterday. Mostly bruises and lingering effects of hysteria and traumatic shock. I'll be back on my feet in no time. Where did you get that gorgeous tan?'

'From a new friend. Listen, I'm about to depart for the Incredibly Dark Forest and I came to say goodbye.'

'The Incredibly Dark Forest!' exclaimed Rubis. 'Why?'

'Hopefully, that's where I'll learn what's going on and how I can escape this dangerous life I've been living recently.'

'The Incredibly Dark Forest is a good place to escape life, period,' said Sapphrina. 'Oh, Jason, don't go there! Come with us!'

'To Caratha?'

'The queen has promised us transportation as soon as Sapphrina is ready to travel. I'm sure you could come too.'

'I'm tempted. But I've still got the Society, the Demon Lords and hordes of bounty hunters to contend with. Once I take care of those matters, I'll come see you. How's that?'

'That's ridiculous,' said Sapphrina. 'You'll be killed and I – we, that is – will never see you again.'

'Thanks for the encouragement.'

'You know what I mean. It's just – come with us! Please?'

'I can't. Not until all this is over with. You two have been in constant danger since you met me. Wolves, bounty hunters, soldiers, demons – you're lucky to have made it this far. I can't escape what's happening, but you can. I don't want your blood on my hands, so this is goodbye until I'm safe to be around.'

'I suppose you're right,' said Rubis, rising and giving me a glancing kiss on the cheek. 'I think I'll conveniently take a walk now.' She handed me the ice-pack and left the room. I took her seat and moved to put the ice-pack in place. Shapphrina caught my hand.

'Enough of that. My face is frozen. Rubis is worse than a mother when I'm ill.' I put the ice-pack down. 'I'm afraid for you,' she said.

'That makes two of us.'

She smiled. 'I've only known you for a few weeks and you've already saved my life half a dozen times at least.'

'You exaggerate.'

'Not by much. Jason, I'm going to miss you. If anything happens to you – and let's not kid ourselves, it probably will – I'll be devastated. At the very least. You're the kindest, the bravest, the best man I've ever known.' She gathered my hands in hers.

'Thank you. By remarkable coincidence, you are the best, bravest and most beautiful woman I've ever met. No slight to your sister, but you've got some extra special spark that makes you . . . that makes you . . .'

'Well?'

'Extra special,' I said at last, raising her hands until they almost brushed my lips as I moved from the chair to sit on the edge of the bed.

'Jason . . .'

'Sapphrina . . .'

'Before you go, I want you to know that—'

'Yes?'

'I've thought about it a great deal, the last few days especially, and I wouldn't say this if I didn't mean it with all my heart. Jason, I – mmmph!'

I cut her off with a kiss. For a woman with a recently dislocated jaw, she was surprisingly energetic in her response. Eventually we came up for air.

'I can guess what you were about to say,' I said. 'But hold that thought until I return. That will give me the most powerful incentive of all to come back alive.'

'Why, Jason! What a romantic thing to say!'

'It just came to me. When I get back, I'll have something more to say.'

Her eyes sparkled. 'I'll look forward to it. Now kiss me again before you go forth to eradicate the forces of evil.'

When that was done, I left the room, trying not to think about the tears glistening in her eyes. Or in mine.

I met Mercury and Raella on the north plaza ten minutes later.

I got a sudden surge of strength as I stepped outside into the full light of the morning sun.

'Whoa!'

'What is it?' asked the queen.

'I feel incredible. Like a juggernaut.'

'Oh,' said Raella. 'That's part of the blessing of Rae. You probably have the strength of ten men when in sunlight, perhaps more. It's fairly standard.'

'Ready to fly?' asked Merc. I imagine torturers use the same tone of voice when asking their victims if they are ready to be flayed alive.

'Sure,' I said with a brave smile. My augmented prowess did nothing for the ominous lightness of my stomach at the prospect of another carpet ride. 'Nothing like soaring hundreds of feet above the ground on an airborne welcome mat.'

'This rug has been thoroughly inspected for defects,' said Raella reassuringly.

'We'll head northwest, over the Longwash and Orphalia, to where the Arbenflow emerges from the southern tip of the Forest,' said Merc.

'What about the invasion?' I asked.

'The latest reports are favourable,' said Raella. 'General Vixen Hotfur commands my northern army and she has halted the Orphalian advance. The Brythalian drive has been blunted as well and order is being restored here in Rae City.'

'We'll be above the battle anyway,' said Merc. 'And Halogen hasn't the wit to have any sort of air corps. I don't expect any problems on that front. So let's quit stalling and go.'

'May the grace of Rae and all The Gods be with you, Jason Cosmo,' said Raella. 'And with you, my love.'

The couple kissed and Merc and I boarded the flying carpet. We shot straight up until we were higher even than the top of the Solar Palace, then sped northwards.

'We can cover fifty miles in an hour,' said Mercury as the wind whipped our faces and his cloak billowed back like an azure banner.

'Wonderful.'

'Shift your clothing to sky blue as I've done. It will make us more difficult to spot from the ground.'

I willed the transition, again marvelling at Raelnan garment magic. 'Just how bad is the Incredibly Dark Forest?'

'The physical environment is not much worse than the usual evil forest, but it's not exactly a resort area. Wild animals, ogres, goblins and the usual assortment of dangerous denizens. We'll be lucky to survive, much less find this shrine.'

'What do you know about the Shrine of Greenleaf?'

'Personally, I've never heard of it. The tales I know say a lost castle filled with treasure lies where the Hidden River joins the Arbenflow. I don't know anything about a holy shrine. It seems like an odd location for one.'

'You think my aura lies?'

'No, I just think The Gods could have picked a better location. No one has ever found the Hidden River. My plan is to skim up the Arbenflow until we find it or get forced to turn back.'

As we flew onwards, we saw the unmistakable signs of war. Geysers of black smoke stained the the northern horizon like dark blood gushing from a chest wound. Ragged streams of refugees clogged the roads to Rae City like rivers of misery, all unaware that the capital itself had nearly been destroyed. In two hours we had almost reached the Longwash and saw clearly that the boiling smoke came from the burnt husks of two river towns and numerous smaller villages which the Orphalians had put to the torch.

The invaders had penetrated several miles into Raelnan territory before their thrust was blunted on a low line of fortified hills held by the Raelnan army, hills the Orphalians had to cross in order to reach the interior of the kingdom. It wouldn't be easy. The Raelnans had built wooden palisades atop earthen ramparts and dug ditches filled with pointed stakes. A barricade of logs and stones blocked the road to

Rae City. Heavy catapults and mobile ack guns pulled by oxen supported these defences.

A pitched battle raged amid the hills. Lacking artillery of their own, the Orphalians hoped to overwhelm the defenders through sheer numbers. They attacked tirelessly, clambering up the slopes and crashing against the barricades, falling back under the withering spears and arrows of the Realnans, and regrouping to charge again. King Halogen's forces resembled a mob in rough green uniforms more than an actual trained army. They fought with courage and animal ferocity, but with little co-ordination of actions. Each little knot of troops attacked and retreated of its own accord, making the battle only a collection of smaller battles on the Orphalian side.

The Raelnans, by contrast, exhibited superb discipline. They left not a single gap in the defensive line and seemed able to anticipate every spontaneous tactic of the enemy. Ack gunners directed their fire where it was most needed, backed up by the powerful catapults. Troops moved efficiently to relieve hard-pressed sections of the line, while medics whisked wounded warriors swiftly away from the front. The Raelnans' boots were polished and their uniforms clean, remarkable in the midst of battle. The Raelnans functioned as one integrated unit; they didn't waste a single sword stroke.

The Orphalian encampment was about two miles north of the hills beside a small creek. Safely out of ack range, it was surrounded by hastily erected palisades and lightly guarded. Only a skeleton force remained behind, mostly supporting personnel, though it seemed a cavalry troop was also being held in reserve.

'See the huge green tent in the middle?' asked Merc, bring-ing the carpet to a halt above the camp.

'The one with the dragon flags all over it?'

'Right. That's where Halogen is, I'll wager. Too cowardly to lead his men in battle. I'd like to swoop down, cut out his black heart, and bring this war to a quick close.' Merc spoke of his rival with an unyielding metallic hatred.

'Is that a good idea?'

'Yes, but we don't have time for personal vendettas now. Maybe on the way back.'

'How wrong you are,' said a hoarse voice behind us. 'Now is a perfect time for vendettas.'

We turned and saw that another magic carpet had silently flown up on us while we studied the scene below. Its rider was covered in deepest crimson, from robes to gloves to hood, with no skin exposed. A silver horn hung from a cord around his neck and an obsidian knife at his belt.

'Isogoras,' said Mercury.

'Mercury,' rasped Isogoras.

They spat one another's names like curses.

'Do you have a sore throat? You sound a little ragged.' Mercury's solicitude was blatantly false.

Isogoras touched the silver horn. 'Do you have any idea how long you have to blow on this thing to summon six hundred winged marauders?'

'The Horn of Hockessin, I presume?'

'The same.'

'I knew it would wind up in your grasping hands eventually.'

'It is my most prized possession.'

'How nice. What inspired you to show your face at last? Run out of incompetent lackeys?' Merc casually reached under his cloak as he spoke.

Isogoras pointed a glowing gloved finger at Merc's chest. 'I wouldn't think about my sunshades just now, Mercury. We must talk.'

'I don't think we have anything to say to each other.'

'I am under direct orders from Erimandras the Overmaster to induce you to join our order. Personally, I would rather see you boiled alive in dragon liver oil.'

'What a coincidence. I would rather be boiled alive in dragon liver oil than join the Society.'

'But the orders of the Overmaster must be obeyed. I must warn you that your potential value to our cause does not justify further recruiting efforts. This will be your last chance.'

'Do you mean if I refuse again you'll finally leave me alone?'

'Of course not. If you refuse again I will finally have the pleasure of killing you, so I hope that you do, but let me run through the benefits of Society membership one more time anyway.'

'Pay attention, Jason. You may find this interesting.'

Isogoras began his recital. 'With your low monthly dues you get access to forbidden arcane knowledge and a new world of excitement. You'll have frequent opportunities to burn, loot, rape and pillage to your heart's content in exotic locations throughout the Eleven Kingdoms. You'll take part in corrupting officials, planning assassinations and plotting the overthrow of mighty monarchs. Men will quake in fear at the mention of your name, because you'll be part of a proud tradition of terror over two thousand years old.'

'This is the good part,' said Merc.

'As a master wizard, you quality for special benefits such as your own complimentary staff of personal slaves. You'll also get an unlimited pass to the exclusive Carnality Club, where you may shamelessly practice any sexual perversion you can imagine with help of a talented staff of lewd and libidinous demonettes. Furthermore, you'll receive a handsome certificate of membership suitable for framing, a free magic ring, and much much more. What do you say?'

'I'd rather burn in hell.'

'As one who has done just that, I'll be happy to help you along.' Isogoras patted the silver horn. 'With this I can send you to the Vilest Vales of Hell, where the demon torturers in the Citadel of Endless Agony will gleefully demonstrate how that fortress got its name.'

'Go for it.'

'First, I have a message for Jason Cosmo.'

'What?' I said.

'The Overmaster of the Dark Magic Society has authorized me to make you this offer. Turn yourself over to me, tell us what we want to know, and no harm will come to you. We do not wish to waste further effort in apprehending you and will look favourably upon your co-operation. We will pay *you* the ten million crowns and give you your own kingdom to rule. If you refuse this generous offer, torture and death will be your lot. What is your answer?'

'It sounds tempting.'

'Of course.'

'But I'll pass.'

'So be it.'

We had hovered in place during this conversation. Now, with the aerial violence about to begin, Mercury willed our carpet to plunge upwards with such speed that we were pressed flat against the fabric. Below us, a stream of toxic yellow jelly flew from Isogoras's finger and filled the space where we had been. Since we were no longer there it fell to earth, to work its nasty effects on the soldiers below.

Merc brought the carpet to a halt and put on the sunshades. 'Stay down. It makes you less of a target. We've got to get the Horn away from him before he calls up reinforcements.'

It was too late for that. Isogoras flew to meet us, sounding the mournful Horn of Hockessin as he came. Small winged demons the colour of blood spewed forth from the instrument. I saw that they were the colour of blood because they had been dipped in the substance, which dripped from their bodies and splattered through the air with every flap of their wings. They were armed with clanging cymbals, shrill whistles and tiny trumpets which made an unholy racket louder than the Horn itself and seriously grated on my nerves.

'Bloody nuisances!' shouted Merc. 'Small, fast and irritating. Probably the best he can do with the condition of his throat, but they can eventually drive us mad with those decibels of damnation!'

'I'll say!'

'Take care of the Horn as we pass!'

We dove into the cloud of nuisances, Mercury crisping as many as he could with bursts from the sunshades. I stayed down until we were almost upon Isogoras, then leaped up and swung my axe. It struck the Horn and snapped the cord, sending it spinning into space. No more little demons emerged from it.

'Good work!'

We still had about seventy of the monsters to contend with, however. They stayed with us through all of Mercury's insane evasive maneuvering, which involved abrupt changes of direction and even flying upside down. We were held in place by the spell of the rug, but I was understandably terrified.

'The sound is making me crazy!'

'Just swing that axe! You're sure to hit some of them!'

Isogoras fell in on our tail and drew the obsidian knife from his belt. Merc fired sunshade shots at him, but he dodged and weaved to deny him a clear shot. Even so, he hit some of the nuisances.

'How's he going to stab us from there?' I asked.

'He's not!'

Isogoras hurled the knife at us. Merc banked into a swift climb. 'The fool! Gravity will pull the knife—'

The knife followed us and was gaining fast. It sliced through a bloody nuisance that got in its way and started to glow red.

'I can't shake it!' said Merc.

The volcanic glass was reverting to its molten form and was now seconds away from catching us. It hit our carpet with a hot splash and the rear of the rug burst into flame.

'We're going down!' said Merc as we lost altitude.

Isogoras soared above us, taunting. 'I'm sure you will get a welcome reception from Halogen of Orphalia, Mercury.'

'We're going down,' repeated Merc. 'And we're taking him with us.'

Isogoras had slowed so that we could hear his words, giving Mercury a clear shot with the sunshades. The spectacles flashed and our enemy's carpet burst into flame and began to plummet as well, falling toward the battlefield. Isogoras had nothing further to say.

'I really ought to think of a good parting line,' said Merc. 'But we've got a bigger problem.'

'Like landing?' I said, beating ineffectually at the flames.

'Crashing gently would be more apt. Response is getting sluggish – I don't think we can reach the river! What else can cushion our fall?'

'The tent?'

Merc smiled wickedly. 'Brilliant idea. I think I can manage that.'

Fire was licking at our backs as we angled towards Halogen's pavilion. The spell holding us in place was weakening, and the unburned portion of the carpet beginning to go limp. We skimmed in low. Excited soldiers shouted and pointed. An archer took a shot at us, missed. We ripped through a dragon banner and crashed into the billowing top of the tent, causing the whole thing to collapse like an imploding green cloud.

15

We hit hard and I was stunned out of my wits. I found myself blanketed in heavy green canvas and I smelled smoke. I heard excited, angry, frightened shouting. My body ached as if I had been used as the ball in a traditional mountain giant game of volleycorpse. It hurt to move. It hurt to think about moving. I lay still and considered the merits of surrendering to unconsciousness. That would free me from this pain, but then I wouldn't find out what all the shouting was about. The sound was muffled by the tent cloth, however, and I really couldn't make much out clearly. I might as well faint.

'Fire!'

I heard that distinctly. It explained the smell of smoke. I briefly wondered just where the fire was, then noticed that it was getting quite warm inside my canvas cocoon. The fire was close by. That was nice. It would keep the wild animals away while I slept and I could cook breakfast when I woke up.

Excited voices reached me.

'Your Royal Supremacy, are you injured?'

'I'm fine, you snivelling cur! But I'll have the incompetent swine who erected this tent flayed alive with toenail clippers!'

That was an interesting exchange. It was difficult to find good help these days. I once had an assistant woodcutter working with me, but he couldn't wedge a tree so that it would fall correctly and never shouted the proper warnings. After nearly being crushed for the third time by toppling timber, I gave him the axe.

'It were assassins from the air, my king!'

'What did you call me?'

'It were assassins from the air, Your Royal Omnipotence!'

'Supremacy, you fool! Royal – no, I like Omnipotence better. A promotion for you. Now what were you saying?'

'They flew in on a magic bath towel, burning like . . . like a campfire.'

'What inspired imagery.'

'Your pardon?'

'Continue, idiot!'

'They headed right for your royal omnipotent tent and brought it down!'

How interesting. The king's tent had been attacked by a burning bath towel from above. It paralleled my own recent past, wherein Mercury had aimed our crashing carpet for the pavilion of King Halogen. How long ago had that been?

I snapped out of my daze. The time was now, this was Halogen's tent, and our ruined rug had set it aflame! We were in the middle of a hostile encampment – I felt about for my battle axe and failed to find it – and I was unarmed. I didn't know where Merc was, or if he had even survived.

'We've got one of them!'

'Bring the dog to me and – by the crown on my brow! Mercury Boltblaster! The vile sorcerer who has bewitched my love delivered into my hands by his own folly! This is going to be a good day, after all!'

I burrowed through the cloth around me until I could peer out and see what was happening. King Halogen was a tall man dressed for a royal ball, not a battlefield. He had a flowing mane of wavy brown hair, a hawkish but handsome face marred mainly by his arrogant sneer, and blue eyes fogged with vanity. He wore a crown made of gold, green velvet and large emeralds surmounted by the figure of a dragon with unfurled wings. He was surrounded by knights in green plate armour.

Two soldiers held Mercury between them. His body was limp and his feet dragged on the ground. He had lost his sunshades, his eyes were glassy, and didn't seem to be in any condition to help himself. Halogen struck him across the face with his sceptre. Merc's head merely lolled to one side.

133

Other soldiers pulled nobles and comrades from the wreckage of the tent while a hastily assembled bucket brigade fought the fire with water relayed from the creek. My position hadn't caught fire yet, but would soon. I couldn't stay here, but if I revealed myself it would mean instant capture.

No it wouldn't! I cursed myself for a fool. No one here knew who I was. I could make my clothing become a copy of the Orphalian uniform and blend right in until I figured out a way to rescue Merc. In the excitement of Mercury's capture, the Orphalians had apparently forgotten that there were two men on the flying carpet. That was one advantage I had.

I emerged from my hiding place and discovered my second advantage. I still had the sun-given strength of ten men, something to keep in mind as I formed my plan. I had to act soon, for I had no idea how long Halogen would keep his most hated enemy alive.

I helped fight the fire so I could be near enough to observe their one-sided confrontation. Halogen smacked Mercury with the sceptre again.

'She loves me, sorcerer, and only your wicked spells have kept her from rushing to my arms all these years!' He struck Merc once more. 'Now that I come to claim her at last, you fear me! You know that my strength and virility can free her from your ensorcelments and so sought to kill me – and now you are mine! Great shall be your suffering this day!' He hit him a fourth time. 'Why don't you answer me?'

'Perhaps if His Supreme Royal Omnipotence would not strike him so, the evil wizard would regain consciousness,' suggested one of the nobles.

'Supreme Royal Omnipotence, eh? I like that. I'll make you a grand duke.'

'I'm already a grand duke.'

'I'll make you a grander duke. Your suggestion has merit. Let him be trussed to a stake. Revive him with cold water and bring me some hot knives, scourges, potato peelers and the like. Well, what are you ignorant ingrates waiting for, a royal decree? Move!'

I abandoned the fire-fighting efforts and slipped through the camp, looking for anything that might be useful in making our escape. I passed the horses, already saddled and barded for immediate mounting by Halogen's noble knights. I stole an unguarded sword and strapped it on. I found the nearest exits from the camp, marked the number of guards at each gate. There were very few. Most were fighting the fire.

By the time I completed my reconnaissance, I had a wild but workable plan in mind. I returned to the spot where Mercury, stripped to the waist, had been bound to a thick wooden post freshly erected in an open space near one of the palisade gates. He was awake now, and fully alert. Good. I would need his help for my plan to work. I edged my way through the crowd gathered around him, mostly nobles and officers who were exempt from the dirty work of fighting fires, until I was directly opposite Merc. I gave a quick wave. He winked in acknowledgment.

Halogen strode forwards, in his hands a whip knotted with shards of glass. 'Today you pay for your many crimes against me, sorcerer. You will soon beg for my mercy, but none shall be forthcoming. Before I am finished, you will rue the day you stole Raella from me with your dark magicks.'

'Halogen, you're still the pompous, preening, pretty-boy, power-mad princeling you were last time we met. Your father's body can't even be cold in the grave and here you are invading a kingdom that has been Orphalia's ally for centuries simply because you can't accept the fact that Raella Shurbenholt is far too wise to wed a psychotic weasel like you.'

'Lies! She is the only woman to ever refuse me, proof enough that she has been put under some foul spell. She is rightfully mine, promised to me from birth for a marriage that will unite our kingdoms for all eternity!'

'It's the land you love, not the lady.'

Halogen cracked the whip, gashing Merc's cheek. It was time to get moving. The fire at the king's tent was almost out, but the Orphalians would soon have more flames to contend with. I snatched a blazing brand from an untended cooking fire I had noted and ran for the horses, raking the torch against every tent I passed. A corporal tried to stop me, but I smacked him in the face with my weapon and he fell heavily to the ground. I mounted a horse which I had already loosened and took off through the camp, merrily igniting tents and scattering bewildered foot soldiers.

My winding path took me past all the nearby tents, which were left burning in my wake. I finally plunged into the crowd around Mercury, trampling knights and nobles.

'Stop him!' screamed Halogen. I clubbed him with the blazing brand, sending his crown flying as he hit the ground.

I drew up beside the stake, wrapped my arms around it, and lifted. Though heavy, it wasn't solidly secured and slid out of the ground without too much difficulty.

'What are you doing?' said Mercury, still bound to it.

'Rescuing you!'

'Like this? Cut me loose!'

'No time!'

I headed for the nearest gate, holding the post before me like a thick lance. Merc's discarded shirt and cloak flew after us. Soldiers tripped over themselves to get out of our path. I hit the gate full tilt, smashing it open with the post.

'That hurt, Jason!'

I set the end of the post on the ground, drew my stolen sword, and cut my partner free. He climbed into the saddle behind me and I turned south.

'Are you okay?' I asked.

'Fine. I was shook up from the crash or they wouldn't have laid a hand on me. Head for the river.'

'I was thinking of running to the Raelnan lines.'

'By going through the entire Orphalian army?'

'Good point.' I headed for the river.

Two dozen noble green knights mounted up and came after us with lowered lances, their mounts churning the turf beneath steel-shod hooves as they galloped across the grassy plain.

'You should have scattered the other horses,' said Merc.

'Sorry. I wasn't thinking.'

'And we could go faster if you'd removed this one's barding.'

'No time.'

136

'You didn't plan this escape very carefully, did you?'

'I was hoping you would have some ideas.'

'Just keep riding.' He glanced back. 'Looks like Halogen himself is coming after us. Didn't even stop to retrieve his crown. He must be angry.'

'They're going to catch us, aren't they?'

'Probably. If they do, be sure to tell them who you are. It might scare them a little before they cut us down.'

It was only two miles to the river at the nearest point, for which we headed. Our lead rapidly evaporated as we rode and by the time we reached the thick reeds on the south bank of the Longwash, Halogen and his knights were just yards behind us. We plunged through the tall grass onto the marshy ground at the water's edge, mud sucking at our horse's hooves, and tensed to leap into the swift brown flood, over a mile wide here. Fully armoured knights would be unable to follow us into the water and by the time the common soldiers arrived to make a full search, we would be too far downstream to be caught. Assuming we didn't drown.

We never took the plunge. Hearing the sudden clamour of crashing armour, surprised shouts and squealing horses, we looked back and saw the Orphalian knights being borne to the ground by men in brown cloaks who had sprung up from the reeds like silent ghosts with spears and axes in hand. The knights and their horses were at a disadvantage on the muddy terrain, and our mysterious rescuers quickly butchered them all – all save Halogen. One of the attackers pulled him from the saddle, slammed him roughly to the ground, and planted her booted foot on his chest and the point of her sabre at his throat.

The woman's cloak flew open to reveal a lean, taut, but full-breasted figure covered by well-worn buckskins. She threw back her hood, laughing. Her long, straight hair was the color of a red fox. The way she moved and the amber of her eyes made me think of quickness and animal cunning.

'What a prize we have here, my boys!' she exclaimed heartily. 'Our little river cruise has proven more fruitful than we hoped!' She bore down with her foot, making the captive king wheeze. 'Bind him!' she ordered, sheathing her sword.

137

'You slatternly trollop—' began Halogen, only to be cut off by a swift kick in the jaw.

'Gag him, too,' she added, stepping away. She nodded in our direction. 'Lord Boltblaster – and you must be Master Cosmo – it was nice of you to bring me this present.'

'Our pleasure,' said Merc smoothly, as if that had been his plan all along. He slid to the ground. 'Jason, meet General Vixen Hotfur, commander of the Raelnan Army of the Long-wash and known to friend and foe alike as the She-Fox.'

'An honour,' I said.

'We're conducting a little commando raid to cut off the Orphalian supply lines,' said Hotfur. 'They've set up a de-pot three miles upstream, just past the ruins of Claymart. Everything comes across there, so we planned to burn it to the ground tonight, sink all the barges we can, and withdraw. Going without food for a couple of days – and knowing we've the capacity to strike at will behind their lines – ought to puncture the enemy morale a bit.' She kicked the now bound king. 'But this is better. I put my base camp here so I could try and snatch this buzzard if conditions looked right. Didn't expect him to come right to me.'

'You knew we were coming,' said Mercury.

'Of course! I've got spies in the camp and scouts all over the area. I knew they had you ten minutes before they did!' She laughed. 'Or something like that. I figured I'd give you living legends a chance to escape on your own before I came to save your hides and I knew with half a measure of sense you'd come right here.'

'Shouldn't you be back leading your troops in battle or something?' I asked, troubled to find a general sneaking about behind enemy lines.

'Boring!' she snorted. 'Standard defensive situation, and we've the high ground. If my colonels can't handle that on their own, they don't deserve to be called soldiers! I leave them the dull chores and take the fun work, like leading this crew of river rats up from Lowpoint to raise merry hell in the backcourt!'

A scout returned and quickly whispered a report to her. 'The opposition is coming in force, so we'll continue this discussion in the boats if you don't mind. I'm scrubbing my torch party, but the day's not a total loss!' She kicked Halogen again. 'Right, sugarplum?'

Hotfur's men uncovered five hidden bark canoes and we piled in, four of the raiders to a craft. Halogen was tossed into one vessel, Merc eased into another. I rode with Hotfur. We left the dead knights lying in the muck and their horses roaming free. It would give the Orphalians something to think about.

'So where are you boys headed?' Hotfur asked as we paddled.

'The Incredibly Dark Forest.'

'Nasty stretch of woods. My father led eight thousand men in there once, chasing ogres. Came out four days later with less than a hundred.'

'Your father?'

'Field Marshal Vulpinus Hotfur of the Third Royal Legion of Ganth. They called him the Grey Fox. Taught me everything I know.'

'He's dead?'

'He was loyal to the crown. When the other generals overthrew the king and formed a military government, he refused to have any part of it. The dictator Myrm Ironglove had him imprisoned and killed.'

'And you escaped and rose to success in the Raelnan service?'

'I've fought for just about everyone, including Orphalia back when old Lanthanide was still alive and hearty. Never cared for Prince Smarmy there, though.' She spat toward the boat carrying Halogen. 'Thinks he's irresistible. I resisted. He's a looker to be sure, but I didn't like his attitude. He got his revenge by spreading slanderous lies about me throughout the court. I couldn't command in such a climate, so I left and signed on with Raella – who's more a monarch than the peacock will ever be. I've half a mind to dump his pretty carcass overboard now.'

'Fine by me,' called Mercury.

'But he's worth more to me alive than dead. With him in hand I can whistle the tune to which the Orphalian army will march. Might even threaten to give him back.'

It was a forty-five minute trip to the river town of Lowpoint, which the invasion hadn't touched. Soldiers and civilians worked side by side on the docks, unloading supply boats bringing food and equipment from down the river. The boats travelled in convoys, escorted by ack-armed cutters. A stone keep on a small island in the middle of the river also bristled with the repeating crossbows.

'You can see why they didn't try to cross here,' said General Hotfur. 'This is a garrison town, our main base for hunting river pirates.'

We landed at the military docks. Ashore were three long barracks, officer quarters, an armoury, and stables, all interconnected and made of stone. Halogen was taken to the stockade under heavy guard. Merc and I followed General Hotfur to her office, a plain room with furnishings of rough-hewn wood.

'I can give you two heroes a cutter which will take you up the Crownbolt and the Arbenflow itself if you wish,' said Hotfur, dropping into her chair and propping her feet on the desk.

'Thank you,' said Mercury. 'That would be helpful since the alternative is riding across Orphalia. I insist, however, that it be crewed only with volunteers. Preferably unmarried volunteers. I hate to be responsible for making more widows than necessary.'

'No problem.'

'How soon can you have it ready?'

'Before you finish eating lunch, if you like.'

'Good. We've still got most of the day ahead of us, and not a moment to waste.' He turned to me. 'From here on out the going gets rough.'

16

'This is it,' said Mercury. 'The edge of sanity.'

The Incredibly Dark Forest loomed ahead of us, a solid wall of leaves rising abruptly from the river plain and reaching two hundred yards into the air, hiding the tree trunks. The leaves sounded ceaseless lethal whispers, as they rustled in the wind, warning those who would enter the Forest to reconsider.

The wall stretched a hundred miles to the east and west, broken only by the shadowy cave-like opening from which the cold and black water of the Arbenflow issued forth. The river was a good eighty feet across at this point, but seemed like a tiny brook next to that vast expanse of vegetation. It was over five hundred miles north to the grey peaks of the Gaedian Range, and the Forest covered the whole way.

It had taken us two weeks to come this far. The river cutter was a twenty-five foot boat with a crew of eight tough, experienced, foolhardy men. The captain was Lufkin Starke, but names didn't matter. We all expected to die in the Forest. It was the only reasonable expectation.

Our course took us down the Longwash to where it met the mighty Gan at the northern fringe of Carathan territory. Then it was a hard pull upstream to the Crownbolt, a wild and boistrous stream with high clay banks, filled with floating debris. It was barely navigable at places and the rowing was hard throughout. We had left it eight miles behind where it bent west to form the north boundary of Ganth and rowed our way up the slow-moving but treacherous Arbenflow, the black artery that flowed from the heart of the Incredibly Dark Forest.

It had been easy so far. The Orphalians didn't bother us. We encountered no pirates. There was no sign of Isogoras or the Society, no problem with the dangerous river monsters that often attacked boats. It was as if fate had given us a respite from trouble, knowing we would get more than our share in the Forest.

'Last chance to bail out,' said Captain Starke. No one replied. He ordered the lanterns lit and we rowed into the mouth of the Forest. Cold, damp air oozed over us like the breath of a corpse. An even deeper chill gripped me, one which had nothing to do with the absence of sunlight. Hostility was in the very fabric of this place and I felt dangerously weak and vulnerable, having grown accustomed to the extra vitality the kiss of the sun goddess gave me. The sun wasn't visible here and hadn't been for centuries.

'It's incredibly dark,' I observed softly. And it was silent. No birds. No insects. Only the splash of our oars. I feared to disturb that silence by speaking loudly.

'Hence the name,' whispered Merc.

The glow of the lanterns at bow and stern barely penetrated the gloom, illuminating only the water directly around the boat. We could distinguish no features on the shadowy banks, which hung over us like the hulking shoulders of a shrugging giant. The captain was steering blind and we progressed slowly. As we rounded a bend I got one last look at the doorway of sunshine leading to the outside world. Then the darkness was complete.

'How are we going to find the Hidden River? We can't even see the one we're on.'

'Well, it doesn't look promising but if The Gods really want you to get there, they'll give us some hints,' said Mercury. 'I hope.'

'Do gods have any power here?'

'Your guess is as good as mine.'

'Look! All round us!'

'Eyes.'

Hundreds of eyes. Pairs of feral red pinpricks on both shores and high above, glaring at us with palpable hatred. My skin crawled and my nape hairs stood stiff. I clutched tightly the haft of my new battle axe for comfort, my sweaty palms staining the wood.

'What do you think they are?'

'We'll find out when they attack,' said Mercury.

'Do you think they will?'

'It's only a matter of time.'

No attack came during the first hour, nor the second. The silent watchers merely watched and grew more numerous until the blackness around us resembled a hellish skyscape filled with demon stars. I had tensely squeezed my axe until my forearms were sore and stiff. We moved even more slowly now, two of the crew having left their oars to man the ack gun.

'What are they waiting for?'

'They're trying to frighten us, keep us on edge,' said Merc.

'They're doing a good job.' I tested my blade for the eighty-seventh time.

The boat ground to a sudden, scraping halt, pitching me forward against the rail.

'We've struck a sandbar,' said the captain. We all knew what that meant. We were immobile and now the attack we dreaded would come. The crew pushed hard at the oars, hoping to free the boat. It was no use. We were stuck fast. They abandoned the oars and took up their weapons.

'Can you move the boat with magic?'

'I'm trying. Something powerful is resisting me.' Merc shook his head. 'Futile. Get ready.'

'I've been ready.'

The first attack came from the water. Three tall and scaly humanoid monsters with long knobby arms, thick chests and cavernous, fang-filled mouths rose up beside the boat and tried to clamber aboard.

'River trolls!' shouted one of the crew.

I leaped at the nearest troll and severed a great, grasping hand with a single blow. Thick grey ichor oozed from the stump of its wrist, but the monster seemed unfazed and continued to pull itself onto the boat with its other hand. I chopped that arm off at the elbow and the troll fell back into the water with a splash. Its severed limb lifelessly continued to clutch the railing.

The ack crew pumped quarrels into the chest of the second troll, but though the shafts sunk deeply into its flesh, it was undisturbed and made it aboard. With talons hard as iron, it ripped open a soldier's torso. Another loosed an arrow into the monster's mouth. That staggered it, and two men were able to knock it off balance, back into the dark water.

Mercury pelted the third troll with levitated sand, beating it back into the water and incidentally loosening the grip of the sandbar on our hull.

The trolls disappeared beneath the surface. A moment later they snapped off the submerged ends of the oars and wrenched the rudder away with a resounding crack. Now they were pounding on the underside of the cutter, every blow making the deck shake. They were going to sink us.

That was when our troubles really began. Unseen attackers in the canopy above hurled rocks, limbs and other heavy objects down upon us. Captain Lufkin was killed by a log that crushed his skull. At the same time, a great chorus of gibbering cries rose up from the river banks, which were here only fifty yards apart, to be followed by massive volleys of little wooden arrows. Poisoned, of course.

Mercury raised a protective umbrella of mystic energy to protect us from the missiles, but was too late to save the crew. They had become grotesque pincushions stuck full of arrows and strewn bloodily across the deck.

'For some reason it doesn't surprise me that we're the only ones left,' said Mercury.

'What do we do now?'

'Head for shore.' Animated by Merc's magic, the boat limped towards the left bank, but the trolls had done their work well and we were taking in water fast. Twenty feet from the shore, Merc and I were perched on the very tip of the bow, our feet dragging in the water and the lantern, which was still burning, swinging crazily above us, dripping hot oil on our heads. The least injured troll pursued us, but I discouraged it by lopping off its ugly head when it got too close. That threw me off balance and I nearly slid into the water, but Merc caught me.

'Can you make it in from here and still hold on to your axe?'

'I think so.'

'Do it.' I swam for the bank while he retrieved a white ball from beneath his soggy cloak and tossed it high into the air. The flare burst into brilliant white light, letting me see my surroundings clearly for the first time.

The high river banks were pocked with holes and gouged through by huge gnarled roots. The great trees were too wide for twenty men with outstretched arms to encircle and almost devoid of branches at the lower levels, instead being crusted with a wide variety of lichens and fungi. The forest floor was carpeted with mushrooms, some taller than a man, and weird grey mosses. A great canopy of intertwined branches formed a black net high above us.

Our attackers, screeching in terror as they fled the light, were revealed as goblins. These are short, shaggy, nocturnal folk, knee-high to a tall man, with pointed ears and saucer eyes. Their food of choice is fried potatoes, but they will settle for the flesh of men. Hundreds of them now scampered away through the mushrooms. Leaves rustled above as those attackers also withdrew.

We scrambled up the embankment and crouched warily amid the mushrooms. Merc put the protective umbrella back under his cloak. 'We're in a bit of a fix,' he said.

'You don't say.'

'The flare spooked the goblins, but they'll be back as soon as it's out – along with every other unfriendly for ten miles around. I've only got a limited supply, so we need to develop some other options quickly.'

Already the glow was dimming. 'How far do you suppose we are from our goal?'

'A couple of hundred miles, at least.'

'I think coming in here with but one boat was just an elaborate form of suicide. We need an army.'

'It wouldn't make any difference. Here one man or a thousand men have the same chance of survival. Next to none. And it doesn't matter how far you plan to travel. One spot is as potentially deadly as another.'

'Meaning we're just as likely to reach Greenleaf as we are to escape the Forest alive if we turn back now, so we may as well push on.'

'Precisely. Look, at least you're safe from bounty hunters here.'

'But what about them?'

The flare had nearly burned out, but it wasn't the goblins which threatened us now. They had yielded to a troop of ogres. Fifteen feet tall, dressed in furs, they had dingy yellow skin and were armed with huge, spiked cudgels. I counted seven. They snorted and drooled as they came. I held my axe at ready.

'Remember how tough Yezgar was?' asked Merc.

'Vividly.'

'He was only half ogre.'

'This axe won't do us much good, will it? Magic?' We broke into a slow jog away from the ogres.

'Anything useful on those jokers would have Isogoras on us within the hour. And I'm sure he'll bring help this time.'

By now we were in a full sprint, whisking through the parasitic undergrowth along the river bank. I thought about diving into the water to escape, but abandoned the notion when I saw the school of river sharks gathering to fight the trolls for the bodies of our companions. Then the flare winked out completely and we could see nothing. We heard the pounding of our feet and the snorting of the long-striding ogres as they lumbered after us.

We heard a heavy thunk, followed rapidly by six more thunks. We heard no more lumbering or snorting. We stopped running.

'They suddenly decided to try stealth?' I suggested.

'An ogre doesn't know the meaning of the word. Let's have a look.'

He sent up another flare and we saw all seven ogres sprawled on the ground, their bodies oddly contorted. A single black arrow protruded from each one's back.

'What kind of archer could hit seven moving targets in the dark?' I asked.

We walked back to examine the nearest corpse. Merc withdrew the arrow and sniffed the point. 'Swangrave. Extracted only from the glands of the Poison Black Swans of Lake Asheron. It kills within seconds of entering the blood.'

'But who?'

Merc held up the arrow. 'See the crescent symbol on the shaft?'

'BlackMoon.'

'I forgot about him when I said you were safe from bounty hunters. For him, a trip through the Forest is like a stroll in the park. He probably vacations here.'

I looked around nervously for a sign of the hunter's location. I saw nothing but tree trunks, moss and mushrooms.

'Don't bother,' said Merc. 'He's only seen when he wants to be seen. Obviously he doesn't want to kill you yet or you'd be dead.'

'What can we do?'

'Hope he doesn't change his mind. If you think of anything better, keep it to yourself. Remember, he can hear every word we say, no matter how softly spoken. But as long as he's guarding our back, we may as well get going.'

'Your plan is still to go up the Arbenflow until we find the Hidden River, assuming it's not too well hidden and we don't get killed along the way?'

'That's the only choice we have.'

'Not so, two-legger mammal-manling!' The cheerful unhuman voice called down to us from above. We looked up and saw almost fifty glowing green spiders as big as ponies descending on phosphorescent green web strands. The one which had spoken was directly above us. I readied my axe, but Merc restrained me. The spider touched ground before us, its companions landing all around to form a protective circle. They gave the whole area an eerie, ghostly light.

'The sharpstick you'll not need,' said the spider. 'I come in peace!'

'That's a relief, considering you have us outnumbered.'

'So we do.' The spider lifted its forelegs and made an almost human flourish. 'The being you're seeing is Luggogosh Longlimberly, King of the Lugs! Lug is shortspeak for you. To say Luminous Green Spiders makes your mandibles ache, should it not? And I may be called Luggo, also for your convenience. You four-limbs are Jason Cosmo and friend, or I'm mistaken.'

'I'm Jason Cosmo. This is the wizard Mercury Boltblaster.'

'Welcome, welcome! This is good. It is you I come to fetch – and you too, wizard. I am sent by the Keeper of the Greenleaf Shrine.'

'I thought you lugs were extinct,' said Mercury.

'Sadly almost so. In great numbers were we slaughtered by murdering two-legger manlings that our body portions might be fashioned for the making of glow-in-the-dark toys to be put in boxes of breakfast cereal. Dwindled greatly, my folk retreated to this big tree-place.'

'Nor did I know you could talk.'

'Of course we talk! Among ourselves with clicking clatter-chatter. But the Keeper now gives me human speech and promises it to all my people when I convey Jason Cosmo safely to him. Time wastes! You must come!'

'Tell us of the Keeper,' said Merc.

'Meet him yourself and I need not tell. Now, Jason Cosmo, ride upon my back. You, Boltblaster wizard, Gokollogriklik will transport. Make the haste! We've far to go.'

Luggo bent low and I climbed onto his furry green back. Merc mounted another spider which scuttled forward at a chittering command from its king. The army of spiders then rose as one, racing up their weblines with quickness and grace. It was almost as bad as flying. Having no strap to keep me from falling, I held tightly to Luggo's spidery skin. It didn't seem to bother him. I worried that BlackMoon would pick me off with an arrow, but the bounty hunter had evidently decided to bide his time and wait for more favourable conditions. Within seconds, we had reached the canopy level and were headed north across a highway of branches and vines.

17

It took three days to reach the fabled Shrine of Greenleaf, at least according to King Luggo. I couldn't distinguish between night and day in the gloom of the Forest, but the spider insisted the darkness was slightly less intense during the day. I saw only the green luminescence of our escorts. Luggo wouldn't take us to the forest roof where the sun shined, saying lugs found its glare unpleasant.

At my suggestion, the spiders spun sticky silk belts to hold Merc and me in place, allowing us to sleep as we rode. Not that it's easy to sleep while gummed to the back of a glowing green spider scuttling through the canopy of the Incredibly Dark Forest. A spider's gait is utterly unlike that of a horse, the only mount I was used to. I particularly disliked those parts of the trip spent in vertical travel. I'd have preferred another magic carpet ride.

Still, none of the dangerous denizens of the Forest molested us on our journey, not wishing to battle with the lugs in force. We reached our destination safely. The lugs deposited us at the edge of a small clearing lit by a warm shaft of welcome sunlight, then withdrew to the comfortable shadows to watch.

The clearing was no more than a neatly clipped lawn surrounding a white wooden gazebo. At this point the Arbenflow was little more than a large creek that widened into a placid pool beside the clearing. Its shining surface reflected the sun and the clouds like a liquid mirror. No other river, not even a trickling stream, was in evidence. If the Hidden River was here, it was still well hidden.

'Luggo! Are you sure this is the place?'

'Yes, two-leg Cosmo,' called the spider. 'Greenleaf, Shrine of. This is the place you are seeking.'

'So where's the Keeper?'

'I do not know. I just got here like you.'

'Hello!' I shouted. No reply.

'It's not very impressive,' said Mercury, sniffing the air. 'The paint is still fresh.'

We approached the structure and Merc touched the rail, getting wet paint on his fingers. The ground near the gazebo was littered with sawdust, wood chips and nails.

'This is not the most ancient of shrines,' I observed.

Mercury stepped into the gazebo, tested the floor, looked up at the ceiling – and stood transfixed.

'What is it, Merc?'

'Excuse me,' he said to the ceiling. 'I'll get him.' He looked at me, bemused. 'It's for you.'

'What's for me?'

He stepped out onto the ground. 'Just stand in the middle and look up.'

I did as he suggested, but instead of the rafters supporting the latticed roof, I saw the dome of a lemon sky and dozens of huge human faces peering down at me as if I was a cricket in a jar. Young and old, male and female, they radiated power – glorious, majestic, infinite power. Divine power.

'Jason Cosmo, welcome to the Gazebo of The Gods,' said one face, that of a man who wore a storm-cloud like a hat. His voice was as the thunder that shatters mountains and I took him to be Great Whoosh, Emperor of the Winds. 'We've been expecting you.'

I glanced at Merc. Normal. Around us the trees, grass, pool. All normal. Eyes back to the ceiling. The clustered gods were still there.

'Well, here I am,' I said, wondering if I should fall to my knees.

'No need to fall to your knees,' said Great Whoosh. 'You have proven your devotion by reaching this point. We have observed you carefully in your travels and are pleased. Your skills, your knowledge, your will – all have grown greatly. You have demonstrated courage, loyalty and resourcefulness. You—'

'Am I late?' said a holy voice I recognized. The goddess Rae forced her way into the assemblege, her face appearing beside Great Whoosh. She smiled down at me. 'Hello again, Jason.'

'Greetings, O Rae.'

'As I was saying,' said Great Whoosh. 'You have become the hero you were meant to be. Now it is time to reveal to you why all that has happened has happened.'

'This should be interesting.'

'Archiva, would you provide the needed background information, please?'

The Goddess of History, a silver-haired old woman with skin the colour of aged parchment, coughed to draw my attention. Her voice was like the turning of ancient, dusty pages. 'In the beginning there were The Gods, who dwell in Paradise. And The Gods grew restless and created the Earth, and it was good, and beautiful, and perfect. But no man dwelt in it then, only the birds of the air and the beasts of the—'

'Excuse me,' said Great Whoosh. 'There's no need to go back quite that far.'

'I like to start at the beginning.'

'Could you skip ahead a bit? He's only a mortal. He hasn't got time to hear it all.'

'Skip ahead how far?'

'To the Age of War.'

'How can you understand the importance of the Age of War if you don't consider the Age of Nature and the Age of Peace first? It's the sharp break with past trends which makes it so significant.'

'Please.'

'Very well. After a millenium of peace came the Age of War. Its origins lie in a complex interaction of such diverse factors as the creation of other intelligent races that competed with humanity, the invention of economics, petty feuds among various gods, and the arrival in our universe of the race of demons. All are important, though the last has the most bearing on the current situation. The demons came from Somewhere Else and constructed the Assorted Hells as a mockery of Paradise, though some speculate that they—'

'Archiva.' Great Whoosh was growing impatient.

'The War of a Thousand Years, involving gods, demons and the mortal races, blasted Arden and ended with the original Great Eternal Pan-Cosmic Holy/Unholy Non-Intervention Pact. In this treaty, all gods and demons promised to leave one another in peace and withdraw totally from mortal affairs. The Gods honoured the agreement. The demons, led by Asmodraxas, did not. Unopposed, they created an Empire of Fear which ruled the world. This was the Age of Despair. After a thousand years, we gods could take no more. We modified the Non-Intervention Pact to allow limited involvement in worldly matters and brought forth a Mighty Champion to free mankind from the yoke of demonic slavery. After a hard struggle, he defeated Asmodraxas, brought down the Evil Empire, and ushered in the current Age of Hope. The important features of this age have been—'

'Stick to the matter at hand,' said Great Whoosh curtly.

'The overall trend to note is that each Age lasts a thousand years. The Age of War ended nine hundred and ninety years ago, making this the critical decade which will determine the character of the Next Age.'

'Thank you Archiva,' said the Wind God quickly as she gathered her breath to continue the history lesson. He turned his attention to me. 'You have already learned that you are a namesake of the Mighty Champion. Know now that you are of his bloodline. It is for this reason that the Dark Magic Society fears you. They hope to release Asmodraxas from his prison and bring an Age of More Despair Than Last Time. They fear you will thwart them in the tradition of your great ancestor. This is why they seek to destroy you.'

'What about the Demon Lords? They seek to preserve the status quo. How does killing me fit their plans?'

'They are Demon Lords. Their first reaction to any problem is to kill it. We have negotiated with them, however, and they have agreed to take no further action against you. They will abide by this agreement only so long as they believe it furthers their purpose of preventing the return of Asmodraxas. You must therefore act quickly.'

'What must I do quickly?'

'Arkayne will explain.'

The God of Magic, his face hidden by a hood the colour of mystery, leaned forward. 'You know it is the Superwand which Erimandras and the Society seek. It is by the power of the wand that Asmodraxas was bound, and it is only by the power of the wand that he can be freed. It follows, then, that Erimandras must not gain possession of the Superwand.'

'So where is it hidden?'

'We don't know. The Mighty Champion hid it and never told us where he put it. Ideally, it should be brought to Paradise for safekeeping.'

'You want me to find the wand and bring it to Paradise?'

'Of course not! Ideal conditions are rarely found. Were the Superwand in Paradise its power would be a constant temptation to all of The Gods. Mistrust would flourish, a godwar would inevitable. If anyone has the wand it creates a dangerous imbalance in the cosmic correlation of forces.'

'So what am I supposed to do?'

'Prevent the Superwand from being found. The Society believes you know its location, a bit of disinformation spread by my colleague Heraldo, God of Propaganda and Journalism. This has diverted them from a direct search for the wand to a manhunt for you. It's up to you to make sure they never return to their abandoned direct search.

'You gods put the Society on my trail?'

'All part of our master plan,' said Great Whoosh soothingly. 'We kept Erimandras preoccupied with you and at the same time created circumstances which would allow you to emerge as a hero and destroy him.'

'So you want me to kill Erimandras the Overmaster?'

'You may not have to kill him,' said Arkayne. 'Just render him and the Society incapable of pursuing their quest for the Superwand. Wherever it is hidden, there must it remain.'

'We have brought you this far,' said Great Whoosh. 'We have prepared you for this moment. We have given you a superb mind, body and will. You have learned the skills a hero needs. Now we charge you with a great heroic mission. Preserve the sanctity of the Next Age. Stop the Society, that it may be an Age of Continued Hope, perhaps even a second Age of Peace.'

'A second Age of Peace? Are you kidding?'

'Well, perhaps that is asking a bit much. Just prevent the Dark Magic Society from plunging the Earth into a long night of evil. That's all we ask of you. That is your duty. Perform it well.'

'Wait a minute!'

'In this place you will find the relics of the Mighty Champion who was your forebearer. Use them in your coming battles.'

'You can't be serious!'

The vision of The Gods vanished and I was looking at the underside of a normal gazebo top.

'What was that all about?' asked Merc. 'I only caught your half of the conversation.'

'I'm supposed to stop the Society from ruling the world for the next thousand years.'

'Oh. Sounds simple enough.'

'Right.'

'Did they offer any suggestions on how you're supposed to do this?'

'The relics of the Mighty Champion are supposed to be around here somewhere.'

'Where?'

'I don't know!'

'Calm down, calm down. The situation isn't all that grim.'

'Not all that grim! Mercury, they expect me to destroy the Dark Magic Society! Me! I'm not even a wizard! I was adjusting to this hero thing pretty well, but this is too much! I can't do it! It's insane!'

'Now think this through rationally. The Society is trying to kill you, right?'

'Right.'

'You can run, fight or surrender. Surrender is certain death. No good. Running and fighting both involve risks, but at least you've got a chance. With me so far?'

'Yes, but what—'

'When we met I agreed to help you in hopes that your aura would tell me how to get the Society to leave me alone. It didn't. So why am I here with you now?'

'You promised to protect me.'

'Only as far as Rae City.'

'Because you're my friend?'

'That's true, but you loan a friend garden tools. You don't escort him through the Incredibly Dark Forest. I'm here because you have become my best hope of survival.'

'I'm *your* best hope? Are you feeling well?'

'Back to run or fight. Both are risky, but running does no damage to the enemy. Your situation never improves. You just keep running until you get caught. That's been my strategy because I haven't had the means to fight – until now. Fighting is only a sensible option if you've got a chance, no matter how slim, of winning. I saw no hope of victory.'

'And now you do?'

'Jason, you've got strength, brains, courage, charisma and character. The Society itself has given you a worldwide reputation as a powerful, dangerous man. The Gods are behind you. You're about to own some powerful relics. Women adore you. You're a leader. You're a hero. Even I, a disillusioned and cynical sorcerer who doesn't believe in heroes, can see that. If anyone can bring the Society down, it's you. I'll help, of course.'

'Thanks. The two of us should be more than enough.'

'I didn't say it would be easy. I said we had a chance. I've gradually come to this realization and now I'm convinced. Any man The Gods will crowd into a gazebo to talk to must have something going for him. I believe in you, Jason, and I haven't believed in anything for a long time.'

'I'm deeply touched, Merc, but you're starting to sound just like the League.'

'No need to be insulting. They're witless incompetents. Excluding Raella, of course. But us – we're an unbeatable combination. We've gone through the Black Bolts, Zaran, Yezgar, the Red Huntsman, numerous demons, Isgoras, Halogen and the Incredibly Dark Forest. We can't be stopped.'

'It's the paint fumes, isn't it?'

'Let's find those relics!'

He dropped to his knees and crawled around the gazebo, minutely examining the turf for clues. Mercury Boltblaster had gone crazy before my very eyes. A practical, pragmatic survivor had become a wild-eyed, suicidal fanatic.

Then again, almost everything I had done since the arrival of Lombardo the Magnificent in Lower Hicksnittle had been suicidal. And Mercury's logic was compelling – as long as the Society was trying to kill me anyway, I might as well strike back. If I was doomed, if there was no chance of victory, if the enemy was just too strong, then why shouldn't I try? The course of history for the next thousand years was at stake! My ancient namesake prevailed, and he fought an enemy that already had total power, an Evil Empire that had ruled Arden unchallenged for a millenium. The Dark Magic Society was nothing compared to that, a pale shadow of what had preceded it. Yes! I would fight! Maybe I would even win.

'What exactly does a relic look like?' I asked Merc, dropping down to join his search.

'No way to tell. It can be anything. Body parts. Weapons. Personal items. Anything that came into contact with a great hero can be a relic. Have you ever heard of the Discarded Tissues of the Sneezing Saint?'

'No.'

'They're relics of Mucosa the Miraculous. Powerful objects, but disgusting to behold.'

'I'd prefer a weapon, I think.'

'Incidentally, this grass is fake.'

We searched the whole clearing, starting at the gazebo and working our way to the edge. We found no sign that anything had been buried here. The lugs could offer no suggestions.

'Maybe we're overlooking the obvious.' I returned to the gazebo. 'This is free-standing, not anchored.' I jammed my fingers under the base of the structure and easily heaved it onto its side. It collapsed into a pile of lumber.

'Shoddy construction,' said Merc. 'I'm just losing all faith in The Gods here.'

'But look!'

Beneath the gazebo was a narrow stone stairway descending into the ground. Cold air that smelled like strawberries oozed up from the opening. I heard the distant sound of dripping water.

'Your relics are probably down there,' said Merc.

'Think so?' I lifted my axe and cautiously descended, Merc right behind me. The stairs went down thirty feet or so and we were soon in complete darkness.

'Could you conjure up some light or something?'

'I could set off a flare it you'd like, but in a confined space that could be unpleasant.'

It proved unnecessary. At the bottom of the stair was an unrusted iron door. It opened soundlessly at my touch, and warm, friendly light spilled out. The strawberry smell was now intense.

We entered the cold chamber beyond. It was a dome, hewn from the rock and polished smooth. There was another iron door in the far wall. The floor was tiled. In the centre of the room was a stone statue of an armoured warrior. The statue held a sword and shield which looked real, as did the armour.

'Look closely at the face,' said Mercury.

I did. The statue had my face. 'An almost perfect likeness.'

'Remarkable! Most remarkable!' I was startled by the cheery new voice, but even more startled when the speaker slid into view. It was a six foot strawberry with big blue eyes and a huge human mouth. 'The likeness is remarkable!'

'Who are you?'

'I'm the Keeper of the Shrine of Greenleaf, of course!'

'But you're a big strawberry!' I protested.

'And you're a big, hairless ape – what of it?'

'Well strawberries don't . . . they can't . . . that is to say . . . I don't believe this.'

'Why should a talking, intelligent strawberry be any more unusual than, say, a talking, intelligent, luminous green spider?' said the Keeper.

'You have a point. But for a place called Greenleaf I'd think a talking tree would be more appropriate.'

'See that tuft of leaves on my top?'

'Yes.'

'What colour are they?'

'Green.'

'There you have it. I admit I'm not quite the typical guardian of a holy shrine, but The Gods put this place together rather hastily and all the talking trees were booked. I'm normally a minor servitor of Freshlord, God of Fruits and Vegetables, but things are slow around the office once most of the spring planting is done, so I got tapped for this duty.'

'Oh. I'm sorry to have inconvenienced you.'

'Don't mention it! I'm getting paid overtime for this. Now I'm supposed to explain these relics to you. I see you already possess the Ring of Raxx.'

'This?' I twisted the ring Timeon gave me. 'What does it do?'

'No one is really sure, but it looks nice. Let's see if I can remember my briefing on the other relics. Ah! The armour is forged of miraculum, light as air, proof against most weapons, and looks like it will fit you nicely.'

'And the sword?'

'The sword. This is the enchanted blade Overwhelm. It will cut through stone like warm butter and has other wondrous properties which I can't recall just now.'

'And this is all mine to keep?' I asked breathlessly.

'If you can pass the test.'

'Why do I have to pass a test?'

'Regulations. We can't be handing out holy relics to just anyone.'

'So what's the test?'

'You must pass through the far door and follow the tunnel beyond. At its far end you will face the test, which you must successfully complete before returning to claim your prizes. Simple, isn't it?'

'Right. Simple. Pass the test, claim the prizes.'

'I will wait here with your friend,' said the Keeper.

Mercury clasped my shoulder. 'Good luck, Jason.'

I gripped my axe nervously and crossed to the far door. It slid open at my touch and I stepped into the steeply sloping dark tunnel beyond. The door closed behind me with a mournful clang.

18

I counted three hundred paces before the tunnel opened onto a small ledge overlooking a great underground cavern softly lit by luminous fungi. A gurgling black river flowed through the chamber; it was some fifty feet below where I stood. This had to be the fabled Hidden River, hidden because it flowed underground! But what was the test?

'Ahem!'

I spun in place and raised my axe. A narrow trail led to a slightly larger ledge a few yards to the right of where I stood. A thin, bespectacled scribe sat at a wooden table. There was a school desk facing him.

'Are you Jason Cosmo?' he said in an officious, nasal voice. 'Here to take the test?'

'Yes.'

'Do you have any identification?'

'I have . . . the Ring of Raxx.'

'Is your name Raxx?'

'No.'

'Then that's no good. Well, I suppose it must be you. Sit down. Did you bring a # 2 pencil?'

'No.' The desk was too small and it wobbled and squeaked with every breath I took.

'Tsk, tsk. Unprepared. Here is a pencil.' He stood and handed me a pencil, then placed on the desk a sheet of paper covered with little lettered circles.

'What is this?'

Reading from a sheet of instructions, pronouncing each word slowly and carefully, he said, 'Grid your name into the appropriate boxes.'

'What do you mean?'

The scribe looked up from the instruction sheet and gave me a snooty appraisal. 'Can you spell?'

'Yes.'

'Then fill in the circles which correspond to the letters of your name.' He began to read again. 'Next fill in your age, date of birth, most recent address, and the name of this testing site, which is Greenleaf.' His voice and manner were more irritating than the screech of a bloody nuisance.

He continued reading. 'I will now give you the test booklet. This is the Standard Heroic Aptitude Test, which will measure your potential for success as a hero. It consists of two thousand multiple choice questions. You are to fill in the blank containing the letter which matches what you think is the best answer to each question. Make no stray marks on the answer sheet. You have one hour.' He handed me the test booklet. 'You may begin.' He turned over an hourglass on the desk.

I feverishly attacked the questions. Some asked me to identify weapons and monsters. There were questions about scholarly essays on heroic ethics, methods, and styles. There were problem questions, asking me to choose the best escape or rescue plan in a given situation. I answered those I knew from experience or common sense, guessed wildly at the rest. My pencil broke twice, and the scribe would only give me a new one after I raised my hand. As the final grains of sand fell, I was filling in blanks randomly, not even bothering to read the questions. I filled in the last one with seconds to spare.

'Time! You shouldn't guess randomly, you know. There is a penalty for wrong answers.'

'I could never have finished them all otherwise.'

'You aren't expected to answer every question.'

'Now you tell me.'

'Let me see your answer sheet so I can grade it. You have to achieve a minimum score to earn the right to keep the relics.'

'Some of those questions weren't fair,' I said as he checked my paper.

'Such as you can't answer questions about sea monsters because you aren't from a seafaring nation? Yes, I've heard these complaints of cultural bias before, but the Standardized Heroic Aptitude Test is still the best measure we have of heroic potential. My, my! This is most irregular.'

'What?'

'You got them all right.' He glared at me over the rims of his spectacles. 'You cheated, didn't you?'

'Of course not! I didn't even know I was going to take this test until I got here. I thought I'd have to fight a horrible monster which, frankly, I'd have preferred.'

'Mr Cosmo, cheating is a very serious matter. I'm afraid I'm going to have to rule the results of this test invalid. You'll have to take it again.'

Never! Not for all the holy relics in creation! 'How would you like to take a swim in that river down there?'

'Are you threatening me?'

I wouldn't really do him bodily harm, but he didn't know that. I snatched up my axe. 'Or better yet, I could—'

'Wait!' he said, quivering like a rabbit. 'Wait! I was observing you the entire time and I saw no evidence of cheating. The results stand! Here is your claim ticket for the relics!'

'Thank you. I appreciate this.'

I jogged back up the tunnel to where Merc and the Keeper waited.

'What took you so long?' asked Mercury.

'It was too horrible to describe,' I said. I flashed the claim ticket before the Keeper. 'But I passed.'

'Excellent! Excellent! You may take it all. I suggest you put the armour on now.'

'Why?'

'Because the Society will attack this place momentarily.'

'What! How did they find us?'

'The presence of The Gods, even indirectly, is like a beacon to them. Well, I must be returning to Paradise now. It's been a pleasure meeting you both.'

'You mean you're not going to help us?'

'I'm just a big strawberry. What can I do?' The Keeper shimmered and vanished. Merc ran up the stairs to ground level while I donned the armour, strapped on the shield and took Overwhelm for my own. The hauberk weighed so little I felt I was wearing a suit of tissue, not chainmail. The helm wore like a felt cap. The sword was light as a broomstick. As I gave it a couple of experimental swings, Merc rushed back into the chamber.

'Jason! Run! Out the other door!'

'What is it?'

'Overwhelming force.'

'How bad can it be?' I asked, feeling confident and cocky with my new armour and the feel of Overwhelm in my hand. I vaulted up the stairs to the surface.

Hundreds of gibbering goblins, their light-sensitive eyes protected by green visors, streamed into the clearing from every direction, waving tiny swords and clubs. They were accompanied by dozens of their larger cousins, the burly bugaboos. Natalia slash hovered above on the back of her purple dragon, Golan. Isogoras the Xornite was seated behind her. They were escorted by Dylan of Ganth and twenty new Black Bolts mounted on sable gryphons and armed with crossbows, all aimed at me. I retreated back down the stairs.

'Merc! Run! Out the other door!'

'I thought you'd be back soon.'

We rushed down the tunnel as the goblins and bugaboos poured into the chamber. I lost my extra strength underground, but we didn't have to deal with Natalia and company. It seemed a fair bargain. We reached the ledge over the Hidden River. The scribe and his furniture were gone.

'We'll hold them off here,' said Merc.

I glanced down at the river below. 'We'll have to.'

'Step aside.'

The first of our pursuers were halfway down the tunnel. Mercury cast a spell which made the floor slippery as greased eels on ice. The lead goblins lost their footing and slid down the slope and right off the ledge to drown in the river below. Goblins can't swim.

But they are surefooted and once those further back realized what was happening and slowed their breakneck pace, they began to reach us on their feet. They could only come a few at a time, however, and I easily sliced them to bits. Mercury stepped aside to watch.

'This sword is wonderful! It almost fights by itself.'

'Considering the way you usually handle a sword, that's probably a good thing.'

The first pair of bugaboos reached me. While I was engaged with one, the other struck me in the head with its spiked mace. My miraculum helm absorbed the full impact of the blow. I didn't even feel it! I dispatched his companion and turned to skewer the one who had struck me.

'I could fight like this all day! The sword weighs so little it's just like waving my arm around.'

'Did you ever try waving your arm around all day?'

'Still, this is easy.'

As the words left my lips, a powerful jet of water struck me in the back and slammed me against the wall. I bounced off and toppled backwards into the river, hitting the surface with a tremendous splash. The weight of normal armour would have dragged me to the bottom, but this suit didn't hamper me at all. In fact, it tended to buoy me up and I was able to use my shield like a float.

The attack had come from a trio of lovely girls on a rock in the river. They held a large hose from which water shot under high pressure. They wore scandalously styled black maillots, gaudy green lipstick, and tacky jewellery.

'Nymphs gone bad!' shouted Merc before he too was blasted from the ledge. When we were both in the water, the nymphs aimed the hose at our heads, making it difficult to stay afloat or even breathe. I lost my grip on both sword and shield, which floated away downstream. To escape the pounding spray, I dove underwater, as did Merc.

That respite would only last as long as we could hold our breath. I have powerful lungs and Mercury has undergone extensive physical conditioning, so we had a couple of minutes before we would have to surface anew. We both had the same idea and made for the rock, coming up on opposite sides.

We took the nymphs by surprise, for they had evidently expected us to flee. I grasped one by the ankles and pulled her in. The others dropped the hose, which whipped about wildly on its own accord, spraying water in every direction.

Pulling a water nymph into the water was not a very good strategy. It offered her no resistance and she was all over me, unlatching my helmet and scratching at my face with long, sharp nails. Yet trying to get a grip on her was like trying to grasp the water itself. A second nymph joined her sister in battling me, and together they forced me under.

The current carried us downstream. One nymph twisted my head back while the other caught me in an embrace and pressed her mouth against mine. The kiss was far from pleasant, for she vomited water down my throat. I flailed helplessly, drowning as surely as the goblins had. The water around us churned wildly and seemed to be flowing upward, in defiance of all common sense. It didn't matter. I was close to senselessness anyway.

We broke the surface of the pool beside the clearing. Sunshine and open air. Not that I got to breathe any of the air. The nymphs were still holding me in place for the kiss of death.

'Enough!' ordered Isogoras from above. 'Leave him to us! Bring the wizard!'

With expressions of profound disappointment, the nymphs released me to bob in the pool with dozens of goblin corpses. One of the Black Bolts swooped down so that his gryphon could pluck me from the water with its talons and deposit me on shore. I lay gasping on the grass like a beached whale. Natalia and Isogoras landed and dismounted.

'Are these yours?' rasped the wizard, dropping my helm, shield, and sword beside me. I coughed and spat in reply. 'Did you think we were unaware of this place?'

'I was,' I wheezed.

'The Society knows all.'

'So you got lucky.'

'Luck had nothing to do with it.' A cloud of prying eyes flew into my view. 'I have observed your every move since you entered the Forest, and you never suspected a thing. I gathered my hirelings and waited for the proper moment. You are mine to deliver to Erimandras the Overmaster. But first . . .' He drew a long, slim dagger from his belt. 'You cost me my most prized possession, the Horn of Hockessin, which it took me years to locate. I was unable to find it after our encounter, so you must pay. The Overmaster won't mind if you are missing a few fingers, an ear, an eye, perhaps your nose.'

Before he could begin his grisly surgery, the three nymphs surfaced with Mercury in their grasp. A Black Bolt snatched him from the water and dropped him beside me.

'What a pleasant surprise,' he gasped.

'Mercury,' said Isogoras. 'This time there is no escape for you.'

Merc ignored the Xornite. 'Natalia . . . keeping low company, aren't you?'

'His gold is good. And I will also gain credit for Cosmo's capture, netting me an easy ten million.'

Merc rolled his head to sneer at Isogoras. 'Didn't care to face me alone again, eh?'

'Too much is at stake for me to take chances,' said the masked wizard. 'Careful planning pays. I have you, I have Cosmo, and I have the relics, all of which gives me the means to depose Erimandras when I return to Fortress Marn!'

Natalia's eyes narrowed in cold calculation as Isogoras spoke, but the wizard appeared not to notice.

'Ever ambitious,' sneered Merc.

'Enough prattle! Bind them, Natalia!'

'Watch your tone when you address me,' she said, but she brought forth heavy steel chains and manacles from her saddlebag and approached us. I glanced at Merc. He winked.

Wizards recover quickly, which is what Merc had been doing as he conversed with our captors, stalling them until he was ready to move. I was ready too, my natural hardiness augmented by the hot rays of the sun. I sprang to my feet and held out my hands. Sword, shield and helm flew into place with Mercury's assistance. He stood at my side, armed with a sabre pulled from his cloak.

Natalia dropped the chains and drew her own sword, the family blade which she had evidently recovered from the Longwash. 'He's mine!' she screamed, scattering the goblins and causing the Black Bolts to hold their fire.

'Drop the sword, Mercury, or I will order my men to slay you,' said Isogoras, indicating the mercenaries. Merc shrugged and plunged his weapon into the ground at Isogoras's feet. 'Let's watch.'

Her attack was swift and brutal, but Overwhelm was equal to it. I certainly wasn't. I just held on tightly to the haft and let the sword guide my arm, praying it was good enough to save me. None of her furious blows struck home, but I was clearly on the defensive and she forced me steadily back towards the river, where the wicked nymphs waited gleefully, hoping for a second go at me.

They would never get the chance. Once I lost my footing in the water, Natalia would win. But there was nothing I could do. The sorcery of Overwhelm, even backed by my strength, was no match for her skill.

While all eyes were upon our duel, Merc stealthily reached into his cloak. He whipped his hand free, releasing his entire stock of flares into the air. Half of them whizzed upward to burst amid the hovering Black Bolts. The spooked gryphons flew out of control in all directions. The rest of the flares went off near the ground. The goblins fled, their visors offering no protection against a light so bright and near. One flare burst in the face of Isogoras and another next to Natalia. Golan collapsed, stunned into numb blindness.

Blinking, I staggered and fell backwards into the pool. The nymphs surged forwards, only to stop at the sight of Mercury's outstretched hands. He helped me to my feet and we ran from the clearing.

'Where are we going?' I asked as we passed a group of goblins. Streamers of light penetrated the gloom beneath the trees.

'I don't know! Just keep running until we think of something better!'

'Isn't this the part where the friendly lugs come to our rescue?'

'We've already done that scene. I think they're gone. They didn't strike me as fools.'

'So we're on our own. Great.'

'It's good exercise.'

Mercury fell flat on his face, twitched and didn't move. I knelt beside him. 'Merc! Are you okay?'

The goblins, back in their element, started to regroup. Avoiding the patches of light, they cautiously headed our way.

'Merc! Get up!' I took off my helmet and bent to listen to his breath. I found none. 'What happened to you?'

I felt a sharp sting on the side of my neck. I reached up and pulled a tiny black dart from my skin, the kind shot from a blowgun. It was marked with the symbol of a crescent moon. That was the last thing I saw before all went dark.

19

I woke. I was lying on my stomach with my hands and feet bound by thick leather thongs. The air was chilly, the snowy ground was hard and stony. My armour had been removed and my tunic and pants provided little protection against the cold. The light was dim, but nothing like the gloom of the Incredibly Dark Forest. I rolled onto my back and got a better view of where I was. The sky was grey and overcast, the sun present but not visible. The landscape to my right was a craggy collection of weathered rocky hills. Mercury lay about a yard away, unconscious and bound as I was, his cloak missing. To my left a dilapidated suspension bridge with frayed ropes and broken footboards spanned a deep chasm. On the far side was the wall of vegetation that unmistakably marked an edge of the Incredibly Dark Forest.

'You awaken. Good. I am BlackMoon.' The soft stiletto voice startled me. I looked up from my sightseeing and saw him standing over me. He was lean and hard, a living dagger of a man with green cat's eyes. I had not heard his approach across the gravel-strewn ground and he had been nowhere in sight a second before. 'I hoped that you would, for I wished to tell you how rewarding this hunt has been.'

'Where are we?'

'Malravia. This is the rendezvous point at which I will deliver you and your companion to the agents of the Dark Magic Society and collect the reward.' He frowned. 'A pity.'

'Why?'

'This has been an enjoyable hunt. It is the pleasure of the chase which I love, not the pecuniary rewards. My skills are such, however, that I am rarely challenged.'

'And I – we – challenged you?'

'No. It was not a matter of skill on your part, but the interesting circumstances through which you led me. I held back, savouring the hunt and waiting for the perfect moment. Stealing you from Natalia Slash and the Xornite wizard in the heart of the Incredibly Dark Forest was a finer experience than I could have asked for. Better even than the fall of that lout the Red Huntsman.'

'If chasing me was so much fun, let me go and we'll do it again.'

'Every hunt must end, and this one has gone on too long. It is time I turned to other pursuits.'

Mercury stirred and mumbled, then rolled onto his back. He quickly took in the situation. 'Malravia. Haven't been here in a while. And you must be BlackMoon.' The bounty hunter nodded. 'I've admired your work,' said Merc sincerely, 'though I'm not too wild about this particular demonstration of your skills.' He strained at his bonds.

'Thank you,' said BlackMoon.

'Incidentally, how did you manage to carry the two of us through the Forest? I am assuming it has been several days since our capture and that you kept us drugged during the journey.'

'It has been a week,' said BlackMoon. 'And you were carried by my porters, a pair of jujula bound to my service.'

'What are jujula?' I asked.

'A breed of minor spirit beings sometimes enslaved by sorcerers in need of cheap labour,' explained Merc. 'But yours, I take it, are bound to serve the wearer of some magic talisman which is in your possession?'

'I do not care to discuss my methods any further.'

'Of course not,' said Merc. 'I assume agents of the Society will be arriving soon to take us into custody?'

'Enough talk. I only allowed you to awaken that I might express my appreciation for giving me a good hunt. It is now time for you to sleep again.' He withdrew a black vial from a pouch on his belt.

'Don't bother,' said Merc, slipping casually out of his bonds. He leaped to his feet and dropped into a fighting stance. BlackMoon reacted instantly, hurling the vial directly at him and ripping a slim, black dagger from its sheath on his thigh. Merc batted the bottle aside. It shattered on the rocks. 'My martial arts training included secret methods for escaping ropes and manacles,' he said.

'I know,' said BlackMoon. 'I had some of the same trainers.'

'You meant for me to get free.'

'Yes. I have long wished to test my fighting skills against yours. This may be my last opportunity. You beat the Red Huntsman with your magic, but you will not defeat me in the same manner. I have dosed you with the powerful spellcasting-inhibitor drug Noarcaine. The synapses of your brain will not function properly for the conduction of magical energies. This will be a fair fight.'

'You have a knife,' noted Merc. 'I don't.'

'You are welcome to take mine. If you can.'

BlackMoon darted forward, leading with the black dagger. Merc deflected the attack and jabbed his stiffened hand at the bounty hunter's throat. BlackMoon dodged to the side and slashed at Merc again. This time Merc tagged his wrist with a hand-numbing blow to the nerve centre there. The knife went skittering across the ground.

'Impressive,' said BlackMoon, snapping a kick at Merc's face. The bounty hunter was taller and had a reach advantage, but Merc was slightly quicker. He sidestepped the kick easily and counter-attacked with one of his own. They continued in this fashion for several minutes, not speaking, rarely landing blows, evenly matched. The only sounds were the scuffle of their feet in the gravel and occasional sharp exhalations of breath.

I knew no secret methods for escaping leather bindings, so I rolled myself over to the dagger, which was unfortunately very near the edge of the gulf separating us from the Incredibly Dark Forest. The drop-off was sharp. The sheer cliff face stretched downward hundreds of feet to the swift flowing waters of the raging River Volkus. I got the dagger in my hands and rolled back a safe distance. As the silent battle continued I rolled onto my back, lifted my hips off the ground, and used the knife to slash the thong binding my ankles together. The knife was sharp and cut through them quickly. Now able to sit up, I tried to get at the bindings on my wrists, but quickly realized that the feat was beyond my dexterity. I would have to make do without my hands. I lurched to my feet and charged toward the combatants. BlackMoon had his back to me. If I could ram him, it would give Merc the opening he needed to finish the fight.

He heard me coming, of course, and stepped aside with the grace of a matador to let me bull on by. I skidded to a halt and turned around for another try. This time I had to run around Merc to get at BlackMoon, but he stopped me with a quick but powerful kick to the chest which sat me down hard. The distraction gave Merc the momentum, however, and he pressed his advantage aggressively, forcing BlackMoon back with a flurry of deadly kicks and punches. I lurched to get behind the bounty hunter, hoping he would trip over me, but he executed a graceful backward leap and landed on the other side of me. I was lying between them now and darting hands and feet whistled above me until Merc leaped across my body as well, still forcing BlackMoon backwards. Inevitably, they moved closer to the edge of the cliff.

Now BlackMoon took the offensive and it was clear that his retreat had been a ploy to draw Merc into this danger zone where the slightest misstep would mean a fatal plummet into the unforgiving rapids. The bounty hunter was much more surefooted than Mercury as a result of his years of pursuing prey through every kind of environment. That advantage might give him victory. And I dared not charge him again lest I inadvertently hurl myself over the edge. His stratagem had locked me out of the battle. I could only watch helplessly.

BlackMoon concentrated on combinations of attacks intended to overbalance the wizard as he defended himself. It wouldn't be long before Merc made an error, however slight, and BlackMoon sent him plunging into the abyss. He would collect no bounty for Merc – but with the reward for my capture he could afford the loss.

Merc extended himself too far deflecting a blow and slipped. As he started to topple, BlackMoon helped him along with a powerful shove. At the same instant, I charged, deciding that Merc, his killer and I would all go down together. I lowered my head and butted BlackMoon in the back between his shoulders, taking him by surprise. He could not have anticipated such a suicidal attack. All three of us tottered on the brink for a frozen instant, then fell.

Mercury reached out desperately and caught himself on a fissure in the rocks less than a yard from the top, wedging both hands into the crack and breaking his fall. Acting instinctively, I scissored my legs around his waist, anchoring myself, albeit upside down. BlackMoon snaked his arms through the circle made by my own bound arms as they hung below me. I stared down past his impassive face at the churning waters far below. It was not a pretty sight from this angle.

'Well, Jason,' said Merc. 'This is another fine mess we're in.'

'Yes,' I agreed. 'How long can you hold on?'

'A minute at most. And I certainly can't climb hauling both of you.'

'What about one of us?' I said, narrowing my eyes at BlackMoon.

'That I might manage.'

'I have a better suggestion,' said BlackMoon.

'I'll bet you do,' I said.

'I see a handhold which will support me. From there I could climb back to level ground and draw you up – with your co-operation. You could easily dislodge me as I climbed if you so desired, but if you allow me to reach safety, I will then draw the two of you up.'

'You expect us to believe this?' I asked.

'The alternative is that we will hang here until Mercury loses his grip and we all die.'

'So instead we should let you climb back up and place ourselves at your mercy?'

'You began this encounter at my mercy. Now I am at yours. You can trust me. You will certainly die if you don't. Co-operate and we can all live.'

'You've got a point,' said Merc. 'But while we're negotiating, I'd like to hear you swear by all The Gods above and the Demon Lords below that you will let us go free and will never hunt either of us again.'

'There is no need for such oaths.'

'I think my fingers are slipping,' said Merc.

'I so swear.'

'Then go to it.'

BlackMoon reached out for the wall, got a handhold, then a toehold, and let go of me completely. He quickly scampered up the wall and pulled himself onto level ground. He extended an arm for Mercury to grasp and slowly pulled both of us up.

'Thanks,' I said, as he expertly unknotted my bonds.

'I have arranged for a delegation from the Dark Magic Society to meet me here this afternoon. I suggest you not be in the vicinity at that time. I won't be. The Noarcane should wear off within an hour, Mercury. Here are your belongings.'

The jujula shimmered into translucent visibility. They were vaguely manlike forms bearing large packs. One handed me Overwhelm and my armour while the other returned Mercury's cloak. They then returned to full invisibility. It was fortunate that jujula were not allowed to directly harm or hinder the living or our battle with BlackMoon might well have ended differently. Invisible foes would be hard to beat.

'And now I must bid you farewell,' said BlackMoon. He started across the bridge and quickly vanished into the forest.

'Now what?' I said as I donned my armour and strapped on Overwhelm.

Mercury fastened his cloak before replying. 'We continue with our original intent. We carry the fight to the Society. We'll start by questioning whoever comes to pick us up. My guess is it won't be Isogoras and Natalia. BlackMoon was probably dealing with another member of the Ruling Conclave. The leaders of the Society compete fiercely for the Overmaster's favour.' He pulled a second cloak from beneath his own. 'Put that over your shiny armour and shade it to match the rocks. We'll sit in the shadow of that boulder over there and see who shows up.'

Two hours passed before a black flying carpet skimmed over-head and settled to a landing near the bridge. The magician controlling the rug was a stooped, emaciated old man cloaked in black. His staff was of sablewood and tipped with a leering silver skull. He was accompanied by two young, strong men wearing black tunics emblazoned with the blood-red sigil for death. The trio remained on the carpet, ready to fly away at the first hint of trouble. They didn't notice the two of us crouch-ed nearby, silent and unmoving.

'Necrophilius the Grave,' Merc whispered in my ear. 'A master of death magic, creator of the prying eyes, a high-ranking member of the Ruling Conclave. The other two are acolytes of the Forbidden Church of Undeath, with which he is associated.'

'Never heard of it.'

'It's a small cult. Hard to gain converts when you're preaching death for all the living. Anyway, we've got to sepa-rate Necrophilius from his staff. It's a killer.'

'You have a plan?'

'A directed burst of strong wind might do the trick. When he drops it, you charge and cut him down. Don't worry about the acolytes. They're probably just along to carry our bodies. Ready?'

Before I could nod my assent, Necrophilius looked directly at us. 'You may come out from your hiding place now Mercury Boltblaster and Jason Cosmo. And please do so slowly and carefully, with your hands above your heads. Any sudden movements might cause me to reduce you to dust with one of my many instant death spells.' His voice was as dry as a sun-bleached skeleton's ligaments. We complied with his instructions. 'Very good, very good. Naturally I have had this entire area under surveillance with my prying eyes for several days. I am aware of your bargain with hunter BlackMoon – and I intend to honour it. Provided we can reach an acceptable understanding.'

'What are you talking about, Deathmaster?' asked Merc as we slowly approached.

'That is close enough,' said the necromancer. 'Kindly sit down and place your hands atop your heads.' We obeyed this command as well, not wishing to chance instant death by making a desperate attack. 'I have some things to tell you. You will listen carefully and then we shall all depart this place in peace. I know that you intend to attack the Overmaster, despite your ignorance of his location. I can provide you with that information.'

'Betraying your leader?' said Merc.

Necrophilius spat. 'That whelp is no leader of mine. He is mad, drowning in the venom of his own megalomania. This search for the Superwand is sheer lunacy. It was lost long ago – let it stay lost. And let Asmodraxas remain in his eternal prison. Erimandras would resurrect the past, but the past is dead. The Society must look to the future, a future in which it rules the world in its own right, not by licking the boots of demons.'

'A future, perhaps, in which Necrophilius is Overmaster?' inquired Mercury.

'Of course. Though I am not alone in opposing the course upon which Erimandras has set our Society, I have been the most effective in thwarting his will. And now I have secured the means of his destruction.'

'And what is that?' I asked.

'The two of you, of course. I supply BlackMoon with many of his deadly poisons at discount rates. In return, I occasionally require him to perform special services – such as bringing the two of you to me before that idiot Isogoras could capture you and take you to the Overmaster. Isogoras made use of my prying eyes to spy on you, but they also transmitted their images to me and I communicated your location to BlackMoon, facilitating his task.'

'So we're here?' said Merc. 'So what's the point?'

'Erimandras is here, in Malravia.'

'Fortress Marn,' said Merc thoughtfully. Marn was a major stronghold of the Empire of Fear a thousand years ago. It had stood deserted for many centuries due to the great evil wrought there – and because of the ghosts which gave it its nickname, the Haunted Citadel. The tortured souls of the Empire's victims who had perished there still roamed the dungeons and corridors of Marn.

'Yes, Marn,' confirmed Necrophilius. 'Erimandras has made it the headquarters of the Society, another demonstration of his preoccupation with past glories. In anticipation of your capture, Jason Cosmo, he has summoned all of the Ruling Conclave to join him there. Unfortunately I, and several others, will be unable to attend. But all of those loyal to Erimandras or too fearful to oppose him are already gathered within the walls of Marn.' He withdrew an ebony scroll case from an inner pocket of his robe. 'This is a map of the secret passages beneath Marn, through which you may covertly enter the citadel. If you succeed in eliminating Erimandras and his followers you will have gained your safety. I can assure you that under my leadership the Dark Magic Society will have no further interest in either of you.'

'And will probably be more dangerous than ever,' I said.

'That is not your concern unless you make it your concern, in which case any bargain made here today is suspended. If you wish to take the crusading perspective, however, consider that it will take us months, perhaps years, to regroup if you succeed, during which time the activities of the Society must of necessity be curtailed. To continue your briefing – the rooms and corridors of the citadel are monitored by more of my prying eyes. They will be under my control, however, and will conveniently fail to detect you. If you are careful, you can reach Erimandras undetected and take him unawares. You will need every advantage you can find.' He dropped the map to the ground. The magic carpet rose several feet into the air. 'That is all. I hope you do not fail.' His carpet streaked away to the east, above the canopy of the Incredibly Dark Forest.

'Sounds like he's got it all figured out for us,' said Merc, picking up the map.

'Can we trust him?'

'Not fully. Somewhere in his scheme is a proviso for our deaths. That is a certainty. But his approach is sound. We creep in, take out Erimandras and his cronies, and then run like hell. Simple.'

'Simple,' I agreed dubiously. We set out for Fortress Marn.

20

The Malravian war chant grew louder and more frenzied with each passing hour. Hundreds of the black-haired, grey-skinned warriors, of both sexes, danced their twisting, jerking dance around the great bonfire. They waved their spears, bows and axes wildly and bellowed their challenges into the night. If they put as much energy into fighting as they did into this dance, we had little to worry about.

After three days of scrabbling up and down rugged ridges, along twisting gullies, and across yawning chasms, Merc and I had reached what looked like a great, broad bowl scooped out of a hilltop by a giant hand. In fact, according to Malravian legends that was exactly what had happened. Their national deity, known appropriately as the Grey God, created this place as a gathering place for all his people. Being a people of few words, the Malravians called it simply the Gathering Place.

'No sense in attacking Marn shorthanded,' said Mercury. 'I spent some time in Malravia a few years back helping the locals fight Ganthians, mountain giants, and nasties out of the Forest. I was made an honorary Malravian for my efforts. That may be enough for us to gain some allies.'

'And if it isn't?'

'We'll be skinned alive and roasted on spits for daring to violate this holy site.'

In the centre of the bowl was a fissure from which seeped noxious fumes. Merc ignited the subterranean gases from a safe distance with his fingerflames and a great plume of fire shot into the sky. The summons was sent. We sat back and waited for the response. For the sake of my skin, I hoped it would be favourable.

The first Malravians arrived that evening, a band of twenty who began the dance. By dawn they had been joined by dozens more. None of them had acknowledged our presence. They simply arrived and joined the growing circle around the fire.

Hundreds of Malravians arrived the next day, hundreds more the day after that. By the end of the week there were over ten thousand warriors at the Gathering Place. It seemed they had done nothing but dance and chant since their arrival. I had seen no one stop to eat or sleep or even rest for a while. No one had asked who issued the summons or why. At least not until now.

Mercury and I stood on a ridge above the circle and conferred with the chieftains of the seven clans of Malravia. Clad in the furs of cave bears and rock tigers, their long hair pulled back into a single war-braid, jaws clenched grimly, eyes glittering fiercely, they were a frightful and imposing sight.

'You and your companion have crossed our land safely because you are accepted as one of the Grey Folk, Brother Mercury, due to your courage and service to the Folk when last you walked this land many years ago. But you dare much by coming to this sacred place and issuing the summons,' said Kogarth, eldest of the chiefs and spokesman for the others. His thin hair was silver with age, his face a craggy mass of wrinkles.

'Such is the right and duty of any of the the Folk,' replied Merc, 'when he learns of a danger to all.'

'And what is this danger?'

'The evil of the Dark Magic Society, which has taken up residence in the Haunted Citadel of Marn.'

'Marn is a shunned place. What transpires there is of no concern to us.'

'Marn is shunned no longer by those who would spread its bloody stain over all the Folk. Surely the dark things of Marn already venture beyond its walls.'

Those clan chiefs with lands closest to Marn nodded grimly at this. Kogarth considered for a moment.

'Even so, Marn is invincible. If defended by sorcerers it is doubly so. To assault it would be folly.'

Merc waved the scroll Necrophilius had given him. 'I know a secret way inside the citadel. And the shamans of the Folk are themselves powers to reckon with.' Kogarth still looked unconvinced. 'Besides,' continued Merc, 'we've got ten thousand mulka-crazed warriors down there. They've got to attack something.'

'That is true,' said Kogarth. He nodded. 'So be it, Brother Mercury. You shall be our war-captain and lead us against Marn. It will be a feat long remembered in our songs – if any of us survive.'

It took five days of swift marching for the Malravian host to reach Marn. The citadel was a hulking mass of black stone crouched like a bloated spider upon a great outcropping of rock halfway up a jagged and desolate peak of harsh grey granite. Its crenellated walls bristled with spires and towers and the stone images of unspeakable monstrosities: demons, gargoyles and things without names. We had threaded our way up a twisting box canyon to reach this point, and the only visible path approaching the fortress was a narrow road winding back and forth up the sheer face of the mountain through more than a dozen gates, all of which were sealed. No defenders were visible, but the very stones of the place radiated cruelty, wickedness and horror. Even the eternal grey mists seemed to avoid the fortress. The first ranks of our host, mulka-mad as they were, recoiled as we drew near. A fearful murmuring swept through the Malravian horde as they realized what we were about to undertake. I heard occasional sharp cries for us to turn back and abandon this mad scheme before it was too late. Looking up at our goal, I wondered if that wasn't a good idea.

'The warriors grumble,' said Kogarth.

'Well they should,' said Merc. 'Many of them may die before this day is through.'

'It is not death they fear, but what may follow death in this place. There are creatures here which swallow souls.'

'Hopefully we won't run into any of those,' said Merc. 'I'll need three shamans and ten warriors to accompany me through the secret way. Preferably not so mulka-sodden that they can no longer think, hear and obey.'

Kogarth quickly selected those who would accompany us. Merc gave them a cursory inspection and nodded his approval. 'Brave Kogarth, this host must provide a diversion to hold the attention of those within. The Society knows we are here for we have seen their creatures scuttling in the shadows as we approached. But they do not know why we are here. Have the warriors scream, chant, dance about, wave their spears and hurl curses for a while. In an hour's time make as if you intend to storm the citadel by main force, but go no higher than the third gate. Should you get that far, withdraw and dance around a while longer before attacking again.' He turned to those who would accompany us inside. 'We have the important task, for we must slaughter the leaders within the citadel, mighty sorcerers all. Yet we have might of our own and, the Grey God willing, we shall prevail.'

'Well spoken,' said Kogarth. 'Go now and destroy the enemies of the Folk.'

Mercury led our band to a narrow cleft in the east wall of the canyon. It was hidden by a protruding lip of rock which made the sheer cliff face seem unbroken, but the path beyond twisted its way into the depths. We were forced to advance in single file. I took the lead with Overwhelm in hand. Merc was right behind me, followed closely by the Malravian shamans and the warriors. We were soon in complete darkness.

'Aren't magic swords supposed to glow in the dark?' I asked.

'Most do,' said Merc.

'This one doesn't.'

'How do you know? You haven't commanded it to.'

'True,' I said sheepishly. 'Let there be light!' The blade Overwhelm instantly shone with a pale pink light. 'Pink?' I said in dismay.

'A trifle unusual, but sufficient,' said Merc. 'I can see the map.'

The ceiling of the passage was no more than a yard above my head at its highest points and frequently was so low that I had to bend over double to advance. The floor sloped downward for the first thousand paces, was more or less level for another few hundred steps, then began to gradually incline upwards. We had gone through so many twists and turns that I was unsure which direction we were facing, but Merc assured me we were almost beneath the fortress. The air was still, dry and cold here and malevolence bled from the walls the further we went.

We eventually reached a wall of solid stone which completely blocked the passage. There was no apparent way to progress further.

'End of the line,' I said grimly.

'Hardly,' said Merc. 'We must locate a hidden door.'

'You didn't say anything about a hidden door.'

'It isn't marked, but since the map shows this passage leading to a blank wall and depicts another passage on the far side of the wall, I am led to assume there must be a hidden door. Extinguish your sword.'

'Why?'

'Because I am about to cast a spell which will make the outline of the door glow with a faint green light which I will not be able to see for this pink glare.'

I commanded Overwhelm to cease giving off light and Mercury made his incantation. Nothing happened, no green lines appeared.

'Well?' I demanded.

'It is possible there is not a hidden door,' said Merc thoughtfully. 'There are spells which allow a man to walk through stone walls as if they were air. Perhaps that is how the wizards of Marn made use of this passage. Unfortunately, I never learned any of those spells.'

'Great. Maybe you could just blast a hole in the wall.'

'I could do that,' mused Mercury. 'Of course, that would probably bring the ceiling down on us as well. Mikla, Rikulf, Iuri – any suggestions?'

The three Malravian tribal priests made negative grunts. It appeared that we were stymied, our secret assault thwarted. I ignited Overwhelm again – and then I remembered.

'Merc! Didn't the Keeper at Greenleaf say this sword would cut through stone like warm butter – or words to that effect?'

'Try it,' said Merc.

I stepped up to the wall and thrust my blade forward. It sank in easily, as if I were stabbing water, not stone. I traced a circle a yard wide, handed Overwhelm to Merc, and pushed hard on the cut-out section. With a harsh scraping it moved forward and fell through on the other side. And kept falling. I stuck my head through the hole and looked down into a seemingly bottomless black shaft. The pit was nearly ten feet across. On its far side was a broad landing and an ascending stairway.

Returning Overwhelm, Merc looked through the hole, then frowned at the map. 'This isn't to scale.'

'Never mind that. How do we get across this pit?'

'Jump.'

'Jump!'

'That's what I said. I think that would be quicker than trying to walk a rope or swing across. I don't see anywhere to attach the grapnel anyway. We'll have to jump.'

'I'm not sure about this.'

'I can easily clear twenty feet in a standing jump, and these Malravians can do better than that. Living in the mountains they constantly have to jump across chasms, gullies and the like. Watch.' With that he stepped through the hole and launched himself through the air, landing on the far side of the pit with room to spare. The Malravians followed in rapid succession, leaving me alone on the wrong side of the shaft.

'What are you waiting for?'

'I don't think I can do this, Merc.'

'What? With those massive thighs? No problem at all. Just jump.'

'Merc—'

'We haven't got all day, hero. You'd best throw me the sword first or you'll have to sheath it and jump in the dark.'

I hurled the blade across and Merc caught it gracefully. With a resigned sigh I crouched in the gap I had made in the wall, bunched the muscles in my legs and sprang forward. I knew instantly that I was going to fall short by several feet. Claws of panic ripped at my gut as I stared down into the onrushing void beneath me. Then I felt an odd upward tug and I flew forward to land on my stomach at Merc's feet.

'Nice jump, Jason.'

I clambered to my feet. 'I think I had a little help. A touch of levitation, perhaps?'

Merc shrugged and returned Overwhelm again. I led the way up the steep stairway. The steps were narrow and numerous. I counted five hundred before we reached the landing at the top where our way was blocked by another stone wall. This time Mercury's spell revealed a secret door and another spell caused it to swing ponderously open. A foul, damp draft swept over us. The evil aura which surrounded us was stronger than ever. My flesh crawled and my hair stood on end. This was worse than enduring the scrutiny of Ouga-Oyg's mirror.

'We are in the lowest levels of the fortress proper,' said Merc. 'Our quarry awaits us in the throneroom many floors above. Let us proceed with stealth and caution. No mulka-chewing yet.'

'Aieee!' cried the Malravians. I thought that an odd response until I noticed that we were surrounded by shimmering, translucent images of broken and bloody men, women and children. They flitted through the air like obscene phantom hummingbirds, passing insubstantially through the walls, the floor, and even our bodies.

'Calm down!' said Merc. 'These poor ghosts mean us no harm, nor have they the means to do us harm except through fear! Are you warriors or frightened sheep?'

I heard a few bleating sounds from somewhere in the back of the group, but something else had my attention. The ghosts were congregating around me and dropping to their substanceless knees in silent homage. Overwhelm's light turned from pink

181

to deep rose to a brilliant scarlet hue and my armour seemed to glow as well. The Malravians fell back in wonder and even Merc looked surprised.

'Merc? What's happening?'

'Amazing. There is a very obscure addendum to the legends about these ghosts which says they will be liberated from their eternal imprisonment here and sent to Paradise when the Mighty Champion walks once more the halls of Marn, where he fought the final battle against the Emperor of Fear, and again vanquishes a great evil. I always thought it was just some silly epilogue tacked on to soften the grimness of the tale, but it appears I was wrong. You are of his line and you bear his relics. I guess that's enough.'

'What does this mean?'

'I assume that if we win these ghosts will be free. If we lose, I suppose we'll be joining them here.'

'Let's win.'

The Society had evidently confined its reoccupation of Marn to the upper floors, for the stony bowels of the citadel were still choked with the dust and debris of ten centuries of neglect. Escorted by a swarm of ghosts, we encountered no living creatures as we ascended through the dark corridors and gloomy chambers of the fortress, nor were we molested by any of the nameless supernatural horrors said to lurk here.

We thrice encountered lone, patrolling prying eyes, but they paid us no heed, true to the words of Necrophilius. Everything was going according to plan until I opened a door and found myself looking at the back of a tall woman holding an ivory wand. She had long black hair, pale white skin, and wore a thin gown of diaphanous violet gauze gathered at her slim waist by a black leather belt studded with steel spikes. In the great hall were assembled dozens of the Society's junior magicians, receiving their orders from her.

'The hillscum without the walls must be taught a severe lesson,' she said. 'We have not yet had the leisure to eradicate them, but since they have come to us we will make the most of the opportunity. You will proceed to the battlements and practise your offensive spells. You may use fireballs, lightning bolts, acid clouds — anything except earthquake spells, which might do damage to Marn. What are you all staring at?' She turned quickly. I smiled and slammed the door in her face. The door promptly vanished in a burst of flame and she levelled the smoking wand at me.

'It's Eufrosinia the Cruel,' said Merc. 'She specializes in pain and torture magic. I'm sorry we can't stay and chat, Eufy, but we've got things to do.' With a gesture from Merc, the ceiling collapsed, forcing Eufrosinia to leap back into the assembly hall and blocking the entrance to the corridor. 'Let's move!' commanded Merc. 'They know we're here now and it won't take long for Eufy and her playmates to break through and give chase.'

Gongs, sirens and other alarms sounded as we ran down the corridor. We turned left at an intersection to avoid a squad of puzzled guardsmen approaching from the right, and quickly found ourselves facing a pair of towering brass doors. The guards were right at our heels. The Malravians shoved huge wads of mulka leaves into their mouths and turned to face the Society's lackeys. I was in the forefront of the skirmish, lopping off heads and limbs as easily as I had sliced through the stone wall earlier.

Merc faced the doors, concentrating on a spell. As he waved his hands in an intricate pattern, the doors glowed red, then white, and finally melted into a bubbling pool which quickly cooled to become a misshapen brass sheet on the floor.

'This way! Quickly!'

I pulled back but the Malravians, now foaming at the mouth, ignored Mercury's command and plunged through the last of the guards to charge at the onrushing magicians led by Eufrosinia.

'Damn!' said Merc. 'They've gone into a battle frenzy. I hoped they'd hold off until we reached the Conclave. No way to control them now.'

'We're on our own again?'

'Again.'

The bronze doors were the entrance to a vast library, half a mile long and almost as wide. We stood on a broad balcony crowded with cluttered desks, which were hastily abandoned by frightened clerks. It hung just above the tops of the monstrous shelves which stretched down out of view and overflowed with books, scrolls and tablets. A series of narrow catwalks connected the balcony to the shelves and the clerks made quick use of them to escape us.

'The main library of the Dark Magic Society,' said Merc smugly. 'All of their knowledge, plans, files and records. An excellent place to produce a diversion.' He made a few passes of incantation. A puff of smoke jetted from his hands and dissipated. He frowned. 'So much for my spectacular fireball. There must be an anti-magic field in here which hampers spellcasting.'

The war cries of the Malravians, mingled with dying shrieks and the explosions of deadly offensive magicks, sounded in the corridor. It was impossible to tell which side was getting the worst of the mêlée.

Merc consulted his map. 'The throne room is up two more levels.' He sprinted out onto one of the catwalks. As I was about to follow, Eufrosinia and three junior mages reached the door. All bled profusely from multiple wounds. The underlings, forgetting about the anti-magic field in the library, projected a selection of weirdly coloured flames and balls of light at me, all of of which fizzled out at the threshold. Eufrosinia merely smiled a wicked smile and flicked her wand.

'She's deactivated the field,' cried Merc, turning in place to defend himself against her next spell. But with another flick of her wand, the catwalk beneath him vanished. He fell from sight. It was a long way down.

I raised Overwhelm to attack. Eufrosinia stood still, letting me get within sword range and swing my blade before raising her hand in a commanding gesture which froze me in mid-swing as if I were made of stone.

She raked her long purple fingernails across my cheeks by way of a caress and hissed, 'It was good of you to join us, Jason Cosmo. The Overmaster is expecting you.'

The ghosts swirled around me in great agitation. Their expected saviour was in no position to save even himself.

184

21

Clad only in a loin cloth, I was suspended on a metal frame in a huge, high-vaulted chamber of dark stone. The air was thick with ancient malice and murky with the thin, grey outlines of the darting ghosts who lost what little faded colour they had here in the heart of Marn's darkness. They flitted around me like pale abstractions, their anguished faces hovering before my eyes in an attitude of hopelessness.

I had been helpless to resist as Eufrosinia's minions brought me here and bound me. I was helpless now, even though the paralysis had worn off.

In the centre of the room was a wide, deep pit filled with charred black lumps that looked disturbingly like human bodies. On the far side was a pyramid of twenty-three thrones. There were twelve at the lowest level, succeeding layers of seven and three, and one throne set above all. Nine were empty. The rest were occupied by men and women of varying age and race, among them Eufrosinia, who sat on the layer of seven. Behind the thrones was a gigantic mirror which covered the entire wall and was surrounded by a wide frame of burnished brass. Between the thrones and the pit was a stone table upon which rested the relics of the Mighty Champion.

'We are the Ruling Conclave of the Dark Magic Society,' said the figure on the highest throne. His hollow voice made my skin creep as if worms burrowed beneath it. 'I am Erimandras, Overmaster of the Society.'

My jaw went slack in horror. He was just a young boy, barely into his teens! The chief architect of all the vile schemes of the Society, the evil genius who led them in their pursuit of world domination, was a mere child! He was seated on a high-backed chair of gold, onyx and malachite. He wore a fine robe the colour of a nightmare and an elaborate horned head-dress. His gaunt face was white as ash, with thin black lips like a line traced in blood from his heart. A slim silver wand tipped with a five-pointed star rested across his knees.

'Aren't you a little young?' I said.

Intense waves of purest agony ripped my body, as if every cell had been pierced with barbed hooks. The feeling was gone by the time the scream reached my throat, but I went ahead and screamed anyway, scattering the ghosts like a flock of frightened pigeons. My innards churned like I had swallowed a cyclone.

'I did not give you leave to speak,' said Erimandras. 'Do not speak out of turn again.'

I was about to tell him not to worry, but thought better of it. I nodded.

'We have gone to great trouble and expense to capture you, but it will all be worthwhile as soon as you reveal what we must know – and that you will surely do. Let us begin. Where is the Superwand?'

'How should I know?'

The agony struck again, this time lasting slightly longer. Erimandras waited until the echoes of my screams had died away before continuing his interrogation. He raised the wand in his lap so that I could see it clearly.

'I seek the Superwand, of which this is a replica. You stole it from my Master a thousand years ago through the basest of deceptions. You stole it and you hid it. Where?'

'I wasn't even born a thousand—'

More agony, longer and more intense, though I wouldn't have thought that possible a few seconds ago. I screamed as if I had lost my soul. The upset ghosts flew madly around the chamber like dry leaves in a storm.

'You are Jason Cosmo, the reincarnation of that earlier Jason Cosmo who ended the Age of Empire. You trapped my Master in a prison from which he cannot escape until what you stole is restored. The Society has searched to the literal ends of the Earth seeking the wand and has found not a clue. Again, where is it?'

'I've never seen a Superwand in this life or any other! I'm not a reincarnation of—'

Agony again. He let me writhe and howl for almost a full minute before ending the pain. I hung in place, limp and breathless, drenched with sweat.

'Do not lie to me. The equation is simple. I need the Superwand to free my Master so that he may reclaim his proper station. Your earlier incarnation hid the wand and the knowledge of its location must therefore be locked away in the depths of your pitiful mind. If it were not, the spineless godlings of Paradise would not have taken such futile pains to protect you. I will pry the information from you if I must strip away every shred of your sanity, every vestige of your humanity, every tender fragment of your soul. Where is the wand?'

'I . . . don't . . . know.'

I blacked out this time. Nothing had changed when I came to and I had no idea how much time had passed.

'Potent as agony matrix is, you should know that it is the weakest of the persuasive devices in our Chamber of Damnation, for our Eufrosinia is most inventive. If it continues to prove ineffective, I shall order one of the truly unpleasant machines brought up. Now tell me where the wand is.'

'I can't.' I braced myself for another blast of pain, but it didn't come.

'I tire of this,' said Erimandras. 'It is time for you to face my Master. We will then see if you continue to resist. Activate the mirror!'

The other wizards shifted nervously at this command. Before anything happened, however, the iron-riveted doors swung open and Natalia Slash entered, dragging Isogoras the Xornite behind her in chains. Both his legs seemed to be broken. The warrior woman halted before the thrones.

'Great Erimandras, as per the terms of our contract, I bring you Isogoras the Xornite.' She threw Isogoras to the floor.

'Ah, yes,' said Erimandras. 'Your timing is somewhat inopportune, Lady Slash, but this gift is most welcome.' He regarded Isogoras coldly. 'Xornite, you have repeatedly failed me. You were given the simple task of bringing a single man into our ranks, yet he consistently refused and eluded me. I then instructed you to eliminate him, and you failed in that. Furthermore, you twice had Cosmo within your grasp, and twice failed to capture him, so that he came into our power through his own folly whilst you thrashed futilely through the

Incredibly Dark Forest ostensibly searching for him. I must wonder at such consistent incompetence. I must wonder if you are not in league with those traitors who dare defy me, whose guilt is made plainly evident by their absence today. Perhaps you are even their ringleader. Perhaps you would set yourself up as Overmaster in my place.'

'I heard him speak words to that effect,' said Natalia helpfully.

'Overmaster, she lies! I—'

'Silence! I did not give you leave to speak. There are no words of explanation or apology which can save you, so best to say nothing. I hired Lady Slash to keep an eye on you and bring you to me in chains once your treachery was apparent to her. She has done well and will be rewarded.' Erimandras paused. 'Let the mirror now be activated – with the traitor as first sacrifice.'

'Overmaster! No!' Isogoras dragged himself towards the thrones, but Natalia yanked him back.

'You are warned once again to hold your tongue lest it be plucked from your mouth. You have failed in so much. Try not to fail in dying with dignity.'

Strong slaves in iron masks entered the chamber and poured vats of oil into the fire pit. A brand was lit and thrown in, lighting the fire. Split tongues of fire leaped high above the floor level and produced tremendous heat. I felt myself slowly roasting, though the members of the Ruling Conclave seemed unaffected by the heat.

Now the slaves lifted Isogoras from the floor and held him motionless at the edge of the pit. Sweat boiled from their bare chest and their skin blistered, but they were oblivious to it all. Isogoras whimpered.

'Now,' said Erimandras. They threw him in. He was engulfed by the flames before he landed amid the remains of the previous victims, his screams overwhelmed by their roar. The flames grew darker. The ghosts of victims past fled the chamber in horror.

'You may make payment to my account at the Bank of Caratha,' said Natalia, turning to leave.

'This shall be done, but stay awhile.'

'I must go. I have business to attend to.' Her back was to the Overmaster.

'I insist,' said Erimandras, his voice becoming hard. Natalia stiffened. 'I will soon have a new mission for you.'

She turned to face him. 'As you wish.'

The slaves brought in more sacrifices, starved and broken men, women and children of every race and nation. All were hurled into the pit. Those that still had tongues screamed, but their screams availed them nothing. I wanted to turn my head, but it was braced in place, forcing me to watch this demonstration of the raw inhumanity of the Society. This was how life had been for all the world in the days of the Empire and how it would be again if the Society was triumphant. This was what The Gods had charged me to prevent.

But I could do nothing now. I was in their power, to be tortured and broken helplessly. Others would have to carry on the fight. All I could do was resolve to take my own life before I would do anything to help these butchers. And I was unable to do even that. Unbidden thoughts of Sapphrina filled my mind. I would miss her and what might have been.

With each sacrifice, the flames darkened, stained by innocent blood until they were as black as the bowels of midnight. At this point Erimandras stood. His throne and the pedestal on which it rested turned so that he faced the mirror. The black hellfire was reflected in the glass. He uttered an incantation that made those reflected flames grow until they filled the whole of the mirror. Then he began the summons. 'Great Asmodraxas, Lord among Lords, King of the Hells, Sweet Prince of Darkness, Dire Master of the Profane, Author of Dread – heed thou the summons of thy servant Erimandras! Thine enemy is now in thy power and the day of thy liberty close at hand!'

The flames in the mirror warped and twisted until they formed a gigantic face, a visage at once beautiful and terrible, inspiring both loathing and love, both a desire to fall down in adoration and to flee in abject fear. The members of the Ruling Conclave bowed their heads. Some trembled. Natalia looked away. The slaves continued their gruesome chore.

The deposed Demon Lord spoke and his voice soothed and stabbed my very soul with its bewitching brutality. 'I see you, Cosmo, most hated of foes. I have long waited for this moment, to see you broken and beaten before me, to extract my vengance for the bitter cup of defeat you hurled in my face so long ago.'

'I don't believe we've met,' I said.

'I know you, Cosmo. I know the outlines of your form, the flavour of your will, the scent of your putridly courageous soul. It is you, Cosmo. You are the one who took from me my dominion and the emblem of that dominion. You are the one who trapped me in this null space where I can neither create nor destroy, where there is nothing to corrupt, no one to rule, and no means of escape. Alone and near madness I endured here for an eternity, unable to perform any act until my servant Erimandras devised this magic mirror as a means of communicating with me and begged for my wisdom. I have guided him in closing the fist of the Society around total victory. I commanded him to cease the fruitless search for my stolen Superwand and instead find the worm who stole it. I knew your spirit would endure in the world, ever fearful of my return.'

'I am not the Jason Cosmo you knew. I bear his name, but that is all. Mere coincidence. I don't know anything about wands or null spaces. You have the wrong man.'

'You are the one. You will reveal the Superwand to Erimandras that he may use it to free me. Then I will be restored to my former glory and I will crush you and the pathetic godlings you serve beneath my iron heel. Erimandras, you may proceed.'

'Yes, O Dark One. Let the perilous pulp-grinder be brought forth!'

That didn't sound promising. I offered up a desperate prayer to The Gods for a miracle. I figured they owed me at least one since they were largely responsible for my being in this situation. Even a slim chance of escape would satisfy me. I could do the rest. But my prayer brought no immediate response, no thunder in the heavens, no splitting asunder of the earth beneath me.

190

As slaves hurried to carry out the Overmaster's command, a messenger rushed breathlessly into the chamber and threw himself before the Ruling Conclave.

'Great Ones, I beg to report that the hill rabble have been pushed back from the gates by the spells of the lesser mages, yet the battle madness is upon them and they gather for yet another assault.'

'The news you bring does not justify this interruption. Our mages are naturally slaughtering the barbarian scum. I have commanded that it be so. And they will continue until the grey-skinned animals are exterminated. You will not disturb me with such trifles again. Throw him in the pit!'

The iron-masked slaves hastened to obey. The ill-fated messenger struggled weakly, but to no avail. He was instantly incinerated.

A second messenger arrived as the slaves set up the perilous pulp-grinder, a massive collection of gears, belts and jagged metal teeth.

'Great Ones, I beg to report that the library is in flames.'

'Impossible!' said Erimandras.

'The protective anti-magic field was deactivated during the capture of Jason Cosmo, Great Ones, and was not reset. Evidently the other intruder, Mercury Boltblaster, succeeded in starting the blaze.'

'Why was he allowed to live?' stormed Erimandras at the cowering Eufrosinia.

'Overmaster, I hastened to bring Cosmo to you and commanded the guards and lesser mages to locate Boltblaster. It is they who have failed you. I—'

'Silence! Find him! All of you – save Lady Slash! He must pay most dearly for this outrage!' The twelve sitting members of the Ruling Conclave rose and rushed from the chamber with disturbing eagerness. A dozen arcane masters, scores of lesser mages, and many slaves and guards beside – if Merc was still alive, the odds did not favour his staying that way for long.

We were crazy to have come here, to have thought we could have ever pulled it off. The Society was just too powerful, had too many resources at its command.

Erimandras shook his head in dismay when his fellow wizards were gone. 'The library is our most precious resource. All our worldwide schemes will be disrupted if it is destroyed.'

'Do not concern yourself with these lesser matters,' admonished Asmodraxas. 'Once we wring the location of the Superwand from Cosmo, books and records will not matter.'

'You are correct, O Master.' The Overmaster quickly regained his composure. By this time the slaves had transferred me from the agony matrix to the pulp-grinder. I was fastened to a conveyer belt by three thick leather straps across my chest, waist and thighs. 'This device will grind your body into an undifferentiated mass of bloody flesh. No bones, no face, no form at all – but you will continue to live and you will feel it all. The liquid pulp you become will be collected in that vat. We will question you and give you the means to reply. If you remain uncooperative, there are a variety of tortures to which we can subject your new form, both chemical and physical. The worst, I think, is feeding you to our slaves. You will make a tasty soup and you will gain an unusual perspective on the process of digestion. Start the machine.'

Two slaves wound a large crank and released it. The belt slowly pulled me toward the clacking iron jaws that would pulverize me. I struggled in my bonds, but the straps were too strong. Erimandras and his demonic master looked on dispassionately, Natalia with grim fascination.

'If you tell us where the wand is now, I will release you,' said Erimandras.

'I wouldn't tell you if I did know, even if I thought your promise was any good.'

'You do know and you will tell,' said Asmodraxas.

'Don't say a word!' said Merc, appearing in the doorway, his red cloak floating around him like a cloud. The slaves rushed at him and flew back lifeless, scattered by an invisible hand. The doors closed behind Merc and I heard the collapse of the ceiling outside. This would be a private confrontation.

'I was wondering if you would show up,' I said.

'I took a wrong turn in one of the secret passages out of the library. But now we can bring this little drama to its conclusion.'

He wasn't a miracle, but he was the next best thing.

22

'Take him,' said Erimandras.

Natalia drew steel and attacked, only to be halted by the same invisible wall of force.

'You've done well in our previous encounters, Natalia,' said Merc. 'Now you're going to be well done.' The invisible wall expanded and slammed her backwards into the fire pit. She didn't scream as she was engulfed by the ebon flames.

'You're the Overmaster?' said Mercury, getting a good look at Erimandras. 'Shouldn't you be home sucking your thumb?'

Erimandras stood and raised the wand. 'Fool! I was an arcane master at the age of five and a grandmaster at seven. I slew the previous Overmaster in my eighth year and began the making of the Mirror of Asmodraxas. It is you who is but a mewling babe before my power and intellect!'

Crimson lightning arced from the simulation Superwand and traced a crackling web in the air around Merc, who crumpled to the floor. He wasn't going to be much help to me from there.

I kept struggling and discovered that the conveyer belt was loose. By thrashing purposefully, I caused it to slip off track and jam the rollers. The pulp-grinder ground to a halt and I hung upside down off the edge of the machine, my head resting on the floor.

Merc rose to his knees and pointed a stiff hand at Erimandras. A sheet of golden flame spread from his fingers, but stopped short of the Overmaster's throne, blocked by protective magic. Still the crimson lightning clung to Mercury like a wreath.

I twisted until the strap around my chest caught on a projecting strut. Using that as resistance, I quickly squirmed my arms and shoulders out. With use of my hands restored, it was easy to unbuckle the other straps. I rolled to the floor and caught my breath.

'Cosmo has freed himself,' said Asmodraxas. 'Stop him.'

Erimandras obeyed, turning the wand on me. I rolled beneath the grinder and crawled out on the other side, crouching beneath the frame of the agony matrix. The magic lightning scorched the floor where I had been.

Mercury used the diversion to reach out with his mind and snatch the wand from the Overmaster's hand. No protective spell countered that tactic and it flew into his possession.

'Now taste your own medicine, brat!' He pointed the wand at the sinister youth. Nothing happened.

'Only I control the wand.'

'Oh.' Mercury bent the wand in two and dropped it. 'So much for that idea.'

I got up and sprinted around the fire pit, heading for the table where the relics lay. Erimandras glared at me and two striking cobras flew from his eyes, sailing directly at me. I reversed course and the snakes hit the floor to slither after me. Erimandras returned his attention to Merc, opening his hand to release a cloud of needles at him. Merc transformed them into harmless safety pins, which bounced off him as he climbed the pyramid of thrones.

I ran all the way around the pit, the serpents at my heels. As I passed the table I snatched up Overwhelm, then turned and killed them. I started to climb the pyramid.

'Face me first, Cosmo.'

Natalia crawled from the pit, her nearly invincible armour glowing as if fresh from the forge, shining against the black flames. The exposed portion of her face was blistered cherry red. Her sword burned like a brand.

My armour still lay on the table and I didn't have time to put it on, not even to snatch up my shield before she was upon me. I ran around the pit again.

Erimandras hurled Merc back with a conjured avalanche of glass marbles that sent him toppling, unable to keep his footing. As he fell he summoned a glowing lasso with which he snared the Overmaster, dragging him down too. They both fell against the stone table and the lasso dissolved. Merc punched Erimandras in the face, bloodying his nose.

'You dare to physically assault my person? I have endured enough. No more petty spells! Now I shall destroy you with the ultimate form of magic – the Cards of Power!' He pulled a pack of playing cards from an inner pocket. The backs were decorated with sneering demons. 'Why do you not quake in abject fear?'

'I play that game as well,' said Merc, drawing his own pack of cards from under his cloak. The backs bore Merc's initials.

'So be it,' said Erimandras, shuffling his deck and spreading it out in his hand. 'Pick a card, any card.'

On the far side of the pit Natalia came at me in all her fury. Overwhelm barely deflected the first blow and it was downhill from there, a repeat of our last encounter. She drove me steadily back, never letting up, forcing me just about anywhere she wanted me to go. The ring of steel was in my ears, my arm was growing numb. She herded me twice around the pulp-grinder, to the far wall and back to the pit again. Every swing was as strong as the first. Overwhelm defended me, but I didn't know how much longer I could maintain my grip on the sword. Already my fingers felt like jelly from the endless impacts of our clashing blades.

'You are nothing, Cosmo. A straw man, a posturing scarecrow.'

'Then why are you so eager to kill me?'

'Your reputation. Undeserved though it is, defeating you will enhance my own prestige. I'll be able to raise my fee.'

'You're going to kill me for the public relations benefits? That's cold.'

'That's business.'

I then realized that my parries were becoming more polished and less desperate as the duel wore on. Even with my layman's grasp of magic I could see that Overwhelm was adapting to my opponent's style. It was learning her moves and tactics, adjusting to counter them more effectively. The enchantment on my blade was more powerful than I had previously realized. Our last bout had been too brief for this aspect to become manifest.

The longer we fought, the more input it would accumulate. And if my sword could find the flaws in her attacks in order to defend against them, it could turn those same attacks back against her – without the flaws. I smiled. Natalia's technique, perfected as she could never perfect it, was mine to use. I couldn't match her strength in this place so far from sunlight, but the advantage of skill, however artificial, was now mine.

I made a conscious effort to take the offensive, surprising her.

'I've toyed with you long enough,' I said, feeling giddy. I could beat her. I was sure of it. It was now she who retreated.

'Impossible. You've gone from incompetence to mastery in minutes, growing more skilful with every exchange. It cannot be, unless . . . the sword!'

She broke off and ran, putting a dozen yards between us in just a few strides. I stood dumbly in place while she hurled one of her many throwing knives at me. Overwhelm deflected it, but they kept coming, five more in rapid succession. I turned aside four. The fifth skewered the biceps of my sword arm. I dropped Overwhelm and pulled the dagger free as Natalia charged again, kicking my sword across the floor and shoving me to the floor with her free hand. Still hot, the gauntlet burned my bare skin and crisped my chest hairs. So did her metal boot as she pinned me and held her sword in a double grip, ready to deliver the *coup de grace*.

'You tire of toying with me, do you? No one toys with Natalia Slash!'

'A joke! A bad joke! In poor taste!'

'Poor taste indeed.'

I wasn't just going to lie there and take it. I grabbed her ankles to pull her off balance. She didn't budge.

'Are you through?'

'It looks that way.'

I wished I had Overwhelm in my hand – and suddenly I did! Another wondrous power of the sword revealed. I was using my left hand, but it didn't matter. I slashed upwards, knocking Natalia's sword from her grasp and gashing both her thighs. She leaped away and I sprang to my feet, kicking her sword away behind me. She launched another flurry of knives, but this time I deflected them all. Overwhelm had learned how to judge her throwing style. I advanced and she backed away as slowly as she dared, too proud to turn her back or otherwise acknowledge defeat.

196

She lunged and grabbed Overwhelm's blade in an attempt to wrest the weapon from my hand. A flick of my arm and her palms dripped blood through sundered gauntlets.

'That was a desperate move. Why don't you just give up?'

'I have never known defeat.'

'Yes, I remember how you soundly trounced Yezgar.'

'I mean I have never been bested by a normal man or woman. Monsters don't really count.'

'Nor do lives when there is a profit to be made by taking them. Right?' She had her back against the wall now. I didn't get too close, just in case she had another trick up her sleeve.

'I am a professional.'

'A beaten professional.'

'Very well. You have defeated me, Jason Cosmo, though you could not have done it without that cursed sword.'

'You're not suggesting it would have been a fair fight otherwise, are you?'

'I'm merely pointing out that it was not your skill which beat me. It was the sword.' She lowered herself to her knees and removed her helm. Her face was proud and beautiful despite the blisters and grime which marred it. Long chestnut hair lay against her head in coiled braids as padding. 'Do it quickly. I will not beg for my life.' Her hard eyes met mine.

'I'm not going to kill you.'

'If you think to make me—'

'Nothing like that. I want you to swear on your professional honour that you will never again serve the Society as long as you live and will, in fact, help me for the duration of this battle, after which you are free to go.'

'You ask much. The Society pays well.'

'Balance that against dying now. Which pays more in the long run?'

'I so swear.'

'Then pick up your sword.' I turned my back to her and went to help Merc. Natalia was utterly ruthless, but honoured any bargain she entered into. At least that was what I hoped.

'Woman,' said Asmodraxas. 'Slay Cosmo now and all you desire shall be yours when I am free.'

I heard her lift her sword and come after me. I half-turned to meet a new attack.

'We are allies for now, Cosmo.'

We approached the table where the wizards dueled, but the powerful sorcery they had unleashed repelled us. Oblivious to all else, they were locked into a deadly struggle which only one could survive. Natalia and I could only watch.

'Is this your card?' said Mercury.

'Yes, curse you!'

'I'm winning.'

'My turn. Cut the deck.'

'Done.'

'Watch carefully. Pick a card, look at it, replace it.' Merc complied. 'I will now set the deck on fire and scatter the ashes.' Erimandras did so.

'What's the trick?'

Erimandras lifted a pinch of ash, which became a whole card in his hand. He laid it face down on the table. 'That is your card.'

Merc turned the card over. 'No it isn't. I had the three of clubs. This is the three of spades.'

'You lie!'

'You lose.'

Erimandras screamed as his body evaporated. Dissipating into wispy streamers, he clawed his way up the pyramid. Merc made no move to pursue him.

Asmodraxas frowned in disgust. 'You have failed me, Erimandras. I am sorely disappointed. I had thought you would free me from my long imprisonment.'

'Master, it is not yet finished.' The Overmaster's form had almost completely boiled away into milky mist. He was almost to his throne.

'Yes it is. You made the ultimate gamble in using the Cards of Power and you were bested.' The Overmaster's robe was empty. 'You, Mercury Boltblaster may take his place as Overmaster. I will share with you my wisdom and you may rule Arden in my name, as one with your power should. You have but to lay low my enemy, Cosmo. Abandon the fruitless path of goodness and join me.'

'Tempting,' said Mercury. 'Your voice almost compels obedience, but I have no wish to rule the world.' The pulp-grinder rose into the air. 'Nor to speak with you further.'

'What are you doing? No! You must not destroy the mirror! You must not leave me once more incommunicado, powerless to influence events. Anything you desire—'

We didn't hear the rest of the Demon Lord's plea. The torture machine slammed into the mirror and it shattered like a glass waterfall. The black flame in the pit winked out.

'Is it over?' I asked.

'Not yet,' said Merc. 'We've still got to get out of here.'

The ghosts returned, this time whole – all wounds healed, all missing body parts restored – and in full living colour. They circled happily around me like a great ectoplasmic carousel and gradually rose to streak through the ceiling, presumably bound for the halls of Paradise.

'That is an encouraging sign,' said Merc.

'What manner of man are you?' said Natalia. I didn't try to answer her question. I wasn't sure I knew the answer.

'The rest of the Ruling Conclave will be back as soon as they realize they were suckered and I slipped past them. I'm sure they sensed the energies of my battle with their master. I'm not up to facing the rest of them. We can be satisfied with what we've already accomplished today. We lopped off the head of the beast.'

I put on the Ring of Raxx and donned my armour. 'So how do we get out?'

'My plan didn't go that far.'

'We can make for the roof and escape on Golan,' said Natalia.

'That sounds like a good suggestion.'

'Here is a better one, cringing maggots – you can die!' The breathless voice came from above, where a translucent image of Erimandras sat on the high throne. 'My dissolution was only temporary. Did you think an arcane grandmaster would not be prepared for the unlikely eventuality

of defeat? I have spells to counter even the Cards of Power.'
All three of us charged up the pyramid as he spoke. 'You
have destroyed the Mirror of Asmodraxas and the library.
The Society is a shambles this day, but you will not live
to savour your victory.' He pressed a hidden panel on the
throne and the entire fortress shook in the jaws of a mighty
earthquake.

Just as we reached the throne it dropped away, descending
straight down a deep shaft. The Overmaster's laughter echoed
from the darkness as the floor cracked, the walls crumbled, and
large blocks of the ceiling crashed around us.

'We'll never reach the roof!' I said.

'That's okay,' said Merc grimly. 'Our job isn't finished yet.
If we can't go up, we'll go down.' With that, he leaped into the
shaft. Natalia and I exchanged curious glances and followed,
hoping we had correctly divined his intent.

23

Mercury slowed our fall with a spell designed for slowing
falls down dark vertical shafts. I assume he used a similar
spell to survive his fall in the library. We floated down like
balls of cotton and landed gently on the empty throne in a
small square chamber far below the fortress. The thunder of
Marn's collapse echoed down the hole, followed by a hurtling
chunk of stone.

'Figures the little urchin would make this escape chute a
deathtrap for any who follow,' snarled Merc, leaping from the
throne.

'You mean we'll be crushed,' I said.

'Only if we stay. I suggest we exit through that door.'

'It's blocked by a gigantic wedge of granite!'

'You're the ones with the invincible swords.'

Natalia and I attacked the barrier, slicing away an opening
large enough to crawl through. Merc went first, Natalia followed. I brought up the rear and therefore took the brunt of
the shockwave that hurled us all against the far wall of the next

room. It was empty except for a few packing crates and what looked like a big glass box with silver frame and a door in the side. No exit was apparent.

'He has eluded us!' said Natalia.

'Maybe not for long,' said Merc. 'Unless I miss my guess, this glass box is a teleportal.'

'Impossible! They never existed!'

'The alternative is that it's just a glass box and we are entombed with it a mile or so beneath the surface of the Earth. Take your pick.'

Natalia studied the box again. 'Perhaps it is a teleportal.'

'Excuse me,' I said. 'What's a teleportal?'

'A box like this. If you know the proper command it will teleport you instantly to a similar box elsewhere. The Empire was rumoured to have a whole secret network of these devices which allowed them to send news or personnel virtually anywhere at any time. The secret of teleportation has since been lost.'

'Then it's our ticket out of here?'

'Right. If we can guess the proper command. Otherwise we suffocate in less than an hour.'

I rummaged through the packing crates, lifting and shaking each one.

'What are you looking for?' asked Merc.

'An instruction manual or something.'

'Don't be absurd.'

A paper booklet fell out of a box and fluttered to the floor. The title was *Teleportal Operation*. It was published by the Imperial Teleportal System Authority.

'You were saying?'

'Let me see that.' Merc quickly leafed through the pages of the manual. 'This chart lists command words for reaching all the teleportals in the system. See, this is teleportal 40468JM and its word is *Mimplecue*.'

'That's great!'

'Not really. This manual is at least ten centuries out of date, we have no idea which teleportals are operational or where they are located, and we don't know which one Erimandras escaped to.'

'Well, I think the important thing is getting out of here. We can look for Erimandras later, after we've had time to rest up.'

Merc and Natalia exchanged glances of dismay. 'That's sensible,' said Merc. 'But that's just not how things are done. When an enemy is down, you finish him if you can. If we take time to recuperate, Erimandras will be restored as well.'

'Boltblaster is correct,' said Natalia. 'We must destroy him now or we will never be safe.'

'I've got a feeling I'll never be safe again anyway, but I see your point. Why don't we just pick a teleportal and try it out?'

'We don't know where we would end up. We could be killed.'

'But we're just going to die if we stay here. What's the harm?'

'You learn quickly,' said Merc, stepping into the teleportal and consulting the manual.

'We should not go all at once,' said Natalia. 'One should go. If he finds safety he may return for the other two. If he perishes the others will still have a chance.'

'I notice your use of the masculine pronoun *he*,' said Merc. 'I take it you aren't volunteering, Natalia.'

'Well . . .'

'I'll go,' I said.

'No one is going anywhere,' said Merc abruptly, touching a metal panel set in the glass wall of the teleportal. The panel had a metal cup in the centre. 'This cup holds a magic crystal which powers the teleportal. I've just noticed that it is empty.'

'Erimandras took it with him,' said Natalia.

'That would be my guess,' said Merc. 'And without it, we're stuck.'

In frustration, I struck my palm with a fist and felt the imprint of the Ring of Raxx. A desperate thought formed in my mind and I lifted up my hand to display the glittering set amethyst. 'I've been wearing this supposedly magical ring for weeks and it's been of no use to me at all so far. Maybe it can provide the power we need.'

Merc gave me a sceptical look. 'Whatever that ring's functions may be, I doubt powering teleportals is one of them –

but what have we got to lose? Come press the ring against the panel.' I joined Merc within the teleportal. Natalia stood without. 'Come on, Natalia.'

'But—'

'A magic ring only works if it's worn. If Jason wears the ring, then it teleports with him. If he dies on the other end, we're stuck here. If he finds safety, he'll have to come back for us anyway, so we might as well go along the first time. Assuming, of course, that this works.'

Natalia joined us within the limited space of the tele-portal. We were crowded together uncomfortably, knees and elbows jammed against one another, Natalia and I stooped over because of our height. I pressed my ring against the panel.

'Tell the ring what you want it to do and concentrate on that,' said Merc.

'Do what?'

'Talk to the ring. I have no idea how to operate it, so you'll just have to try an exercise of pure will. Be forceful.'

'Right. Forceful. Ring of Raxx, I want you to give power to this teleportal!'

'Now concentrate! Imagine the power flowing from the ring! Exert your will!'

'I'm exerting!'

'Okay, here's a command word. Ready? Gablazook!'

I felt a draining surge of energy, saw a hot purple flash, and was suddenly swallowing black saltwater. The darkness was broken by another purple flash and we were back in the chamber beneath Marn, falling out on the floor and gasping for air as the water which had come back with us flowed from the teleportal.

'I think we can rule that one out,' said Merc, sitting up. 'It's obviously submerged. I was able to get us back because you maintained your concentration, Jason. Good thing you didn't panic.'

'I didn't have time.'

'At least we know the ring will work. Unfortunately, the manual is now a mass of wet pulp. We're left only with the command words I happen to recall. Ready to try again?'

'This is madness!' said Natalia.

'You don't have to come with us,' said Merc. 'But if we make it to safety we aren't coming back.'

'Let's go,' said the warrior woman, standing.

We crammed ourselves into the teleportal again and I resumed my concentration.

'We ought to be more successful this time, just on general principle,' said Merc. 'Here we go. Garihart!'

Another surge of energy and flash of purple light brought us to a teleportal in what looked like an abandoned sitting room. The teleportal was against one wall and faced fine quality couches, chairs and other furnishings, including iron statues of animals. Dark green curtains concealed the walls and a golden brown rug covered the floor. Everything in the room was coated with a thick layer of dust. Boy-sized footprints led from the teleportal to the oaken door across the room.

'Maybe we got lucky,' said Merc, as we emerged from the teleportal. 'This could be the place.'

Natalia and I drew our swords.

'Where are we?' I asked.

'Wherever unit 22169VS is,' said Merc, reading the serial number from the teleportal. 'That could be anywhere, though I'd venture to say we're not underwater.'

One of the animal statues, a big iron frog, winked at me.

'Merc, that frog statue winked at me.'

'Are you sure?'

The frog opened its mouth, bellowed a rusty croak, and shot its tongue at me. The iron muscle struck my chest like a hammer and sat me down hard. 'I'm pretty sure.'

The frog croaked again and leapt across the room, tracing a dusty trail through the air and landing full on my chest. It must have been completely solid, for it nearly crushed my ribs to powder. Only my magic armour saved me from immediate harm, but I lay helplessly on my back, unable to take a breath with that weight upon me.

The frog was joined in its attack by the other statues. An iron butterfly the size of an eagle flew at Natalia to batter her with its wings. A metal war dog snarled at Merc and was joined by an iron ant as big as a dog. A life-size grizzly bear statue growled and sniffed, as if deciding which of us to attack. Choking dust filled the air in grey clouds.

'Sorcery!' said Natalia, as she deftly sliced the butterfly into fluttering foil.

'So?' said Merc, leaping atop a cabinet to escape the jaws of the iron dog. 'What have you got against sorcery?'

'It means Erimandras must be near.'

'Gah . . . gah . . . gah . . .' I wheezed, trying futilely to push the kicking frog off me.

'Not necessarily,' said Merc, pulling a dull rock from beneath his cloak and shoving it into the maw of the ant before the artificial insect could sever his darting arm with its mandibles. The ant lost its grip on the cabinet and fell to its back to twitch erratically. 'These statues could be enchanted to attack all intruders without being specifically animated and controlled.' He peered down at the ant. 'I thought a piece of lodestone might bring interesting results.'

'Gah!' I responded.

Natalia decapitated the dog and then snatched up the frog by one of its hind legs and hurled it across the room. It shattered the teleportal and went on through the wall. She pulled me to my feet.

Only the bear remained. It stood on its hind legs and towered over all of us, dust whirling around it like a wreath of hellsmoke. If the frog was any guide this bear was about a dozen tons of solid iron. It growled a metallic growl.

'Cocky monster, isn't it?' said Merc. 'It waited until we finished the others.'

'It doesn't look like it needs help,' I said. 'Do you have another lodestone to feed it?'

'Sorry. I'm all out.'

'We'll have to fight it directly,' said Natalia.

'You first.'

The bear took the initiative, charging and knocking us all over the room with a single sweep of its club-like paw. Natalia fell across a couch. Merc stuck to a far wall. I landed on my face amid the broken glass of the teleportal.

'Round one to the bear,' I said.

'But not round two!' Natalia hurled the couch at the statue. It broke harmlessly across the beast's thick body. Merc peeled himself off the wall and rubbed his hands together while trying to think of a useful spell.

I ran at the bear, swinging Overwhelm in a great arc and severing one of its paws. With the stump of its foreleg it shoved me to the floor and pounced. Knowing I did not want to be crushed beneath an iron bear, I rolled out of harm's way.

Natalia attacked from the other side and hacked at one of its hind legs, only to be slapped across the room once more. The bear continued after me and I skittered fearfully across the floor until I reached the wall and willed Overwhelm into my hand.

'Get back!' said Merc. The body of the dog rose into the air and flew at the bear like a missile, striking it in the head with a tremendous clang. The bear caught the dog in its jaws, chewed it up and swallowed it. It spit a dog leg at me. I deflected the missile.

'This is not going well,' I said.

'I'll levitate the bear!' exclaimed Merc, proud of himself at this new idea. His face took on an expression of intense, painful concentration. 'Maybe.'

The bear stopped moving towards me and seemed puzzled. Its feet rose a fraction of an inch off the floor. Unable to walk or otherwise approach me, it roared in frustration.

'Now what?'

'Kill it! I . . . can't hold it up . . . for long.'

I approached the bear. It snarled and raked the air with its claws. I edged back. 'Merc, I don't think this thing *can* be killed. We could hack it up, but even with our swords, it would take a while.'

'Then get behind it and help me push it through the door.'

Natalia and I sheathed our swords and approached the bear from the rear. Lacking contact with the floor, it was unable to turn and attack us. We put our hands on its haunches and pushed, aided by Merc's telekinesis. The bear drifted slowly across the room, gathering speed as we went and roaring all the while. It hit the door and went right through it, taking most of the wall with it. We went on into the carpeted corridor beyond and sent it through the far wall into a wine cellar, sending casks and barrels hurtling in all directions.

'I'm losing it!' said Merc. The bear fell to the flagstones, turned to face us, and promptly fell from sight as the floor collapsed beneath its great weight. It was followed by a dozen barrels of wine. We heard a great splash and smelled the foul odour of sewage drifting up from the hole.

'Good plan, Merc! How did you know the floor was weaker in this wine cellar on the far side of two walls?'

'It seemed reasonable that the floors of any adjoining chambers wouldn't be reinforced to bear such a weight.'

'We're beneath a city,' said Natalia.

'Obviously,' said Merc. 'But what city?' He examined one of the wine casks. 'This is Plum Sparkle from the Trebor Trig Winery – sold exclusively in Caratha.'

'We're in Caratha?' I asked.

'No, we're under Caratha.' Merc led the way back into the corridor and located the footprints we hoped belonged to Erimandras. 'It looks like the Overbrat has a hidden series of apartments here as his escape of last resort.'

Swords ready, Natalia and I flanked Merc as we explored the complex. In addition to the room where we had entered, we found a kitchen, a storeroom, a small study and several closets. Everything was dusty and untended. At length, only one door remained unopened.

Merc and Natalia crouched in readiness as I kicked it in. The room beyond was dimly lit by red lanterns in the shape of demon heads. Erimandras reclined on a large bed, propped up on several cushions, his hands out of sight beneath a blanket decorated with pictures of skulls. He was slightly more opaque than he had been when we last saw him, but he still looked fairly insubstantial.

'I've been expecting you,' he said.

'Liar,' said Merc. 'You expected us to die beneath Fortress Marn.'

'True. But I heard your battle with my guardian statues and I've been expecting you since then.'

'That's more like it. This is the end, Erimandras.'

'Fools! I am Overmaster of the Dark Magic Society. I can never be defeated. I anticipate every exigency. I am your superior in every respect.'

'Then why are we tracking you down and not the other way around?' I asked. 'Your minions hunted me across practically the whole of the Eleven Kingdoms. Hundreds of innocent people died and many more were endangered in your search for me. You hounded me, wounded me, tortured me, destroyed my quiet life. By all rights, I should be dead, but I'm not. The only thing keeping me on my feet at this moment, despite all my wounds and pain, is the desire to see justice done, Erimandras. Justice for me, justice for all your countless victims. You're finished.'

'If this is so,' hissed Erimandras, 'then why do you fear to tread this chamber? I lie here defenceless before you – why don't you come and slay me?' He glared at us disdainfully. 'It is because you fear me still. You know you can never win.'

'This is crazy,' said Merc. 'You're bluffing. The Cards of Power should have dissolved you permanently. Despite your survival you can't be anywhere near your full strength.'

'Then come for me, Mercury Boltblaster. Come for me all of you – come and die!' Erimandras's face was livid. 'Or else be wise. Fall upon your knees now and swear loyalty to me. I will make you a king over half the world, Jason Cosmo. I will teach you arcane secrets you could not learn elsewhere, Mercury Boltblaster. I will forgive your betrayal, Natalia Slash, and make you queen over the other half of the world. Swear now and all in yours.'

Mercury laughed. 'If you thought you could kill us, you'd have done so by now instead of wasting time with these blandishments. We call your bluff.'

The three of us stepped into Erimandras's bedroom. The evil wizard threw back the blanket and held forth a perfect set of human teeth, wired together as if still in the mouth. 'Behold the Jaws of Death!'

Merc and Natalia drew back with expressions of alarm. I picked up the cue and retreated as well.

'You're still bluffing,' said Merc, but he didn't sound certain. 'Using such a powerful talisman as the true Jaws of Death in your weakened state would bring your instant destruction.'

'Perhaps. Perhaps not. But it will certainly bring yours.'

The jaws flew from his hand and came at us, expanding to monstrous proportions and opening wide to engulf us all:

24

We scattered as Erimandras laughed his thin, airless laugh and the Jaws of Death snapped their way through the wall of his bedchamber, reducing the stone wall to weathered dust. Natalia turned left and sprinted down the corridor, Merc and I went to the right.

Mercury explained the threat we faced as he halted to cast a protective spell. He looked more fearful than I had yet seen him. 'Death lost his jaws in a wager with Vanah, Goddess of Fortune and Chance, a couple of ages back. It was his teeth against the life of the mortal wizard Sajahk the Smiling, whom she favoured. The obvious moral is that you should never gamble with the Goddess of Chance.'

The jaws broke clear of the wall and turned from side to side slowly like a Ganthian bloodhawk searching for its prey. Merc and I had spotted an adjoining passage and ducked around the corner.

'Vanah had no real use for the teeth, so she buried them beneath a mountain and surrounded them with mighty guardians – magic, monsters, traps. Naturally, when the necromancers of the world got wind of this, they were beside themselves with joy. Many expeditions were mounted to recover the jaws, eventually one succeeded.'

The clenched jaws decided to move in our direction, stalking slowly but purposefully through the air like a hound stalking a scent. The scent of life. Our scent.

'Dreadful Dwarkanath was the one who succeeded. I think he's one of the dark saints of the Church of Undeath now. He used to have a castle staffed entirely by animated corpses and worked closely with ghosts, wraiths, vampires and the like. But when he tried to gain control of the jaws they swallowed him whole, reduced his entire castle to ruins, and went on a killing spree across six kingdoms before finally being banished by a large band of priests and master mages called together for that purpose. But seven thousand people had already been killed, including all those wizards and priests.'

'Seven thousand?'

He looked me dead in the eye. 'I think it's about to be seven thousand and three. No one knew where the jaws went after the battle. They were never seen again. Some suggested Death had reclaimed them. Looks like they wound up with the Overbrat instead.'

The Jaws of Death rounded the corner and streaked towards us, opening wide as they flew. We turned to flee and discovered belatedly that we had chosen a dead-end corridor. The irony did not amuse me.

Mercury stood forth and cast the spell he had prepared. A huge bolt of crackling red energy flew from his outstretched hands and met the jaws in mid-flight, only to vanish into that black maw between the dreadful teeth as the jaws flew onwards, undisturbed. Mercury never had a chance of getting out of the way in time, and nowhere to go anyway. He was swallowed whole, gulped into the great beyond with a moribund snap. The jaws stopped, momentarily sated, but still facing me.

Natalia appeared at the other end of the corridor, behind the jaws, and shouted for their attention. I thought that very brave and considerate of her since she could have been long gone by now, but her tactic was useless. The jaws ignored her and opened slightly, advancing on me. I was cornered, a sword and shield my only defence against a monstrous apparition which had just killed one of the most powerful wizards I knew of.

Powerful wizards? 'Natalia!' I shouted. 'Get Erimandras! He's unprotected while the jaws are busy with me!' She turned to obey, but the stricken Overmaster must have heard me, for the jaws turned in place and streaked away in pursuit of her. I was right behind them and rounded the corner just in time to see Natalia swing her sword in a swift, brutal stroke that chipped one of the incisors. Before she could swing again, the dental destroyer had her in its grip, swallowing her down like a grave does a coffin. I was all alone.

The sinister jaws stalked me slowly, herding me against the wall across from Erimandras's door. I held Overwhelm out before me, but knew it was a futile gesture.

'You need not perish as your companions have done,' called Erimandras from his chamber. 'Reveal to me the location of the Superwand.'

'I told you before and I'm telling you now – I don't know where it is and if I did know, I wouldn't tell.'

The Jaws of Death opened wide and I stared down the metaphysical throat beyond, seeing only the cold, eternal blackness of a tomb. The mingled scents of attar and carrion blew over me and I heard the faint sound of a faraway funeral dirge.

'It is total, endless, eternal oblivion you stare in the face,' said Erimandras.

'I'm not afraid to die. After all I've been through, how could I be?'

The jaws moved closer until the chilling teeth were almost touching me. I had nowhere to retreat. Every hair on my body stood stiff, goosebumps marched across my skin, my own teeth chattered like dice in a cup. But these reactions were purely physical, instinctive. My heart and mind were calm. This supernatural apparition held no threat for me that I hadn't already faced. If this was how my life was to end, so be it. I had done my duty to The Gods and humankind as best I could.

'Consider carefully. There is no return from the Jaws of Death.'

'The hell there isn't,' said Mercury.

Shocked, I looked down to the source of the voice. He was clinging to the Lower Left Cuspid of Death, quaking uncontrollably, his beard and hair shocked white as chalk, his face drained of all colour.

'Merc! You're alive!'

'Let's keep it that way.'

'Impossible!' spat Erimandras. The teeth snapped at me. I

blunted the bite with my shield and lopped off the point of the lower cuspid on the right. Merc held his place tenaciously.

The teeth closed to make a wall of enamel and shot forward, ramming me through the corridor wall. I lost my footing and fell to my back in the next chamber. The jaws snatched me up like a dog going for meat. I dropped Overwhelm and my shield and wriggled free, hitting the floor and rolling to my feet. The jaws came at me again and this time I caught them in mid-bite, preventing them from closing fully.

'Merc! Get out!'

'Gladly.' My friend pulled himself out of the abyss and crumpled to the floor like a corpse. I continued to pit my strength against the Jaws of Death, pushing them back down the corridor and into the Overmaster's bedroom.

'What you attempt is impossible,' said Erimandras. 'The certainty of Death is inexorable.'

'I don't doubt it. But the Jaws of Death . . . are not Death itself . . . and they depend . . . on your power . . . which is dwindling.'

'Fool! You cannot defeat Death! You cannot!'

'I don't have to defeat Death – just you.'

'I am Erimandras the Overmaster! I am—'

'Fading fast.'

He was. The will and energy he was pouring into forcing the jaws shut was undoing his recovery from the Cards of Power. His thin form was growing less solid by the second. At the same time, the force of the teeth decreased and I began to not only check them, but force them open.

'You cannot defeat me.' His protest was almost inaudible.

'Fine. We'll just pretend.'

'Fool! If it means my utter dissolution I will summon the strength to defeat you!'

But instead, the Jaws of Death abruptly retreated, spun in place to face Erimandras, opened wide, and flew to engulf him and his entire bed before vanishing into thin air. He had become too weak to control them. The jaws had turned on him and destroyed him.

'Good show,' said Merc, crawling to the doorway. He gave me a thumbs up sign and collapsed.

'Thanks.' I fell to my knees and joined him in oblivion, the strain of being tortured, teleported, crushed by an iron frog, and nearly swallowed by the Jaws of Death all in one day finally catching up with me.

I dreamed. Or at least it seemed a dream to me, for I floated weightlessly upward, up through the streets of Caratha, through the clouds, through the blue veil of the sky. Up and up to a place of light and beauty and music and majesty. Up until I stood upon a sward of fresh green grass and breathed sweet, pure air while brightly plumed birds flitted around me, chirping joyously. Before me was a great open gate fashioned from gold, platinum and silver. It was decorated with shining bands of diamond, ruby, sapphire, amethyst, pearl, beryl, topaz, opal and dozens of other gems I could not name. Beyond the gate was a street paved with gold and lined with fabulous gleaming mansions and palaces. Three people advanced towards me on foot. When they drew near, I recognized the goddess Rae, who wore a low-cut golden gown. Her companions were Arkayne, the God of Magic, and the wise and wonderful Great Whoosh. I fell to my knees.

'Arise, Jason Cosmo,' said Great Whoosh. 'Even here in the outskirts of Paradise there is no need to humble yourself before us.'

'We are pleased with your accomplishments,' said Arkayne. 'Erimandras the Overmaster is dead, the Citadel of Marn in ruins, the Dark Magic Society crippled by the loss of its leaders, its records and the prospect of internal warfare. Most importantly, the threat of Asmodraxas has been checked. He shall not return.'

'And you have reminded me of the nation which honours me and reunited me with the line that is descended from me,' said Rae. 'I'm so glad I became your patron goddess.'

'As am I, O Rae. But if I am in Paradise, does this mean I am dead?'

'You're semi-dead,' said Rae.

'Indeed,' said Great Whoosh. 'The toll upon your body has been great and you hover now twixt life and death. You could go either way but, as a reward to you, we grant you the power to choose. You may continue to live in Arden below or you may enter Paradise now.'

'And you will live in my palace, remaining by my side for eternity,' said Rae, which pretty much settled the question in my mind.

'I choose to live, O Gracious Gods.'

'So be it,' said Great Whoosh.

'But, if I may, I would like to ask you some questions before I go back.' Arkayne and Great Whoosh exchanged glances.

'You may ask,' said Arkayne.

'Am I truly the Mighty Champion of old? You told me that I am of his line, but am I some manner of reincarnation?'

'Reincarnation is not our policy,' said Arkayne. 'We grant to each mortal one life to live, for good or ill. You are very like your ancestor in courage and spirit, but you are not a reincarnation. You are yourself.'

'May I meet him? The original Champion?'

'Impossible,' said Great Whoosh firmly. 'Have you further questions?'

'The Superwand,' I said. 'Where is it?'

'That we do not know,' said Arkayne, 'as we explained to you before. It was hidden even from us, such is its power, its danger.'

'How can anything be hidden from The Gods?'

'We have not inquired deeply into the matter,' said the God of Magic. 'We have made it our law that no god or man shall seek that talisman. I would speculate that the Mighty Champion, the original Jason Cosmo, hid it in a place beyond our power.'

'Beyond your power?'

'We are The Gods of this world, this universe, but there are a multitude of others in which we hold no sway. Perhaps the Champion took the Superwand to such a place. I do not know. Inquire no further on this matter.'

214

'As you command. I have no further questions.' I bowed.

'Then we shall leave you with your patron,' said Great Whoosh, and he turned to accompany Arkayne back through the gates of Paradise.

Rae gathered me in for a warm, godly hug. 'You are the most marvellous mortal I've known in years. You should have seen the look on Lucinda's face when she found out I was your sponsor. She was positively green. Especially after you destroyed Marn and bested Erimandras.'

'Merc did most of that.'

'Whatever.' She caressed my cheek. 'Your tan looks good. Try to keep it by getting plenty of sun. That way I can keep an eye on you too.'

'I'll do that.'

'That mortal girl you were running around with has a lovely tan too. The two of you look good together.'

'Sapphrina! Where is she?'

'In Caratha, which is where you are too. Or were. Or will be. That is where your body is, I mean, as opposed to your soul, which is here. Anyway, I'm sure you'll see her soon.'

'Yes. I hope so.'

'Be sure to drop by my temple from time to time. Of course, the one in Caratha is really much too small. They don't really appreciate me as much as they should there. They favour the gods of commerce and the sea – as if there would be either without the sun. It really makes my blood boil. Of course, I have been neglecting my worshippers for a few hundred years, but you'd think they would remember me anyway. Which reminds me, I must remember to schedule another eclipse soon. I haven't done one in ages and they are such fun. I wonder if Lune is busy today. We have to coordinate these—'

'Goddess?'

'Yes?'

'Could I go back now?'

'Oh, yes! Of course. Silly of me to ramble on so.' She kissed me lightly on the cheek. 'Return to life, Jason. Return to life – now!'

25

I opened my eyes and saw Mercury (his hair still white), Raella, Rubis and Sapphrina hovering over me. I was lying in a firm bed in a small pleasant room filled with flowers.

'He's awake!' said Sapphrina, who immediately filled my mouth with a wet kiss.

'So glad you could join us,' said Merc when she was finished. 'True to form, you've been unconscious for—'

'Three days?' I guessed.

'Exactly. I recovered a few hours after our battle, as wizards tend to do, and dragged you up to street level to find a healer. I went to the Raelnan embassy to send word of our whereabouts to Raella. Then I located the twins through the city directory. Since then we've been waiting for you to wake up. The healers said you were in a Paradise coma, conferring with The Gods.'

'How did they know that?'

'You were smiling. Of course, there was nothing they could do if you elected to remain in Paradise and nothing for them to do if you didn't, so we moved you from the healing house here to the embassy. Now that you're back we can tie up loose ends and Raella and I can get back to Rae City. I assume you'll be staying in Caratha for a while.'

I glanced at Sapphirina. 'Yes. What loose ends?'

'Well, for example, you may wonder how the war in Raelna turned out.'

'Now that you mention it.'

'Raella?'

The queen smiled knowingly at Merc. 'Orphalia surrendered and withdrew when they realized we had Halogen. The nobles also renounced him and elected his cousin Stron Astatine as their new king. Halogen is now in Raelnan custody, imprisoned in the Bronze Tower where he can do no harm. With that matter closed, we turned our full might against

Brythalia and drove them back beyond their own borders. But I have more welcome news than even that. Mercury and I are free to wed at long last.'

'That's incredible! How does this come about?'

'The Goddess Rae has given me a special dispensation suspending the dictates of tradition and sanctioning our marriage. There is nothing the nobles can say now, no way they can force me to abdicate.'

'Then – congratulations to both of you.'

'You will come to Rae City for the wedding, of course. All three of you.'

'Of course. When is the ceremony to be held?'

'In three months' time,' said the queen. 'A state wedding requires a great deal of preparation.'

'Now get out of bed,' said Merc. 'You're fully healed and we have something important to do before I leave.'

'What do you mean?'

'I'll explain on the way.'

I strode boldly into the offices of the attorney Periglio, tastefully decorated with red leather walls and a glossy ebonwood floor. Mercury was right beside me and casually rendered the lawyer's two bodyguards unconscious as we swept past the wide-eyed receptionist into the inner office.

Periglio was seated at his desk. He was a small, furtive man with rodent eyes and greasy, slicked back hair. Gold and diamond rings glittered on his fingers and his tunic and doublet were well-made.

'Who are you?' he demanded. 'How did you get in here?'

I dropped one of the Society's bounty notices on the desk. 'Are you the selfsame Periglio who is the designated agent in Caratha of those who posted this bounty?'

'Yeah. So what? Get out of here before I summon my bodyguards and have you thrown out.'

'You probably don't get many walk-in clients, do you?' observed Merc.

'No, I don't. Strictly by appointment. Now if you will excuse me. Harak! Rothar! Are you guys asleep out there, letting these clowns barge in like this?'

'They'll wake up in an hour or so,' said Merc. 'We'll have completed our business with you by then.'

'I . . . see,' said Periglio. 'So what do you want?'

'I'm here to claim the bounty,' I said.

'What!'

'I'm Jason Cosmo. I've brought myself to the designated agent and I want my letter of credit for ten million crowns to be placed in an account at the Bank of Caratha.'

'You're crazy! You're no more Jason Cosmo than I am. Get the hell out of here!'

I drew Overwhelm and sliced his desk in half like a watermelon and scattering his papers across the floor. 'This is my enchanted sword Overwhelm.'

'So? Proves nothing. And desks cost money, you know.'

Merc grabbed the lawyer by his collar and yanked him to his feet. 'Let me make things a little clearer for you. We know that you handle the legal interests of the Dark Magic Society in Caratha. We know the Society posted the reward on my friend here. We also know that we just returned from killing the Overmaster of the Society and a good many of his minions. One more won't make much difference to me. The bounty offer still stands and Jason has just fulfilled its conditions. So what is the problem?'

Periglio squinted at me. 'You know, he does seem to be Jason Cosmo. Of course, the idea was that he be brought in as a prisoner, but going solely by the offer as it is worded he has fair claim to the money. I see no problem here at all.'

'Good.' Merc released him. The attorney opened a drawer in his sundered desk and produced the letter of credit, which he signed over to me.

'Thank you,' I said. 'Have a wonderful day.'

With ten million crowns in the bank, I was suddenly one of the wealthiest men in Caratha, apart from the great merchants and noble families. Word of my presence in the city would quickly spread after my appearance at the Bank of Caratha. Claiming my own bounty would only add to the fame – or infamy – I already had due to my supposed criminal exploits. But, as Merc explained, the news of the deed would free me from constantly having to worry about the legions of bounty hunters and other fortune seekers who were still looking for me.

Mercury and Raella returned to her kingdom to prepare for their wedding. The twins and I would follow in three months time, but meanwhile they were helping me get oriented in Caratha. With their expert guidance I bought a small villa in the wealthy residential section of the city and purchased a wardrobe they deemed suitable for a conquering hero/rogue.

They also advised me on how I should invest my fortune in order to increase it. It seemed to me that ten million crowns was enough to live on for a lifetime, but they assured me that Dinarmark's Law of Fortune Accumulation or Dispersal, an arcane money theory I had never heard of, demanded that such large sums are either dispersed almost overnight due to bad luck and mismanagement or increase at a prodigious rate due to wise investment. The latter course seemed preferable.

Once these chores were out of the way, Sapphrina and Rubis took me on the grand tour of the city, showing me such sights as Alcazara Palace, the Consolidated Temple of The Gods, the colourful bazaars of the trade district, the public baths, and the ivy-covered campus of the University of Caratha. Caratha was huge, dwarfing even Rae City. It teemed with people of every description engaged in ceaseless activity. Its products were exotic, varied and abundant as befitted the City at the Centre of the World. It would take years to see and experience it all.

But years I had. My quest was completed, though Mercury warned me that factions of the Society would certainly seek revenge and reminded me that with the Next Age still ten years away it was likely The Gods would call on me to again serve their purposes. Furthermore, my own prominence would invite trouble to my door from virtually every quarter. I should be prepared for anything that might develop.

Meanwhile, I enjoyed what was developing between me and Sapphrina. In the two weeks since my arrival in Caratha we had not continued our uncompleted conversation begun in Rae City, allowing it to hang over us like a hovering dove, both of us enjoying the suspense until, on a midnight walk through the garden of my villa, we decided we could delay no longer.

'Let's do this properly,' I said, whirling her about to face me and taking her in my arms.

'Okay.'

'Sapphrina . . .'

'Jason . . .'

'I love you.'

'And I love you. And now I melt into your arms and you will kiss me – but then we must go inside because mosquitos are biting me."

'Me too. I'll have to call a pest control mage tomorrow.'

'Yes,' she said, snuggling closer. 'Tomorrow.'

Our lips met and for long moments we were oblivious to the bloodsucking insects, but eventually they could be ignored no longer. I led the way inside and up the stairs.

The hero business was tough, much more perilous than woodcutting or turnip farming. But, after all the foes were laid low, the dangers surpassed, and the obstacles overcome, the rewards were sweet indeed.

Douglas Adams
The Long Dark Tea-Time of the Soul £3.99

When a passenger check-in desk at Terminal Two, Heathrow
Airport, shot up through the roof engulfed in a ball of orange
flame the usual people tried to claim responsibility. First the
IRA, then the PLO and the Gas Board. Even British Nuclear
Fuels rushed out a statement to the effect that the situation was
completely under control, that it was a one in a million chance,
that there was hardly any radioactive leakage at all and that the
site of the explosion would make a nice location for a day out with
the kids and a picnic, before finally having to admit that it wasn't
actually anything to do with them at all.

No rational cause could be found for the explosion – it was simply
designated an act of God. But, thinks Dirk Gently, which God?
And why? What God would be hanging around Terminal Two of
Heathrow Airport trying to catch the 15.37 to Oslo?

Funnier than *Psycho* . .more chilling than *Jeeves Takes
Charge*. . .shorter than *War and Peace*. . .the new Dirk Gently
novel, *The Long Dark Tea-Time of the Soul*.